Nothing's fair in Love & Marriage

Lena Knight

A note from the Author

Please note that this is a work of fiction, created by my imagination. Naturally, some scenes were inspired by personal events. The story may also entail some triggering subjects, so be advised.

Thank you in advance for giving my story a chance. Hope you like it… Happy reading.

Trigger warnings: mention of loss, child abuse, emotional abuse

Something I find important to tell you, even though it's a spoiler, is that **this book has NO infidelity** despite it being somewhat of a love triangle.

This book is special to me for two reasons. One, I am a proud mama of a child with autism, and two, I know what it's like to lose oneself. And even though I was lucky enough to marry my Luka, I know there are a lot of women out there who aren't as lucky. I hope this book finds you, gives you a voice, and the strength you need to believe in yourself.

Lena

This one is for all the special lioness mothers out there.

Playlist - *available on* ***Spotify***

Everleave - Alexandra Kay
28 - Dean Lewis ft. Ruth B.
Hate you - Jim Yosef, RIELL
Last thing on my mind - Ronan Keating ft. LeAnn Rimes
Overthinking - Zoe Wess
I told you things - Gracie Abrams
Gravity - Pixie Lott
Am I Enough - Loi
Nothing's Forever - Zoe Wees
Roommates - Hilary Duff
How would it be - Lene Marlin
I'm the problem - Morgan Wallen
Disaster - JoJo
Don't give up - Zoe Wees
The heart never lies - McFly
Almost here - Brian McFadden ft. Delta Goodrem
Broken Arrow - Pixie Lott
Not ok - Robert Grace
Fix it to break it - Clinton Kane
Idle Strangers - Miccoli
Every day is a song - BUNT ft. Austin Jenckes
Hello, my old lover - Dove Cameron
Sky - DROP
Room for 2 - Benson Boone
Fall into me - Forest Blakk
Seasons of Love - from the musical RENT
Can I be him - James Arthur
Everywhere - Michelle Branch

Goodbye looks good on you - Alana Springsteen ft Mitchell Tenpenny
You take me home - Walk off the Earth
You set me free - Michelle Branch
More than a feeling - Declan J Donovan
On my way (Folktales) - Leah Haywood, BUNT
What's left of you - Chord Overstreet
Love you now - Luke Grimes

Prologue

Nora

The clock on the microwave blinks 02:14 AM in neon green. The house is quiet, save for the occasional groan of our old refrigerator and the snore coming from Rick's nostrils. I am in the kitchen, laptop open, words staring right at me. One glance at his feet hanging over the couch armrest is all it takes for the knot in my chest to tighten.

When was the last time we shared a bed?

I exhale through my nose, letting my eyes fall shut for a moment.

If you go to any search bar and type in one particular set of letters, you get a large number of different variations on the subject. This is not my first time searching for the meaning of the word.

- marriage

/ˈmarɪdʒ/

noun: **marriage**; plural noun: **marriages**

  1. The legally or formally recognized union of two people as partners in a personal relationship

It's all right there, straightforward, to the point, and oh so simple. Something very much expected. Yet, if you add one word, the definition itself changes completely. For example, if you put the 'happy' followed by 'marriage,' you'll likely find articles with phrases like mutual respect, love, understanding, compromise, strong communications, and shared values.

With one press of the Enter button, my eyes read out all the words spread across the screen. Right there, in black and white, every word presumptuous and logical. I didn't expect how I would react after reading the various ideas about what a happy marriage should be.

So to say I am more than surprised that my whole body trembled with so much ache and that my eyes formed a whole new set of tears would be an understatement.

My head turns to the wall on my right, where my favorite photo of us stands as a reminder. We look so happy in it, so much in love that it hurts to look.

Ten years. I have been part of a legally recognized union with another person for ten years, and not a single word comes to mind to describe it.

Sure, there is love; sometimes mutual, mostly one-sided, but it's there. At the beginning, there was an abundance of it; today, not so much…

It got lost on the way, ran away to spare itself from all the suffering. So, yeah, marriage - a broad spectrum of possibilities - and somehow I am stuck in one of them, on a loop, going nowhere.

We built a life; that much is true—a home, routine, a history. But lately, it feels more like cohabiting with a stranger. I twist my wedding ring once, twice, looking at something that doesn't feel like a symbol anymore, more like a question…

When did we lose each other?

Each tear that slides down my face feels heavier, like my heart is taking inventory of all the truths I was too tired to admit.

I wonder if he ever thought the same.

I wonder if he ever would.

Closing the laptop with a sigh, I stand up and quietly go upstairs, one thought looming…

Is love enough?

Chapter 1

Luka

The transition from spring to summer is the worst part of the year for me. Work is in full bloom, overloading my already heavy shoulders, and the mixture of heat and humidity is a whole different kind of hell.

Sweating through every inch of my workwear, I take off my hard hat with the sole purpose of taking a breather. Two guys called in sick today, so I had to step up to keep the timeline on track. Naturally, they picked today to get sick, leaving me to do all the heavy lifting on this damned heat.

Superstition wasn't part of my upbringing. I usually don't pay it much mind. But today feels like it's working against me. A black cat must have crossed my path, or maybe a mirror shattered nearby. That's the only explanation for all the bad luck I've had so far.

Aside from the two guys on my payroll who called in sick, my truck broke down, leaving me at the mercy of public transportation. I stepped in some stinky dog shit, which got me barefoot, while I furiously scrubbed my boots, cursing under my breath. So, to sum it all up, today was not one of the good ones.

As I chug my practically boiling water, I glance at the workers, panic in their eyes, shearing around the site. I've come a long way... Started out as a boy doing odd jobs for my neighbor for some extra allowance. Now, I run my own business. Over the last few years, I worked hard, learning everything I could about the craft. Over time, my skills and knowledge grew, so I felt ready to bet on myself.

Unlike my brothers, I was not much of a bookworm. I enjoyed spending my free time with my nose between the pages, but I wasn't one to study. There was no lack of intelligence; I just never craved or needed to prove it with a piece of paper. I am more of a hands-on guy, something that the rough skin and blisters around my fingers can prove. The fact that I was profusely called '*The Hulk*' came in handy during my specific kind of education. I could carry a load in my weight well before I learned to jerk myself off, so there's that.

The constant nickname is not hated as much as begrudged. People see my exterior and think I'm an impenetrable shell without feelings. Much to their dismay, I am far from it. I also bleed, have a steady heartbeat, and am the opposite of the tank everyone around me labels me to be. Everyone, that is, outside of my family. My mother and my brothers know me better than that.

The last clang of metal echoes across the site as the crew packs up for the day. Tools are being tossed into bins, boots scrape clean. The sun is sinking low behind the crane, reflecting over the windows we put in today. I wipe the sweat from my brow with a gloved hand and lean on a stack of wooden beams. This part of the day is my favorite, when the noise dies down, and everything stills… when I can just breathe.

Some of the guys are still laughing near the gate, making

plans. We share a nod in passing as I head to the container. My phone buzzes, and I know who the message is from before I bring the screen to life. I smile when Mak's name appears, asking if I need him to pick me up. I quickly reply to my older brother that I will take the company truck and lock the screen.

This place, my life, is everything I once wanted. I am successful, healthy, don't owe anybody anything… by every external measure—content. On paper, it's all solid. No one from the outside looking in would think I was missing a damn thing. But at the end of the day, the empty space in my bed tells a different story.

I am lonely.

I run a hand through my hair, leaning back to stare at the sky like it might have an answer.

It doesn't.

It never did.

I tried dating, swiping, flings, but none of it stuck. They all wanted something shinier than what I am, more polished, less worn out. Someone without calloused hands or stories that lack happy endings. I look at the empty frame of the rising building. Someday, people will live here. Laugh here… Love here.

I wonder how it would feel to come home to someone who notices when you walk through the door… who cares how your day went, not just out of politeness but because they need to know.

Knowing I have an overwhelming number of agonizing emails to go through, I decide to bail, too drained. Who knew that emails would turn out to be the most frustrating part of my job? Mateo, brother two out of four, keeps saying I should hire an assistant. But honestly, I can't bear to put anyone through that kind of torture.

As I lock the container, my eyes trace a single beam of light to a vision in yellow.

A few steps reveal another figure, a much smaller one. It's the cutest little boy, his eyes fixed on the spinning barrel. Without a blink in sight, he focuses on the truck, eyes locked, mouth hanging open. One hand swings while the other grips something delicate.

He's wearing a blue shirt and matching shorts, his feet hidden inside rain boots. A hat on top of his head, a couple of stray light brown locks escaping from the sides. Slowly, my eyes roam to the person the other hand belongs to. From her red sneakers, bare legs, a sundress reaching her knees, up to the chest, exposed neckline, right to the most beautiful face I've ever seen. Oval-shaped, set of full peach lips, hazel eyes by the looks of it, and wavy hair falling down her side, light brown, like honey.

"Oh, sorry. We didn't expect anyone here. He's obsessed with that mixer." She gives me a shy smile, but the fear in her eyes is impossible not to catch. It wasn't so much her being scared of me as it was the expression a kid would have when caught red-handed, fingers in the cookie jar.

"It's no problem, the site is closed down for the day," I deadpan.

I soak in more of her details, unable to unglue my eyes from her, too mesmerized. Curiosity gets the best of me, so I indulge it. There's not a single shred of imperfection there, apart from the pain that seems to penetrate the kind smile she puts on. Freckles cover her face, even her forehead, but mostly around her nose and cheeks. They play around her skin with every sun ray that illuminates all of her glory. Ready to get myself out of this weird, creepy state she pulled me into, I kneel in front of the boy who is still all into the mixer behind me.

"What's your name, little fella?"

Fella?

Where did that come from?

"It's Declan," she cuts in, and I look up at her. "He doesn't speak much." A genuine smile lights up her face as she adds, "He has autism." The way she's expressed it, with pride, strikes me right in the chest. I turn my focus to Declan, understanding his hand movement and the lack of interest in me. Kids are often the only humans who see beyond my exterior, but this guy appears indifferent to my presence.

I stay on my knees and hold out my hand. He meets my gaze, then gives me a strong high five. A zing of pride rushes through me, and I stand up, buzzing from the contact I've been gifted.

"He is verbal, mostly when he needs something," she chuckles, "but he doesn't fully get communication. For example, he didn't understand your question, though he does know his name."

I nod, standing up, not able to look away. She's breathtaking.

"TMI, I'm sorry, I don't have a filter, it's a character flaw, and usually someone needs to gag me."

She smacks her hand over her mouth so hard that the sound echoes around the site.

"That came out wrong, sorry again. Just tell me to shut up and I will, otherwise a whole lot of word vomit will come, and by the sound of it so far, it won't come out good."

One thing's for sure: this one is a fast talker. That whole sentence lasted a second.

She takes a deep breath and shakes her head, making me straight out laugh, head tossed back and all.

I take in their similarities. They share the same mouth and the exact shape of their eyes, though hers have more green in them. He also has freckles, but not to the same extent, more as if they are just starting to manifest. Desperate for more information, I extend my hand. "My name is Luka."

"Do you live on the second floor?"

I cock a brow.

"It's a song." She shakes her head again, smiling, right hand holding Declan, her expression apologetic as she offers me her left hand. "I'm Nora."

I grab it tight, feeling the piece of metal on her finger, one that shatters whatever I was starting to envelop.

Chapter 2

Nora

Sweet mother of all mercy!

Luka.

I mentally repeat it on a loop, not fully understanding why, but it's out of my control at this point.

I can't confirm or deny, but there might be some full-on drooling happening on my side of the fence. I am staring at a muscled wall, and then out of the blue, he turns around. Why would he do that? My eyes immediately go south. Someone shot me because I am checking someone else's ass, me, a married woman…

And what a fine ass it is…

What the melon is wrong with me?

He turns around to face me again, and I stop breathing.

Those eyes, my Lord…

I am not a fan of whiskey, yet all I want to do is drown in a pool of it. The sun isn't helpful at all; it intensifies the color.

I must be staring because his lips curve upward.

Oh, my God… are those dimples at the side of his smile?

I think I died and went to heaven!

No, stupid—the only place you are going to is the deepest part of the inferno. What the melon is wrong with you, Nora?

The little angel on my shoulder speaks out, but the devil wants to come out and play.

I don't usually look at other men. Sure, I might glance at a handsome guy now and then. I also comment on attractive actors, but I always do this in front of my husband. I know Rick wouldn't like me noticing any of the details. Luka's jaw is tight, his lips are wide, and he looks a bit pale. That's probably from dehydration. His brows and lashes are thick, too. His skin is the color of a cappuccino, and yes, I do my tones in coffee references, sue me! He gives off the whole Jack Reacher vibe, and I don't mean the Tom Cruise one…

After I disclosed that Dec had autism, Luka shared no comment, something I deeply appreciate. Usually, people go with three different strategies when I share the diagnosis. First one is '*But he looks normal*', second '*was it because of the vaccine*?', and third, which is also my personal favorite, '*everyone is a bit autistic*'.

And when Dec gave him a high five, my heart short-circuited. I wasn't even there anymore. A blabbermouth took my place, and at some point, I lost track of what the melon I was talking about.

His eyes turn to mine, though I have to tilt my head up to meet his gaze fully. He's tall, so tall, towering over me. If we lined up, my nose would be right between his nipples. Now I can't help but think about them. What in the melon is wrong with me?

Help! Please!

A chuckle escapes him, and I flinch at it, petrified that he might have read my mind somehow, which causes my cheeks to blush—one of my many character flaws. My cheeks are sneaky little bastards in full-on betrayal mode. Whenever I feel nervous, put on the spot, horny, or sad, my cheeks demonstrate all the reds on the palette. I can feel the warmth covering the flesh on my face, and that's my cue to escape the situation.

"Does he want to sit in it?" Luka's ruffled yet gentle voice snaps me out of the current trance only to put me in another, more dangerous one…

Boy, am I demented!

"Hm?"

"The truck, would he want to sit in it?"

"Oh," I mumble, sounding like I am disappointed or something. I have to give myself a mental slap because my mind went somewhere it definitely shouldn't have gone.

Bad girl!

"That's ok, you don't have to do it. He likes to watch."

"It's not a problem, all the workers are already gone, and since I am the boss, I am allowed to do whatever I want."

The way he's said the word *'boss'* tingles in my ear, and I quickly erase it from my brain cells.

"Well, if that's the case, we'd much prefer the crane. He loves them, but they are on the inside, so he usually looks from afar."

That gets him to share a smile, and fudge me if it isn't a mixture of pants dropping and heart melting.

A sharp pang of guilt hits deep because in no way am I in any capacity supposed to like anybody else's smile other than my husband's, even if I haven't seen one in a while.

"I could arrange that, but you would have to put a hard hat on."

"Thought you said all the workers left." Why I am arguing with him is beyond me, and I flinch, preparing for him to lash out.

To my surprise, his voice remains calm and steady. "Safety first. I wouldn't want anything to happen to the two of you."

Protective. Great.

Well, I might as well start digging my grave.

"Ok, I guess." I shrug as he goes to unlock the gate. He opens it for us to enter and tells us to wait there before he disappears into one of the containers. A minute later, he's back with one hard hat in each hand.

"Luckily, I have student workers, so we have small ones." He hands one to me, then gets down in a squat and places the other on Dec's head. I prepare for a protest that never comes, which stuns me.

That's new.

Dec doesn't like people, especially men. It takes him a long time to adjust to others, yet he seems at ease around Luka.

Wrapped up in the yellow HDPE, we stride further around the site and halt in front of the smallest of the three cranes. Luka turns to face me with wonder in his eyes, a bit of mischief in them as well, before he bubbles, "Do you want to go up?"

"What?" I can feel my eyes widening at his question.

"Do you want to climb up? I would be with both of you every step of the way."

Something about him, the way he carries himself, and his calming voice, makes him seem trustworthy. I don't know how it's possible to have that sort of trust over a person I met—what was it—ten, fifteen minutes ago? Without much overthinking, I nod, and he makes way for me to pass him.

"You go first, then Declan and I will follow." He motions with his hand in the direction of the stairs.

I give him another nod and wrap my hands around the railing, ceasing my foot mid-air, rethinking.

"It's ok, I got him," he reassures.

That confirms it. The guy is a mind reader. Great! Just what I need. The second my ring clinks on the steel, shame consumes me. I shake it all away and start my climb, looking over my shoulder with each step, checking on Dec, with a glance at Luka.

When we reach the operator's cab, my discoverer takes over the controls, and I immediately try to pull him away, but am stopped by a chuckle. It is the softest sound that somehow vibrates through my entire body.

"It's ok, let him. It's turned off, so he can play with the buttons."

"Oh," I murmur, letting go of Dec, allowing him to enter his explorer mode. He opens everything possible, presses all the buttons, and experiments with the entire turntable or whatever the correct terminology is. My smile gets to its full extension at the look of one very amused and happy little boy, who is my whole life. Somehow, I can feel Luka's eyes on me, but I brush the thought away. I focus everything I have on my son, so oblivious to his mother being the worst person in the world.

Chapter 3

Luka

If someone told me that a simple smile would turn my day around, I would've laughed in their face. And yet, here I am, transfixed by a beam that lit up something within me, I thought was long extinguished. I always wanted a family of my own—a house full of kids that I'd raise with the love of my life. But along the way, those dreams faded, only for them to come back, sparked by the purity of one boy.

Blindsided by the pair occupying the cab of the crane, my mind races with hope.

She's married with a kid!

My newest mantra isn't working. Even with the notion hovering, pretty much screaming at me, I am unable to look away. That smile, the wrinkles at the sides of her eyes as she watches Declan play around the consoles. She seems happy, but if you look deeply enough, there's an overwhelming sense that she is putting effort into hiding the sadness and pain. Not physical pain, but something holding her back, or eating her from the inside. A big part of me wants to figure it out.

In some way, spending the last 30 minutes in her vicinity changed my whole chemistry. The fact that she trusted me without hesitation rattles me. From the first moment our eyes met, she was right there looking into my eyes like they were open doors. I felt her stare in all the right places.

"Spaceship," Declan shouts, his voice a bit robotic. His mother laughs next to him and doesn't correct him. It makes me feel all warm and fuzzy…

Why?

"Yeah, buddy, feels like it, doesn't it?" She squats down just as he lifts his hand and points with a crooked finger.

"Mama, crane!"

"Yeah, Bug, you're inside a crane," she bubbles, rubbing a hand over his upper back.

They laugh together, and it's the best song ever to exist. Why the hell is this happening to me? Why does a simple sound of someone's laughter make me feel so alive?

Perhaps because you'll be going home alone, with no one waiting for you.

Okay, my mother and my brothers will be there, but they don't count.

"Let's go to the cement mixer and then home, it's getting late." Her soft voice makes me blink, and I realize the day has slipped away from us.

How did that happen?

As we go down, I take the lead. It helps me control things if someone slips.

This day feels like a Twilight Zone episode. It started as one of my worst days, but ended up being one of my favorites. I can't help but grin widely.

"Thank you for this. You made his day." She smiles at me in that genuine way, and yet, it doesn't reach her eyes.

"It was nothing, really."

I should be the one thanking you.

That's what I want to say, but I bite my tongue.

"So you do this often? Prowling around construction sites, I mean?"

"When we have one on the way, sure. We discovered this one a month ago; it's on our route home from his therapy." She looks at Declan, pure love screaming out of her. "Usually it's closed when we get here, so I deemed it to be perfect." She shrugs, adding, "We don't like to get in other people's way."

"You're always welcome here! But it's best to avoid busy hours. Things can get pretty hectic."

"I bet. It looks like it's going to be huge."

"Yeah, an apartment complex, 12 stories high."

"Wow, big commitment right there." She bobs her head, showing genuine intrigue.

We have entered small talk mode, great. If you haven't picked up on that, that's sarcasm…

"How can I thank you?"

"No need, it was my pleasure, honest." And I mean it. The look on Declan's face is something I never knew I needed, skyrocketing this day to the top.

Without warning, rain starts pouring, making me groan. She lets out a loud, hearty laugh just as Declan starts jumping up and down, mouth open and tongue out. Not much can be done to cover ourselves, but judging by the looks of the two of them, they don't want any cover-up.

Her head falls back, welcoming each drop like a gift from the sky. I take a deep breath, drinking it all in. Looking at her feels freeing.

"Do you need a ride?" I blurt, rethinking my offer because I'm not sure if Declan would be safe in my work truck without a kid's car seat.

"Oh no, it's not necessary, we like walking in the rain."

"Seriously?" My question comes out more like a squeal.

"Oh yeah, and we also like jumping in puddles."

"Puddleeeee," Declan exalts, causing a flutter inside my chest.

"Thank God I predicted the weather and got him into his rain boots."

"You predicted?"

"Yeah, I'm like the Lorelai Gilmore of rain."

I chuckle, and her eyebrows flare upward as her jaw drops.

"You understood the reference?"

"You mean how you can smell rain as opposed to her smelling the snow?"

"Oh my God, I can't believe you got that."

You would if you knew my mother. I keep that thought to myself, thankful my Mama made me watch all her shows with her.

"One of my many talents." I give a playful shrug.

"Well, now I'm all sorts of curious," she marvels, unbothered by the darn rain. I take a moment to try and see what she's seeing. Feel what she's feeling. The droplets are warm, and it's as if my brain rewires. I always thought rain was cold. My shirt clings to my skin, something that would bother me on any given day. Not now. Not today.

"Perhaps we could leave it to our next encounter?" I let the question out into the universe.

Hopefully sooner rather than later.

"Perhaps." She lifts her face to the sky again, allowing the droplets to wash her face. We're soaking wet, except they are happy about it.

"Thank you again for everything."

"You're welcome. I guess I'll see you around."

"Guess so."

She turns around holding Declan's hand tightly, but I can't get myself to do the same. I watch their slow walk turn into a skipping session, and I let out a chuckle.

In that moment, something happens to my heart, something I am pretty sure never happened before.

It starts to beat.

Just before they're about to turn around the corner, Nora yells, "Hey, Luka?"

"Hm?" I yell-humm.

"How do you like your coffee?"

"Black?" It ends up sounding like I posed a question.

"Sugar?"

Where is she going with this?

"None."

"Thanks, Bye!"

"Bye." I wave, puzzled.

"Bye." Declan waves with his little hand as well, and then they're gone.

Chapter 4

Nora

I wrestle the door open with one hand, the other holding Dec, who is damp and giggling into my hip. My dress clings to my skin, soaked through, and my hair is all frizzy, but I don't care.

"We're home," I shout. "We got ambushed," I add with a breathless laugh, kicking the door shut behind me.

No answer.

"Total downpour, plus every puddle was ours."

Nothing.

I help Dec wiggle out of his wet clothes and send him butt-naked to the bathroom.

"Rick?"

I find him in his usual spot, the far end of the couch. Arms crossed, eyes fixed on the TV.

"It's almost seven," he remarks, giving me a sideways glance.

"The clouds rolled in, and you know how Dec likes the rain, plus you're never gonna believe it... We got to play in the crane, the owner, Luka—"

Killing my excitement, he interrupts with a scowl, "What's for dinner?"

Is he blind?

I am still soaking wet, evident by the water dripping all over the floor.

"You did see that I just got home, right? I haven't made any dinner yet," I point out. He's not even looking at me; the TV is more interesting, as per usual.

"You didn't text."

"Since when do I need to text?"

Considering he can't even be bothered to memorize a simple weekly schedule.

"Since I came home, no dinner, no idea where you are."

And there it is.

I stand there, shivering. "So you're mad because there was no dinner, or that I stayed longer outside with our son instead of rushing home to meet your expectations?"

I see the tension in his jaw. "Don't twist this into some noble parenting thing. It's about respect."

As if you know anything about respect.

"Rick, I get that you're tired. I was out in the rain, chasing every drop, watching him light up. That counts for something, right?"

"Great, you had fun," he scoffs, flipping through the channels. "Meanwhile, I come home to an empty house with nothing to eat."

I stare at him, the ache creeping behind my eyes—not from this fight, but from the fact that this is where we are—*again*. Like nothing I do counts unless it fits into his idea of what a good wife should be.

"I'm gonna change Dec," I say quietly, "and then I'll make you something."

A grunt followed by some loud huffing and puffing coming

from his spot on the couch gets every hair on my body to rise. I clench my teeth, commanding my mouth to stay shut because I don't want to spend the evening fighting over nothing. I go into my usual wife mode, faking my smile. "What do you want?"

Silence.

"Sandwich it is," is the last thing I say before I walk away.

After dinner, we dove into our nighttime routine. I read Dec his daily Disney story and cashed in my ten kisses before giving him ten of my own. Turning on the nightlight and switching off the main one, I said goodnight and closed the door. When I walked into the living room, I felt relieved to find Rick lying on the couch, comatose.

It has been like this for quite some time, and as much as I don't want to seem or sound malicious, I can't help but feel like such. It started over a year ago, when Dec figured out how to get out of his crib and come to our bed. He'd get nightmares and wake us up. So Rick took over the couch, and he's been sleeping there ever since. I still sleep on my side of the bed, hoping that he will fill the space beside me.

With both my boys sound asleep, I clog the drain. I turn on the faucet and let the tub fill with water, creating bubbles. My current read in hand, I slowly assume my relaxation pose on the ceramic.

The water is as hot as I can take it, which does wonders for my back, one of many chronic pains in my ass—another side effect of being a stubborn, self-reliant person.

Growing up, I was often left to my own devices, which fed my independence. So, I'm used to managing everything myself, even home improvements. Rick could've helped, but only on weekends, and I'm an impatient little sucker. My own hands did all the furniture assembly, something I refrain from in public, so that he could keep his macho card.

Don't get me wrong, Rick is a hard worker, our sole provider, the reason we have a roof over our heads and can afford all of Declan's therapies. I love the man with all my heart, but that doesn't change the fact that I've surrendered. The process was slow, diminishing everything that used to be me.

The past me, the one before the '*I does*' would sucker punch the current version of me. Probably do some real damage to the face, break some fingers, bitch slap or two... I have only myself to blame, and I know it, yet I still choose to live it, let it define me as nothing but a wife and a mother. Hide the pitchforks and put out the fire. I love being a mother; it's my dream come true, challenges and all. But being a wife? That didn't pan out as I had hoped.

Soaking in the bathtub, surrounded by foam, I read the same paragraph over and over. As I do, I feel another crack. I toss the paperback, and it hits the tiled wall with a thwack before it falls face-first on the floor.

I miss my husband, who is sleeping just down the stairs.

How messed up is that? He's right there, and I miss him.

I am embarrassed to say I can't even remember the last time we kissed.

I know he loves me, but the problem here is that I am not so sure it's enough, at least not for me, not anymore. How can it be, when he makes me feel unappreciated and unvalued, and that hurts me more than I dare to admit.

Cinderella

Stuck between the dust and cinder
Lost in the havoc of that one splinter
The torn in my heart
The one you put deep inside

The dreams of a prince, they're long gone
A castle turned into a prison of my own
No throne for me, just the shackles
That never seem to disappear

In the middle of the floor, I'm dancing alone
Empty and hopeless, all dreams gone
No one to hold my hand, no one at all
For Cinderella, I remain
Dusting all my love away
Hoping it would somehow stay

Powerless and weak is my new name
Everything I had you put to shame
Walls built up and here to stay
Turning everyone far away

No white horse or carriage
No pumpkin and no magic
Fairy godmother left me behind
Leaving me alone to rewind

In the middle of the floor, I am dancing alone
Empty and hopeless, all dreams gone
No one to hold my hand, no one at all
For Cinderella, I remain

Lena Knight

Dusting all my love away
No more hoping for it to stay

Chapter 5

Luka

"Morning," I say through a yawn. The only person who wakes up around the same time I do is Mak. He's doing his residency and has the worst working hours, though you'll never hear him complain. With the rest of the house silent, Mak pours two cups of coffee and hands me mine with a breathy "morning."

Two sips in and he finally looks up, frowning, "You look flushed; everything ok?"

No. I barely slept; the little high five haunted my dreams, mixed with Nora's smile in the rain.

"Yeah, please don't doctor me, at least not for another five more sips." It sounds like I'm begging, my eyes fighting to stay open.

"No, dude, this doesn't look medical, though it does seem chronic," he tells me with a straightforward tone.

"Just tired, work's a pain, and drowning," I respond, the level of my energy too low to come up with anything better.

"Doesn't look work-related." He tilts his head to the side, giving me a once-over.

"Stop analyzing me," I snap, dropping my head.

"Morning," Tristan, our youngest brother, joins us in the kitchen wearing his PJs.

"Why are you up so early?" Mak asks him with raised

brows.

Tristan likes his beauty sleep, so it's a valid question.

"Early practice. Coach mad. Played bad."

He is in his last year of high school, a big-shot quarterback with many prospects. He's the second athlete in the family, after Tyler, who's a college basketball player on his way to the pros.

Mak hands Tristan a freshly filled mug, and he chugs it like it's pure H2O. With the last drop, his eyes flare, and his signature grin appears on his jock face.

"No way?" he gasps. It sounds like a question, a very annoying question.

"What?" Mak sputters.

"No way!" This time, Tristan makes it a point.

"What?" Mak jabs it again and then shares a look with Tristan.

I'm fucked.

"Spill, who's the girl?"

"I don't know what you're talking about," I feign ignorance.

They both turn to face me, crossing their arms over their chest while still holding their mugs. I know what's coming. It's a routine we have whenever one of us feels a spark. It started in Tyler's junior year, when he turned into a heartbreaker.

"Hair?" Tristan with the first stab.

I give in with a sigh. "Brownish, like a light caramel meets honey."

"Eyes?" down to Mak.

"Hazel."

"Mouth?" Tristan again.

"Belong to her husband."

"Oh shit!" Tristan exclaims just as Mak growls a "Damn."

"Yup," popping the P, I nod without stopping, like the action will make it sink in more.

"How did that happen?" Mak wonders with genuine concern.

"Her kid's obsessed with the cement mixer; they were at the site when I was locking up." I go soft, smiling at the memory, those brown eyes locked on the baller, a twinkle in them. A warm feeling rushes through me.

"She's got a kid?" they both blurt out at the same time, down to the tone and volume.

"Yeah, he's so cute," I gush, "has autism. Gave me a high five." I puff out my chest, like it's some big deal, which it is—to me.

"Good for you, big brother, but what the heck?" Tristan shrieks, finishing it off with a tsk.

"What?"

"You can't go there, you know that, right?" Mak jumps in with his two cents.

As if I need another reminder. I spent the whole night trying to convince myself of the same thing, but only ended up dreaming of an impossible happy ending.

"I know, don't worry. It just took me by surprise, that's all," I disclose.

"Right," he drags it out, not convinced, much like me.

Checking my watch, I sigh in relief when I note the time that gives me an actual excuse to leave this conversation. I wave goodbye to my nosy brothers and head out.

I get my pick-up back today from the shop, so at least I have that going for me.

My drive is quick, with little traffic, the radio in the background, and the volume low. My work truck doesn't have Bluetooth, so I can't connect it to my phone, leaving me at the mercy of whatever is on the FM.

When I arrive at the site, a couple of guys are already in the middle of their morning gossip.

"Morning, boss."

"Morning, Rick, Morty."

That one gets a laugh out of both of them. Thankfully, most of my workers are around my age, born in the year starting with 19, so they understand most of what I'm saying. These kids today wouldn't know a pun if it smacked them in the nose.

"What's with the faces?" They have bizarre looks on them, something between a grin and the *'I know something you don't'* scorning smile.

"Nothing," they chuckle, and that reaction gets my jaw tense.

"Oh, hi," the familiar soft voice comes from behind me, and when I turn, it suddenly all makes sense.

"Hi," I greet her back as I take her in. Her hair is pulled back into a ponytail, and she's wearing the same red sneakers she had the first time I saw her, except this time she's not wearing a dress. She has a simple blue oversized shirt that covers the upper portion of her short leggings. Declan doesn't notice me, looking around like he's seeing the place for the first time.

"I brought you coffee to say thanks for yesterday. Those two got jealous, so I got them some too," she spills. I turn to glare at them, ready to threaten. They freeze, reading my expression immediately.

Good!

She walks toward them, tray in one hand, the other holding her son.

"The big ones are yours," she tells them softly, offering the tray so they can take their cups. Then she turns around and closes in on me, a full smile plastered on her face.

"I got you another one in case the first one got cold."

"Why?" I utter, regretting the question as soon as it escaped my mouth.

Why? Why?

That's all I could come up with? Seriously?

Just say thank you.

My inner thoughts are more refined than my actual self.

When I take the tray, our fingers brush, and it shouldn't cause my entire body to light up, but it does. It was the slightest of touches, yet I felt its potency, its strength deep inside.

"Like I said…" she hesitates, combing a strand of hair behind her ear. "To say thank you for yesterday."

How is this woman real?

"So you got here at this hour and got me coffee?" Great, now I'm scolding. What is this woman doing to me?

"Oh, don't worry, Declan wakes up at six on the dot every single day… has been since he was two. Yay for me!" She looks at her boy with a twinkle in her eye and lifts her hands midway, performing a shy, celebratory wave.

"You didn't have to do that."

"I know, I wanted to."

That's nice of her, platonic nice, nothing to read into.

Nothing at all.

"Thank you."

"You're welcome."

She turns her wrist and checks the time. The watch face is on the underside where the pulse line is. It shows something hidden under the strap. Curious, I practically whoop out, "What's that?"

She wiggles her wrist, letting the watch slide down a bit. Then, she lifts it to my eye level. I check out the details and breathe in her perfume, vanilla, and something else. Her tattoo is as simple as it is complicated. The infinity sign is composed of puzzle pieces in a spectrum of colors.

"The colored puzzles are a symbol for autism, and the infinity is the love I have for the dude," she explains with a beam. Of course, she would mark her love and wear it proudly. I wonder if there are others.

"Do you have more tattoos?"

"Oh yes!" she exclaims, "I have one around my ankle, one behind my neck, one under my left boob, and one down my right lateral side."

I heard everything she said, honest, but somehow the image of something under her left boob stuck.

"Do you have any?"

"Luka!"

"Hm?"

"You were thinking about my left boob, weren't you?"

She wasn't angry about it, more like playful, teasing. It's not lost on me, this comfort level we have around each other, even after only one brief encounter.

"Do you have any?" she repeats, and I clear my throat.

"Right… Yeah."

A large percentage of my skin is covered with ink, mainly to conceal my past. But I'm not going to tell her that. "I have a couple spread across my chest, one on my back, one on my shoulder, and one on each calf."

One tilt of a head, raking of the lower lip, and narrowed eyes would indicate her doing some heavy imagining.

"Chest?" I probe, and she shakes her head.

"Calves, actually," she drags it out.

I raise one brow. "Really?"

"I'm as surprised as you are."

"Hm."

"Hm." She tilts her head to the other side and smirks. That action isn't supposed to cause a flutter within, and most definitely not make my cheeks burn.

I am a man, for crying out loud, I don't blush.

"So what are you up to?"

"I'm gonna grab a coffee for myself and take Dec to the playground."

"Playground? This early?"

"Yeah, I prefer it that way. It's usually deserted this time of day, so it allows him to do whatever he wants and me actually to sit down while he plays."

"What's it like when it's full?" I ask, curious.

"Terrible. Most parents don't pay too much attention, so I have to keep an eye on every kid out there, interfere when necessary, not to mention shadow my kid."

I can't even imagine what it must be like for her to be in a constant state of worry and alertness.

"Wow, intense."

"Tell me about it."

"You're amazing," I mutter, my filter deciding to malfunction.

"Where did that come from?"

"Just an observation."

"Well, stop observing, it's giving me the heebie-jeebies."

"Noted," I chortle.

"Good… Bye, Luka."

"Bye, Nora. Bye, Declan."

"Bye, guys," she hollers, giving my workers a wave. I provide them a firm scowl.

"Bye, Nora," they both yell back with a grin and a wave.

Two coffees in hand, one warm-ish, one cold, I beeline to my office for the time being. Placing the two cups on the desk, I take a seat, dropping my head in my hands.

What the hell is wrong with me? It's the question of the day. My heart is still pounding. The weight on my chest is like a large rock pressing on my lungs, not giving me any room for breathing, driving me insane. On the bright side, I might not see her again. But on the flip side, there's a good chance I'll never see her again.

Chapter 6

Nora

Oh, the playground... how I love the playground in the morning, all deserted and quiet. Declan's favorite toy—monkey bars, mine—the bench. The playground we vacate is my favorite. Why, you ask? It's secluded and gated, which gives me a sense of safety. The barrier keeps my little daredevil on the inside, letting me loosen the imaginary leash.

The sun is starting to warm up the day, and I take my seat on the corner bench just as Dec starts his sprint in the direction of the spiral slide. Right here is where he feels most free, having the entire area to himself. He has the freedom to explore, be himself, and me? I can breathe, drink my coffee hot, listen to my book... and all that while keeping my eye on the happiest kid on this planet.

After going over all the stations for one hour straight, he finally settles into the sandbox. This is the only activity I am allowed to join. I sit beside him and start building a sandcastle, knowing damn well it will be destroyed the second I remove the bucket. That's us. I build. He tears down. But he does it with the widest smile, and that's good enough for me.

Overstimulated by the sand, we walk home, hand in hand, enjoying the hot rays on our skin. It's times like these that I'm grateful for our small entryway. It's the perfect spot to leave behind anything from the outside, like rain, snow, or, in this case, sand.

We dispose of our clothes and head straight to the bathroom. This calls for a quick shared shower, something Dec is not the biggest fan of. He likes his bubble baths, and he likes them long, just like his mama. Much to his dismay, today is not a bath-time day; it's more of a 'get rinsed as fast as possible' day.

We get into the tub, and I turn on the shower, letting the warm water spray us from above. It takes some extra time, getting rid of all the sand from Dec's hair since it's super thick, and thankfully, he's not complaining. All clean, we step outside together, and I work the large towel, getting him dried, while we both sing our favorite bath-time song from Cocomelon. We get dressed and head downstairs, where I turn on the TV and put on our favorite show, Bluey. And yes, I do mean our. It's not only for the kids but also for the parents, and I am grateful that such a thing exists. I can't tell you how many times I cried watching it. Funny thing, some episodes make me feel appreciated as a parent, and I find it bittersweet that something animated can accomplish what my husband never has.

We watch two episodes before Dec's eyes start closing involuntarily, so I pick him up and carry him to his room. He doesn't stir when I tuck him in, not even when I kiss his little forehead. I grab the baby monitor and head down to work on lunch.

I open the fridge with a sigh, scanning its contents. After a quick inventory, the decision is made.

Risotto it is.

The vibration of my phone halts my intense carrot-chopping, and I check the screen. I smile when my Discord app lights it up again.

Sunny: *Are you serious with this?*

Last year, I found an online group of mothers with children with disabilities. It felt good not to feel alone. We shared stories, experiences, workings of medications… pretty much everything. There was one mother in the group I felt most connected with, so after a while, we started DM-ing.

I wipe my hands and send out a quick reply.

Me: *Chapter 25?*

Sunny: *Was the point of this book recommendation to have someone to share the trauma or something?*

Yes.

Me: *Maybe*

Sunny: *Tell me it gets better*

Me: *Isn't life's favorite thing to make things worse before they get better?*

I toss the chopped carrots into the pot and turn to the meat. Halfway through slicing it into perfect little cubes, my phone dings.

Sunny: *Oh no, you're in your philosophical era. I can't with that.*

I smile and mix the meat with the carrots and onion, stirring it all with a wooden spoon. As soon as the pork starts releasing its juices, I add water and reduce the heat to let it simmer.

Me: *I'm trying to get you distracted. But to answer your question, it gets better in the end; you just have to endure some more pain in the meantime.*

Sunny: *I am never trusting your recommendations again. EVER*

Me: *We'll get back to it when you finish*

Sunny: *Anyway, how's your week been*

Me: *We fought again*

Sunny: *What was it this time?*

It took me a while to open up to Sunny, especially since I couldn't do it with my best friends. It's hard. As it happens, my best friend is married to my husband's sister, who is my other best friend, by the way. So I can't just go on and tell them that I am miserable, now, can I? As much as I love the people closest to me, there are some parts of my life I can never share. Aside from the embarrassment, it's the guilt that keeps my mouth shut. Even on the hardest days, all I can allow myself is to put it on paper. I have a box of letters, an inspiration I got from a book, all waiting to be read. A few months ago, I actually grew a pair and gave one to Rick. I poured myself into the words, my pen taking all the emotions with it, while my soul begged for his effort. The hardest words come back in a flash.

I'm not asking for grand gestures. I'm just asking for us. I know we've both changed over the years, but love isn't about staying the same, right? It's about choosing each other, again and again, even as we change. I don't just want to live with you; I want to <u>live</u> with you.

I underlined the last line three times. He cried, I cried, and he promised to try, which he did, for about a week before turning back to his regular self.

Me: *Same old, same old. How's your week going?*

Sunny: *Well, I got the job.*

Sunny is a psychologist. She put her career on hold to take care of her daughter with Down Syndrome. She's a single mom; her ex left them right after she gave birth. The bastard. Ana, her daughter, will be starting school in September, giving Sunny the free time to work.

Me: *I knew you would. I am so proud of you.*

Sunny: *Thank you, that means the world to me.*

When Dec wakes up, he goes straight to the playroom. It was originally designed as a walk-in pantry, but we converted it into a small playroom. It has a cozy reading nook, an IKEA Trofast storage combination with all of Dec's favorite toys, and a security camera connected to my phone so I can keep an eye on him at all times.

While Dec plays, I quickly go to check on lunch. Just as I'm about to have a taste, a loud thunk makes me jolt.

I rush to the playroom and turn on my CSI brain. After a quick check over his body, I let out a breath: no blood, no bruises, nothing.

Whoosh!

I wipe my forehead and continue scanning. His dinosaur encyclopedia on the third shelf is sticking out, as if he tried to grab it but failed. The stack of blocks is scattered across the floor, telling me he got angry and tossed them aside. I slide the book out and hand it to him, but he doesn't take it; instead, he gives me a frown.

"Oh, I get it. You wanted the one next to it," I conclude, going back to the shelf to return the book. When I try to take out the one he wanted, it takes a bit of force to slide it out, so I understand his frustration. I hand him the one about the horses, and I get a jump with a smile so wide, my heart sparks up. I can't quite explain it, that feeling I get anytime I understand his needs, wants, or wishes. I give myself a pat on the back, figuratively, and go to the kitchen to finish lunch, pleased with myself, fulfilled even.

Your World

Empty eyes, no blink in sight
Arms ready for the longest flight
Empty eyes, pupils wide
Not a shred of fear to hide

Could you show me how you see the stars?
How strong are the bars
Could you show me the way you feel it all?
Let me in, I won't let you fall.

Please let me step on the bridge
Allow me to get closer
To be a part of what matters
A part of your world

Empty eyes, never fading.
Gazing, searching, anticipating
Empty eyes that never fade
Whatever imagination has made

Please let me step on the bridge
Allow me to get closer
To be a part of what matters
A part of your world

Chapter 7

Nora

My early mornings are routined.

Get the meal for Rick packed for work, make coffee, keep an eye on Declan, forget you made said coffee, and end up drinking it cold.

Rinse and repeat.

My little bugger is already awake—full throttle, jumping all over me. I hear a clunking noise coming from the kitchen. Rubbing my eyes, I drag myself to check the cause, only to be welcomed by one angry Rick.

Great, what did I do now?

"Why didn't you pack my lunch?" he snaps, and I immediately recoil.

Shoot! Fudge! Shoot!

"I'm sorry, but you did witness last night, right?" That one makes his nostrils flare, and my blood boil.

After a short visit to the doctor's office for his regular monthly quick blood check, Declan wouldn't stop screaming the entire ride home... It kept going the rest of the evening, until he finally collapsed in my lap.

My hair is a mess, and I smell due to another night without a shower, and, yes, I haven't even had a chance to brush my teeth.

"It took him forever to calm down. It was way past one when he finally closed his eyes, and I collapsed right there with him on his bed."

My back sure feels the consequences of the night.

"So?"

Don't do it! Don't do it!

You have hands. I want to yell. *All you have to do is get a container out and put the contents of the pot into it.*

But per usual, that is not what I do. No, I open the cabinet, take out the Tupperware, fill it, and hand it to the angriest man alive.

And there goes the cold shoulder.

He tosses the container into the sink and disappears, leaving me frozen in place. A year ago, I would've cried about it, cuddled myself in the corner, and sobbed through. Nowadays, I can't seem to find any tears; I guess they've stopped caring, too. Once again, I am left with my thoughts spinning around in my head. Wrong kinds of thoughts, like '*Why didn't I wake up sooner?*' or my personal favorite, '*Why can't I do anything right?*'

Before, I would put up a fight, try to reason with him, make him understand. It would turn out to be pointless, since he couldn't seem to hear or understand my pleas. 'Cause the devil doesn't bargain, right? Now, I go for the usual—I give up, and get rewarded with the silent treatment.

Is it wrong of me to welcome his blackballing? Sure, yet here I am, happy to get it because it gives me some peace of mind.

My little man runs into the kitchen, demanding milk, which in Declan's talk means cereal. He has a special way of naming things. For example, he loves eating those jerky sticks and calls them logs. I find it innovative; I mean, they do look like logs. There are also those soup pearls, which he calls acorns. Again, hats off for his logic there.

He is my heart, and I am his voice, i.e., interpreter. Few have the privilege of understanding the language he speaks, but I am fluent and proud of it. I graduated in everything that is Declan, down to his unspoken intentions and wants. I can understand his one look better than any movie with audio description. It's both a gift and a curse. I don't mean to sound evil, cruel, or anything like it, but the life of a mother of a special needs child is not an easy one. There is a lot of resentment felt daily, not to mention the constant fear of failure.

Through a yawn, I fill a bowl with milk and warm it up in the microwave. Unlike me, Declan is a morning person, waking up at the same time every day, like clockwork. No matter if he falls asleep at eight, ten, or one in the morning, he'll be waking up at six sharp.

Sleep deprivation is now part of my DNA, since I have no idea what actual sleep looks like anymore. My body has adjusted to the rhythm, and coffee provides the energy I need to continue. Before Dec, I wasn't a coffee fan. Now, I need it more than water—no, screw that, I need it more than I need air.

From my spot across the table, I watch him eat, a few drops of milk falling around the bowl. He cleans it up, leaving no trace.

We've come a long way.

Dec is a force of nature, in the best way possible. His

energy, unfortunately, never matches mine, since mine is nonexistent. The recently turned five little bundle of havoc is my life and soul.

I love the kid with all my heart. That love can't chase away the demons. I worry I'm not good enough for him. Anger, guilt, and fear of the worst haunt me. And let's not forget about the ten different scenarios my mind conjures each minute, thinking of all the worst outcomes. It's something of an art form that comes with the territory. The things that come to Declan's mind are downright menacing, and I am the one in charge of hampering them.

Looking at him, it's hard not to rewind. The day he was born was the happiest day of my life; the day we got the written confirmation of our doubts was my worst. My thoughts when I read his diagnosis were filled with dread. All the dreams shattered, all the hopes faded at the simple written word, and all the negativity took over. So many tears were shed in all the wrong ways. I still hate that version of me. She went to the worst places, believing her child would never be normal.

Normal - oh, how I hate that word.

My head went through a rollercoaster of emotions, all directed toward a three-year-old and all he might miss out on. Thankfully, I snapped myself out of such thoughts and turned all my attention to doing what was best for him. All of my efforts were directed toward his happiness, and I am proud to say that, despite everything, Dec is one happy kid. Sure, he stacks his cars rather than rides them, prefers spinning the ball to bouncing it, and is more interested in turning the wheel of a bike than riding it, but that makes him more fun to look at.

I embrace anything out of the norm, skipping all that is labeled as typical. I buy him toys he can stack and spin, and watch him in awe as he does just that. Not one moment of his childhood post-diagnosis was spent by me telling him 'not like that' or 'do it like this'. I am the one following his lead, not the other way around. Slowly, that mindset allowed me to be welcomed in.

We have a special bond, one that I am so thankful for. Unlike most people with the same diagnosis, Declan is a cuddly little thing. He loves my hugs and never escapes my touch, and it's the one thing I prayed for. My love language is physical touch, and when I read about what autism stood for, down to all the bad things about it, the lack of physical contact was the thing that caught my eye. It was a selfish thing, but thinking back, I wouldn't change the silent prayers I sent out to the universe. The day he said 'mama' turned out to be the second-best day of my life, one I never thought would happen.

Every milestone is celebrated. It may seem over the top to outsiders, but we don't care. His accomplishments are greatly appreciated, and every day with him is a gift, even the bad ones.

"Playground?"

I don't even finish my question; he's on his feet so fast, jumping up and down in excitement. We get ready together, and I can see his impatience taking over, so I work faster. Outside, we start our walk to our favorite place. The traffic light turns red, and we halt next to a woman pushing a stroller. A cute baby girl peeks out, clapping her hands.

My mind takes me back to Declan around that age, when

I first began to have suspicions. Even as a baby, I knew something was off, but everyone told me I was overreacting. As he grew, so did my intuition, and by the time he turned one, I was sure, though the official confirmation came way later.

The light turns green, and we cross the street, my hand tightening the grip holding his delicate one.

"I love you just the way you are, my perfect little prince," I coo, the exact words I tell him every night before I put him to bed, and I know he understands them.

Chapter 8

Luka

The site is quiet. Everyone has already left, and I am in the middle of doing the safety check.

My phone buzzes in my pocket. I pull off my gloves, flex my fingers, and grab it. Mateo's name lights up the screen.

"Wanna grab a beer?" The bad signal makes his voice static over the line.

"Maybe later," I reply, checking the time. I can hear his smirk over the line. "Still chasing the ghost, huh?"

I don't answer. Let him think whatever he wants. I shouldn't be waiting around, but I do, a bit longer, every single day.

"I'll call you when I'm done here." I leave it at that and hang up in the middle of his chuckle. He knows me well, too well.

With the sun spreading the heat, I step out from under the scaffold, my boots crunching over the gravel. Everything in me is tired, not just my muscles.

Then I see them.

I rub my eyes, pinch myself even, then blink profusely to make sure it isn't a mirage. Right there, across the street, Nora is kneeling, tying Declan's shoelace. No rush, taking her time to make sure it's tight. And just like that, I forget about the ache in my back.

I straighten up and cross the street.

She looks up as I step onto the curb.

"Hey," I say, my nerves making my breath uneven.

"Hi." She blinks like she hasn't expected me, then smiles. A genuine smile, small, almost reaching her eyes.

We stand there for a second. The quiet second when no one talks, but the silence speaks.

"You guys coming from therapy?" I ask, taking a knee in front of Declan, the green dinosaur set he's wearing, making his eyes pop.

"Yeah. They played with the shaving cream during therapy; it's a sensory thing." She points to his hair, and I note the residue, making it look gooey. I lift my hand, and Declan smacks it with his without blinking. The contact sends a shock to my heart, like a defibrillator bringing me back to life.

"Sounds messy." I lift my gaze to her and straighten up.

"Yeah, but he'll get a bath out of it, so it makes him happy."

I smile at that. How she simplifies everything, all the while turning it to her advantage. Remembering how the two acted in the rain, I quip, "Big fan of water?"

"Yeah, in every shape or form."

"That's not a thing."

"Sure, it is."

"I don't think so."

"Okay, mister smarty-pants."

I want to scold her, but it's impossible; she's too cute for it.

"Working late again?" she asks, her eyes locked on mine.

Her gaze shows all the colors—dominant green, honey red around the black circle, and brown in the corners. It's as if her eyes have three different halos in them, making it impossible to look away.

"Yeah, bad things keep happening, and I have to fix them."

"Hazard of being the boss man."

"Yeah, I guess," I say with a shrug.

"Well, good thing we caught you, then," she rattles on, "Would ice cream fix the mood?"

What mood? I thought I was being nice.

"Ice cream vanilla, walk, blue ice cream," Declan yells, jumping up and down, his hand in full swing mode.

"Well, now we have to go," I thunder, smiling at him. I can't help it; the way his eyes glint pulls my mouth wider.

"There's an ice cream shop around the corner, if you want to join us for a walk."

I don't even hesitate. "I would love that."

I match their pace, and we round the building, the ice cream shop coming into view. It's one of those tiny, family-owned spots with a chalkboard menu and a bell over the door. It smells like childhood.

She orders a scoop of vanilla and one of bubble gum, each in a separate cone. She hands Declan one and holds the other before turning to face me. She nudges me to order, so I glance at the choices. I order a mint chocolate chip, and she gives a little silent scoff.

"What?" I cock a brow.

"You're basically eating toothpaste."

"Have you ever tried it?" I probe, and she shakes her

head. I take the little spoon from a bowl on the counter and fill it with the green cream. I offer it to her, but her hands are full; one cradles Declan while the other grips her cone. Without thinking, I bring it to her mouth, and she takes it without hesitation. I try not to read too much into it, tossing all wrong thoughts aside, and wait.

"Definitely toothpasty," she mocks, and I chuckle.

"Oh," Nora gasps, like she just remembered something. She turns to the elderly woman behind the counter. "Can I have two scoops of chocolate in a to-go container, please?" A minute later, a container is placed between us, and the lady rounds up the bill. I take out my wallet, but Nora stops me. She works fast, handing me her cone so she can pull her phone from her back pocket. She pays with it, leaving no room for negotiation, and stuffs the container into the small bag hanging over her shoulder. We say goodbye before stepping out into the sun. We walk for a while in silence when I notice the lack of licking on her part. Declan is already halfway through his ice cream.

"Why aren't you eating?"

"Oh, this is Dec's. He doesn't like mixing the two flavors, so this is the solution."

"You don't want any?"

"My hands are kinda full." She lifts them for emphasis. Now I feel like a jerk for not figuring this out sooner.

"I'm happy to go back and get you some," I offer, but she shakes her head with a smile.

"That's ok. I'm not much of an ice cream person," she mutters, and I know it's a lie. I let it slide, but file it away for the future.

We cross the street, and Nora lifts her hand to thank the driver for stopping for us at the crosswalk. It's a simple gesture, but it sparks something inside of me. And it gets me thinking. This woman is remarkably selfless and caring. I mean, she brought coffee not only for me, but for my workers, so they wouldn't feel excluded. She holds the door for others… deprives herself of having ice cream just so her son can have two.

As I think of something clever to say, Nora lifts a finger and walks away. She goes directly to the homeless man sitting on a tattered blanket. Right away, I notice he's missing a lower limb.

"Hi, Larry. I brought you your favorite." She squats in front of him, and his face lights up.

"There are my two favorite people," the guy, Larry, beams. She hugs him. His clothes have holes, and he wears an old, worn-out hat. She doesn't mind, though.

She takes the container out of her bag and hands it to him. He waves at Declan, who waves right back before turning to his mother. She reads his expression, and they exchange cones. Declan goes right into his ice cream, and Larry looks right at me, one brow lifting in assessment.

"Am I finally meeting the husband?"

I choke on nothing. And Nora looks flushed, embarrassed maybe!?

"Oh, no. This is my friend Luka," she clarifies, getting back to her feet, and I must say, I'm really starting to hate that word.

I extend my hand, and he takes it. Firmly. "Nice to meet you, Larry."

His smile is honest, his grip almost a plea I see right through. *Take care of her.*

"How is my favorite human?"

I know he's asking about Declan, which only proves my first impression of him. Larry is one of the good ones.

"He's great. It has been a good week," she bubbles, and I wonder how rare those are for her. How often does she have bad ones? How bad do they get? And mostly, why do I care so much? I can't help it, though, no matter how hard I try.

"How are you?" She changes the subject, causing the guy to scoff, as if he expected it.

"Just another day I woke up to," he sighs. Sadness overwhelms me at his words. I don't know his story, but there's so much written in his expression. Loss overpowering it all.

"And what a nice day it is," she quips. He snickers, and I join.

That's Nora for you, turning everything into positive. I step back, giving them some space to catch up, all the while keeping my eyes on their interaction. There's familiarity there, comfort, and I can't help but notice how Nora is different around him, relaxed. They talk for another five minutes or so, and then we say goodbye.

When we turn the corner, I break the silence, blurting out, "That was nice of you."

"It's the least I could do. He's the one who defended our country, lost his leg, only for the same country to turn on him."

Tale as old as time. Good people get stomped on. I have so many questions, so I start with the most obvious one: "Is there not a place he could go or something?"

"Yeah, he only goes there to shower, or when the police make him leave. He always comes back, though."

Trying to wrap my mind around it, I open my mouth, but shut it when she continues, "You know that song 'The man who can't be moved'?" She waits for confirmation, so I nod. "It's like that for him. Before he went to war, he had a girl; she told him she'd wait."

I hear the sadness in her voice, but I ask anyway. "She didn't?"

Nora shakes her head. It's impossible not to see it in her eyes, how much she truly cares for him.

"That was the stop where the bus picked him up, where they said goodbye. So he comes here every day hoping she'd find a way back to him."

"Wow, that's..." I trail off, unable to find the right words to say. But I do know my heart is breaking for him.

"I tried finding her for him, but there are no records with the name he gave me. I think she remarried, but he refuses that notion."

That doesn't surprise me one bit.

"How crazy it must be to love someone so much to wait."

"When it's the right kind of love, I think the wait is worth it, don't you?"

I mull over her words and wonder if I'll ever experience such love.

"Yeah, I guess you're right."

We stop at a crossroad when Declan starts pulling Nora in the opposite direction.

"No Dec, no playground today," she tells him in a soft voice. He starts screaming, punching himself in the chest with his free hand.

I watch in shock as she gets down on her knees, grabs his shoulders, and demands eye contact. Then she starts whisper-screaming, rubbing his arms up and down in a soothing motion. Soon enough, the volume of his scream dials down, and he matches her whispering one.

I am in awe of her. How calm she is, how in tune with him. I would've one hundred percent lost it, panicked, and done the wrong thing.

Nora takes a deep breath, waiting for her son to do the same. He does. Then they exhale together. They repeat the action three times before she stands up again.

"Sorry. His favorite playground is that way," she says, patting Declan's head. "This guy has a great cognitive map and can't be fooled."

Who uses words like 'cognitive map' and 'heebie-jeebies'?

Nora. Nora does.

Chapter 9

Nora

I got him to calm down, but Dec's still pulling me.

"My arm is about to be ripped out of the socket," I grunt.

"Ok, then let's go to the park," Luka says matter-of-factly. Terror washes over me, and he must see it. The playground in the afternoon is my worst nightmare.

"I know it's probably too crowded right now, but I'll be your extra set of eyes and hands."

"Oh no, we should head back, we already dragged you out of your way," I mumble, "and we've taken enough of your time already." I tick a strand of hair behind my ear, averting my gaze to the ground. There's an ant trail crossing my path, taking all the focus.

"You haven't," he argues, "not really."

I lift my head, trying to get a good read on him. He's too nice for his own good.

"I got him; you can trust me."

I do trust you. I want to say it, but think better of it. I barely know him, and yet, there's a bond, like the one I have with Ryan, my best friend since we were five.

I switch my gaze from him to Dec's pleading eyes and back to Luka, all calm and collected, and when he flashes those dimples at me, I can't help but buckle.

The walk to the park is short, and when I open the gate, my boy bolts straight for the monkey bars. Luka rushes after him, yelling over his shoulder, "You stay."

I do as I'm told, finding a spot that gives me the perfect view of my surroundings. I watch as Luka keeps a protective stance while Dec swings from one bar to the other, his laugh echoing throughout the entire park.

Then my son starts sprinting, with Luka following suit and keeping up with ease. I bet he won't even break a sweat, unlike me. You'd think that having a fast kid means I have great lung capacity and fettle. Wrong. I've got none of that.

The boys reach the grown-up monkey bars, causing another turmoil within. I can't tell you how many times he's begged me with his eyes to lift him so he could reach them. I am too short, not to mention too weak, to give him the push he needed, so we never got around to it. It's another thing in my overstuffed failure pile. Luka does it one-handedly. I watch Dec hold to dear life on the bar, while Luka trails his every move, protective hands at the ready under him. My chest tightens, my smile fades, and I have to fight back my tears. I've asked Rick many times to join us and help make Dec's wish come true. He always has an excuse—too tired, not in the mood, or busy with something else. If only he could see the joy on our son's face.

Declan deserves this feeling, the happiness this simple accomplishment brings. So once again, I compel my heart not to dwell, not to break. It takes three deep breaths to turn up the frown.

As I walk toward them, I can't help but notice the number of women drooling, their sights set on Luka. I get the appeal;

there's no denying it. He's got that tall, handsome thing, but it's the way he is with Declan that adds to the allure.

"You've got a fan club," I disclose when I get close enough.

He doesn't acknowledge my remark, so I keep going, "I'll be your wingwoman, all you have to do is point."

He chuckles, but it's tame. "Not interested."

Oh, shoot. It never occurred to me to ask if Luka was seeing someone. There's no ring on his finger, so naturally, I have to feed my curiosity.

"You got a girl waiting for you?"

"No," he deadpans, a bit of a bite in his tone. Shoot, maybe I've offended him. Maybe he's not into women, which, frankly, I have trouble believing. I ask anyway.

"A man?"

He turns to face me then, a full death glare piercing through me. Ok, wrong thing to say. Duly noted. I lift my hands in surrender, mouthing a 'Sorry'.

"Is that the vibe I give out?" he mutters, his eyes turning soft, almost as if they're pleading. What for, I can't say for sure!?

"No. Luka, you don't give off that vibe."

"Good."

I feel his smile, but I decide to look at my Bug instead, swinging back and forth. The little monkey is ecstatic. The power of that twinkle in his eyes consumes me so much that it spreads warmth through my entire body. At the end of the day, he is the only thing that matters.

"Can you dress him? I need to clean the bathroom." I place the clothes on the couch, and sit Dec next to him. Rick nods, and I beeline upstairs.

After our little adventure at the playground, we took a shower together, which led to a lot of water spillage. Using a towel, I double the speed and dry the floor, then the wall tiles. All done, I sprint downstairs, expecting Dec on the couch with Rick, but he's not there. I head to the playroom, only to find Declan covered in shit, literally. And not just him, the carpet, and a part of the wall.

The urge to scream is strong, but I swallow it down with three deep breaths. It's not my son's fault; I know that. He doesn't know any better. My husband, on the other hand…

"Rick, dang it, I told you to dress him."

Dec is smiling ear to ear, oblivious to the mess he's produced; it's all a game to him. To say that potty training with him was my biggest challenge would be an understatement. Now and again, he forgets that he has to go to the bathroom to do number two and ends up going in his pants. That I can deal with; however, when he decides to play with what comes out of him… now, that's a whole other level of hell. I believe we hold the record for the number of thrown-away carpets over the years. At first, I'd scrub them clean, but eventually got tired of it and opted for the trash instead.

I take in the scene of the crime once again, strategizing

my best course of action. Thankfully, the playroom has a small window, so I open it to let in the fresh air. It's too high for Dec to sneak through. He also can't fit, so it's the only window without a child lock.

That's when it gets to my head that Rick hasn't answered me, so I grab Dec's hand and drag him to the living room. As expected, Rick is on the couch, nose to his phone.

"Rick?"

"Hm?"

"I told you to get him dressed, look."

He does, a quick glance, two seconds long, before he turns back to his screen. Since I have more pressing matters at hand, I carry my feces-covered son upstairs to the bathroom.

It takes a few rounds of intense scrubbing to get rid of the stench. I give him one last scrub for good measure. Then, I take him out of the tub and dry him off.

I give him a piggyback ride downstairs, where I quickly clothe him before picking him up so he wouldn't dare run into the playroom.

With Dec on my hip, I stand in front of Rick and wait until he graces me with eye contact. He does, and I go all in, "One thing, Rick. I asked you for one thing: get him dressed. You didn't, and now the entire room stinks."

Actually, the entire house does, but that's beside the point.

"You didn't specify I had to get it done right away, so it's not on me."

Sure, turn the blame on me. What did I expect anyway? This is his go-to...

"It was implied," I aim to reason with him, knowing it's useless.

"Nor, I am not a mind reader," he retorts, and I try and fail not to scoff. It comes out loud and resentful. That's when he gets up. My husband has a good 9 inches on me, so I lift my head for a full face-to-face.

"It's not my fault you didn't think it through," he deadpans, his face devoid of any emotion.

And now I feel like a failure—yet again. How does he do that?

I should make him clean up the mess, I should yell or scream at him. But that's not what I do. Instead, I drop my head, turn around, and walk away. In the playroom, I set Dec down in the corner, hand him his blocks, and get to work. First, I roll up the small round carpet; then, using the cleaning wipes, I unsoil the wall, leaving it spotless.

Next, the act of tossing the carpet. I pass Rick by, unbothered as ever, and get outside feeling happy that tomorrow is trash day. Mrs. and Mr. Jordan waved from across the street. They are both sitting in their rocking chairs, enjoying the quiet. I wave back, smiling. It soon falters when my mind goes into its overthinking. Will Rick and I ever get there? White picket fence, two rocking chairs next to one another, gray hair, wrinkles on our faces… will we make it?

Taking slow steps back, that all too familiar pressure on my chest manifests. For the first time since I said 'I do', I fear that my future might not have the happy ever after I've always dreamed of. And what a dream it is. Was. A one-story white house. A big yard for kids to run free. A piano inside for me to play, and the love of my life beside me, hearts in his eyes as he watches me create something new. It seems so unreachable that I can barely picture it anymore. And that pains me more than I would like to admit.

Sighing, I step into our home, and suddenly it, too, feels empty, much like me.

How did we get here? I wonder, expecting the tears to form. None come, and it's as much a relief as it is agony.

I walk into the playroom and sit on the floor by Dec. He's building a block tower, so I start one right next to his. He makes eye contact with me, and it goes straight to my heart. I know how lucky I am, that I should be happy, yet a part of me is far from it. That's why I focus on the other part, the one that belongs to my son. My sun. He's the only light I need, and I'll be danged if I don't give him my all. Rick might not deserve it right now, but my world sure does.

Chapter 10

Luka

Today sucks!

Scratch that, this whole week so far has sucked.

I'm beyond overwhelmed, having to do damage control on two separate sites. There's a virus going around, so four of my men called in sick, which caused havoc of its own. I had to call in reinforcements and hire outside contractors to help with the mess before it piles up.

I shut the door of my container behind me when I get ambushed.

"Luka, my man," my best friend Ryan beams, practically jumping me.

One bear hug later, I ask, "What are you doing here? Aren't you supposed to be by Tessa's side?"

Ryan's wife had a baby a week ago, their fourth child, a little girl. The Martins moved here from Canada just over two years ago. They followed Tessa's brother, who had already settled in. We worked together at my last construction job and became close; over time, we grew to feel like family.

"She kicked me out," he deadpans.

I gasp in disbelief, "What?"

"Not like that. She demanded I get back to work. I believe the word 'useless' was involved."

I chuckle, imagining his wife yelling at him.

Last weekend, when I visited Tessa in the hospital, she asked me to be the co-godparent to their newest member. I get to share the title with her sister-in-law, and I plan to take that role very seriously.

"Can't say I blame her."

"Hey," he whines with a push to my chest. "I didn't know we contracted with your firm. I was actually going to ask the new boss for a favor."

"You're not even on the clock." Scowling, I tap my wristwatch for emphasis.

"I work fast." He shrugs.

"Don't say that in front of your wife," I tease, opening the door of my office so we can finish the conversation without my men eavesdropping. You'd think that a bunch of construction workers would be all macho and shit, but no. My men turn into gossip girls the moment there's tea, as they like to call it.

"Four kids, dude, just saying."

We both laugh as he drops his ass in my desk chair. I cross my arms over my chest, my patience wavering. Ryan straightens a bit and gets down to business. "Anyway, you know my best friend, El?"

I know of her, sure. His whole family won't shut up about her, especially the kids. I haven't had a chance to meet her yet.

"Your sister-in-law, El?" I point out her second title.

Not only is she his sister-in-law, but they've been best friends since childhood. Ryan talks about her so much that I feel like I know her better than he does at this point.

He snaps his fingers and points his index at me. "That's

the one. Soooo," he drags, "their patio roof collapsed, and she called me for help."

"Oh, shit." I scratch the back of my head. "Was anyone hurt?"

"No, thank God. But she does have a kid running around and asked if I could fix it sooner rather than later."

"Take whatever you need, the company truck is…" I stop myself, remembering he mentioned a kid. "You know what, I'm free now. You'll get more work done with an extra set of hands."

He doesn't argue, rather takes it, jumping to his feet. "Thanks, man."

"Anytime."

He follows me out back and helps load up the truck with everything we might need. I leave him to stock the rest while I discuss work with Peter, my second-in-command. I hear Ryan grunt behind me, the little baby, and I chuckle under my breath. Thankfully, I've already sorted everything out, so leaving Peter in charge won't cause a headache.

I take the wheel, and Ryan joins me, slamming the passenger door with unnecessary force. With a loud growl, I turn to face him, and he already has his puppy dog eyes, mouthing his apology. Yes, I am sensitive when others mistreat my stuff; sue me, why don't ya!?

As I back out of the site, Ryan clears his throat.

"I should warn you. El is a stickler for favors, so she'll want this on the books, pay full price, and all."

"Don't you dare charge her," I insist, turning up the AC. By the looks of it, it's gonna be a helluva hot day.

"Trust me, she will ask for a receipt for every used

screw."

"Doesn't sound like Auntie El."

If I am to trust his kids, Auntie El is the best, most fun-est person alive.

"She has a lot of layers."

Can't say I wasn't curious about her. The more they sold her praises, the more my interest grew.

I can't believe I finally get to meet her.

About ten minutes later, we arrive in front of a blue, two-story townhouse. The driveway is empty, so I park my truck there, thinking it'd be easier to haul the stuff inside. Stepping out, I give the house another look, wondering how many stories it holds.

We fill our hands with the arsenal and make our way to the front porch. When the door swings open, my heart tries to jump out of my chest.

"Luka?"

"Nora?"

God, she's beautiful, even with the black circles under her eyes that make her look exhausted. Her hair is tied in a messy bun, a few strands falling down the sides of her face.

"What are you doing here?" we both gasp out just as Ryan yells, "You two know each other??"

"He's the guy I told you about, the one who got Dec on the crane."

She talked about me? I think I'm blushing.

"Wait," Ryan gawks at me, "you're the crane guy Tessa raves about?"

I give him a playful shrug, puffing out my chest like a person deserving of the aforementioned rave. Then, to my surprise, Ryan adds, "That makes sense, Luka's totally the guy to do that."

"So you're Auntie El? How?"

"My full name is Eleonora, and the kids couldn't pronounce it when they were little, so El stuck." She lifts her pointer and plays off all serious, "They are the only ones allowed to call me that, for the record."

"Noted."

"You two work together?"

"Yeah, I mentioned him."

"No, you never mentioned a *Luka*."

The way she said it, inclining like it would be a name to remember, buzzes right through me.

Ryan lets out a laugh, then gives her an intense stare, giving her time to connect the dots I have no notion of. When her jaw drops, he gives me a transparent wink.

"Ooooohhhh, it all makes so much sense now."

"It wasn't your first guess when you saw him?" Ryan gawks, shaking his head.

"Not really," she shrugs, then brings those beautiful eyes to meet mine.

"How's that even possible? Have you looked at him?"

Crimson covers her cheeks, but she bypasses it quickly.

"I have, but it was not my first thought, or the second."

I keep turning my head back and forth between the two blabbermouths who are busy keeping me in suspense. At my frustration's peak, Nora throws me a bone.

"When they talk about you, they refer to you as," she puts on air quotes, "*The Hulk*."

"Of course they do."

"But Tessa calls you a ten-foot Teddy bear."

"I don't know which one is worse."

"Teddy bear suits you more."

There goes that flutter that has no business manifesting.

"Anyway, are you gonna let us in?" Ryan exasperates.

"Oh, right, sorry." She steps aside, and we enter her home, my heart beating at full speed.

"Thank you for coming so soon. It's hard to keep Dec away from the back."

"How did it happen?" I ask as I sneak a peek around her home, overflowing with framed pictures.

"Without a warning! Thankfully, we were not outside. I was brushing Dec's teeth when the loud boom scared the shit out of me."

She walks us to the back and opens the sliding door.

"I didn't expect you to come so soon, so I didn't move all the beams back."

Suddenly, her tired eyes make so much sense.

"You moved the beams? By yourself?" I bark, and Ryan gives me a 'you better shut up' look.

"Yeah, just in case Dec got out. Not that he could, there's a child-proof lock, but I couldn't risk it," she says it like it's no big deal.

"And you moved them by yourself?" I hiss this time. Ryan keeps looking at me, so I snap at him, "What?"

"Nothing," he gulps, "something in my throat." He widens his eyes, trying to communicate without words, but at the moment, I can't concentrate on reading him. I am fuming so hard that my blood is boiling.

"Why would you do that on your own?"

It's a fair question, and not at all discriminatory. I was raised a feminist, and I am all for girl power, but that doesn't mean that you actually have to do the heavy lifting all by yourself.

"It's not like I could ask someone's help in the middle of the night."

A weak argument, in my opinion. Thankfully, Ryan jumps in, "You should've called me."

I nod in agreement.

She shakes her head. "And wake up Tessa, or the baby? No, thank you," she drags, trying to play it out. On this, I see her reasoning, but that doesn't stop me from asking the obvious.

"And your husband?"

"Rick was sleeping."

My eyes dart to her hands, fidgeting. Not buying it, I roar, "He was sleeping?"

"Yes," she falters, but I won't budge, not on this.

"The loud *boom* didn't wake him?"

She drops her head, and now I'm certain she's lying. Ryan digs his elbow into my ribs. I ignore it.

"He's a heavy sleeper. Plus, I was closer to the noise," she adds, playing with her necklace and biting her inner cheek. The fact that she's this nervous says it all.

"Whatever," I huff, "we'll handle the beams, don't worry. We'll be out of your hair ASAP."

We step out onto the patio, and as soon as she closes the door, I explode, "What the fuck?"

"Rick is..." Ryan trails off, his mouth opening and closing more times than I could count.

"Whatever. Let's fix this mess," I grumble.

We both assess the damage and plan the course of action. Obviously, we have to move the beams first, and we get right to it. With each piece I move, my anger intensifies. She fucking carried these beams alone. There are over a dozen of them, each heavier than the last. And her husband was sleeping? That doesn't sit right with me.

I hear the sliding door, but I don't bother stopping to look. I catch her soft voice, though. "One with creamer, and one black, no sugar."

Of course, she remembers how I like my coffee…

Chapter 11

Nora

I don't want to go back there.

Tough, as if you have a choice.

With Declan clinging to my back in a piggy ride, I lift my chin and suck it up. We spent two hours at the playground, and his battery has been drained.

I couldn't get out of my house fast enough. So after I made them coffee, I excused myself and bolted. My head has been spinning with the revelation that Luka is 'The Hulk'. The freaking Hulk is Luka.

What the melon?

All the stories I've heard in the last year keep replaying.

Hulk is a softy

He has the biggest heart

Kids love him

He's amazing

He spent the night building them a treehouse all by himself

Tessa always goes above and beyond selling his praises, like I wasn't sold already. I get it now. I've witnessed his kindness up close and personal.

We reach the driveway, and I feel the drop of Dec's weight—a clear sign he has entered a snooze. Slowly, I open the door and tiptoe upstairs. In his room, I gently put him to bed and linger for a beat, watching the motion of his chest. With a quick peck on his chubby cheek, I tuck him in, then make my way out. The baby monitor is already in the kitchen.

Downstairs, I wave at the guys through the door, letting them know I'm back. I quickly tidy up the living room, mainly toys, when I hear my name being called.

"Nora?"

I turn around with a hum.

"Where do I put these?" Luka lifts his hands in front of him, one empty mug in each.

"I'll take that," I say, as I try and fail to pry the mugs from his hold. He doesn't budge, only stares at me with that intensity of his, which I am somehow accustomed to way too soon.

"Where's Declan?"

I smile at his question, ignoring the odd fluttering in my stomach.

"Napping upstairs."

He gives me a quick nod, dropping his shoulders. I take the opportunity to snatch the mugs from his hold. Triumphantly, I glee right at him, and he shakes his head before turning to walk back outside. He stops abruptly, then takes a step back, his focus on the couch, where the folded blanket lies over a big pillow.

Panic strikes.

Oh, fudge. I got distracted and forgot to hide the evidence.

Rookie mistake.

We don't have guests often, but when we do, I make sure

to get the stuff upstairs, too embarrassed for anyone to know about our sleeping arrangement.

Raging eyes fire imaginary daggers, maybe even something bigger, heavier, right at me.

"Where's the bathroom?"

Knowing what he's getting at, my defense system activates. "It's not like that."

"Where. Is. The. Bathroom?" he seethes, eyes filled with anger and something else, pity maybe.

"Upstairs," I blow the lid off.

The moment stretches, complete silence, with me trying to read his face, unable to find any excuse. I know what he's thinking, and he's right. Rick was downstairs when the beams collapsed. He did nothing. After I put Dec to bed, I moved the beams all by myself while my husband snored on the couch. *'Can you be quiet? I'm trying to sleep,'* was what he said after an hour of me dragging the damned things across the grass.

The gut-wrenching feeling from last night is nothing compared to Luka's damning stare. It clenches my heart to the point of breakage. It wasn't pity I saw before; it was pure disappointment. His silent judgment cuts deeper than words, stirring something within me.

Four blinks later, he gives me the bare minimum of a nod before he walks away. But his look remains, causing a whole new set of pain I never knew existed.

I've been hiding in the kitchen for the past hour, deliberately avoiding the guys. Lunch is done, the table is set, meaning it's time to face my demons. Considering Ryan did me a huge favor by coming by so fast, I decided to make his favorite.

The baby monitor stirs to life. Perfect timing. I run upstairs just as the bedroom door swings open. Dec rubs his eyes, then lifts his head. "Mama."

Oh, how I love the sound of that.

I open my arms, and he jumps on me like the monkey he is. Together, we take the necessary steps until we reach the back patio. My nerves are all over the place. I take a deep breath, grip the handle, and slide.

Sniffing the air, Ryan gurgles, "You didn't!?"

I grin at him, my very best friend in the whole wide world, as he smiles back with that familiar look on his face. He crashed into my life with a bang, literally. Somewhere around my fifth birthday, he threw a firecracker under my feet while I was in the middle of building my fort. He took a good look at my handiwork, asked if I wanted to be his friend, and the rest was history. I was the one who introduced him to Tessa, something I proudly mention in my best man speech at their wedding. She introduced me to her brother in return, sealing the already formed family.

Being an only child, with a not-so-great relationship with my parents, gaining some new family members was a blessing—until it wasn't. I get along with my mother-in-law better than I ever did with my own. My bond with Rick's family makes it tough to hide behind the lie. Besides, the mask I wear is for their benefit, not mine.

"Come on, let's eat," I state, my eyes on Luka. I can see the workings of his jaw muscles, and his reaction wounds me as if the sound of my voice nauseates him. With a heavy heart, I step back inside, leaving the door wide open for them.

We all take our seats, and I grab a spatula-full of casserole and place it on Dec's suction plate. The guys dig in next, stuffing theirs to the brim.

Working the fork, I spread out the food to cool faster. When I'm certain it's tongue-burn free, I set the plate in front of Dec and give him his fork. That's when Luka decides to finally speak to me. "You're not eating?"

"I already ate," I say at the same time Ryan blurts, "She's allergic to corn. Like, deadly allergic."

I shake my head in amusement. Luckily, I'm not a fan of corn, so it didn't cause much devastation.

Luka's features soften, and his eyes meet mine, causing instant goosebumps.

No. Go away! You are not welcome here!

Too late, my body is already covered. I hope he doesn't notice.

"So you made whatever this is, knowing you won't be eating it?"

"It's Ryan's favorite," I deadpan. "It's called Pâté chinois, the Canadian version of the Shepard's pie," I add. Luka looks at me with a piercing gaze, and I swear I can feel his stare penetrating somewhere deep. He hums to himself before getting back to his food.

We munch in silence, save for a few moans from Ryan,

accompanied by mumbled words that sound a lot like 'omigod', 'thank you', and 'amazing'. Every few seconds, I notice Luka's gaze turn to my son, his lips forming a slight curve.

"I have to take Dec to therapy. If you finish before we come back, could you lock up?"

"Of course, I have my key, don't worry about it," my best friend belts out.

I glance at Declan, taking his last bite. A single corn kernel lands onto his plate, but he doesn't get flustered; he lowers his head and sucks it into his mouth, causing the table to laugh.

"Thank you for lunch," Luka mutters, standing up, his plate in hand.

I follow suit, getting on my feet with a flat, "The least I could do." I reach to grab the plate from him, but he twists his body, shielding it from me. I cock a brow as Dec runs to the playroom, likely to complete his LEGO tower. I watch as Luka stacks the remaining plates and brings them into the kitchen. Ryan does the same with the cutlery.

I do not move, though. I don't think I'm even blinking.

Movement makes me lose my balance, and I look down to find Luka's hand trying to pry my plate. Swallowing a lump, I lift my head, meeting his stare. There's a question in his eyes, I can see it clearly, but I don't want to answer it. It takes a couple of beats for my grip to loosen, and Luka takes advantage, snatching the dish from me.

Numbness takes over, that empty feeling I am way too acquainted with, building up. I press my lips together, shaking my head, and get to work, cleaning up the table. I don't need these thoughts to infiltrate right now. Or ever.

Rick never did that.

Dang it.

Ten years, and not once has Rick picked up his plate.

The knot in my chest tightens at the thought, and I hate that their actions make me draw comparisons to my husband. Using the dishes as a distraction, I start scrubbing the pot when the first tear strikes.

Chapter 12

Nora

"Has Ryan already been here?" Rick takes his spot on the couch, and I feel a flicker of anxiety as I glance out the back, the beams standing horizontally for the first time since the whole thing broke down, much like my life.

"Yeah, he and Luka got here pretty early, and they did most of the work. I think it'll be finished tomorrow."

"Who's Luka?"

"Ryan's friend. Funny story, he's actually—" my explanation gets interrupted by a grumble.

"And why do you know his name?"

Great, it's the Jimmy situation all over again. God forbid I be nice to people. I close my eyes and sigh, thinking about the last time I made that mistake.

Rick is not a jealous person. He's downright possessive, and not the good kind, the kind you read about in romance novels. He didn't speak to me for three days straight when we ran into our postman on the street. Jimmy, a couple of months shy of retirement, is a kind older man who goes the extra mile to get our mail first. This way, I don't have to face the post office, a place Dec really dislikes.

The same thing happened when he overheard me talking with the Amazon delivery guy, named Paul, who kindly noted it had been a while since my last order.

Keeping my anger at bay, I take a deep breath. "Why do you always do that?"

"What exactly?"

"Make a scene for me being polite?"

"When have I ever done that?"

I open my mouth to retort, but nothing comes.

Just like that—memory wiped!

How is it that one sentence has the power to do that?

For the life of me, I can't think of anything, fully aware that a mere minute ago, I had the whole scenario playing out in my head.

"Forget it." Trying to settle the tension, I disclose, "he's Ryan's friend. He's gonna be the godfather to the baby."

"Whatever," his jaw ticks, "what's for lunch?"

"Pâté chinois."

The loud sigh he let out tells me he's not happy with my choice.

"I made it as a thank you to Ryan. He got here the same day I called him."

And once again, I am defending myself. Why? Why do I do this???

"Whatever," he says with indifference, but I know the tone, understand every thought behind it.

"I'm sorry, do you want me to make you something else?"

Great, now I'm groveling.

Stupid, stupid woman!

"It's fine," he mumbles, standing up. He gets to the table and takes a seat, waiting. I quickly glance at Dec, who is focused on building a house with magnetic tiles in the playroom, so I stick Rick's plate in the microwave. I count down the seconds, watching the food rotate. My mind goes blank, and I appreciate the distraction. I can see why Dec likes it so much.

"How was work?" I set the plate before him and take a seat opposite my husband.

"Fine."

"Do you want to do something this weekend? Maybe the forest, we haven't gone in forever," I hope.

"Nor, after a long week, all I want is rest," he deadpans, not lifting his gaze from his phone.

"Oh, yeah, you're right," I respond sluggishly, my eyelids heavy. I can't remember the last time I felt so tired, so I get it. I do. He's out there, every day, working his ass off for us. Of course, he wants to take it easy in his free time.

"Dec mastered the zipper," I beam, changing the subject to something more upbeat.

"That's good," he nods absentmindedly, taking a huge bite, not sharing much emotion over something that I consider to be huge. We've been working on it for over a month, so it was a big accomplishment.

"Yeah, he did this thing today, it was so cute…" Just as my heart starts pounding in excitement, he flatlines it with a harsh tone. "Can you just let me eat in peace? I am tired."

There he goes, adding another set of weights to my chest. Frankly, I don't know how much more of it I can take. Dropping my head, I stand up. "Of course, sorry. We'll go for our walk."

I swear the kid has superhuman hearing because as soon as the last word leaves my mouth, he's next to me, jumping up and down.

With a skip in his step, he goes straight to the shoe cabinet and gets out his boots. I follow suit, putting on my sneakers.

Today is our therapy-free day (excluding the weekends), so I opt for a long walk. Declan, naturally, has different plans because he starts pulling me in the opposite direction.

"Cement mixer," he shouts, and my shoulder protests at the jolt. I don't have the energy to fight him on it, so I suck it up and take him to his favorite place.

Standing before the truck, we both watch the barrel turn. We stay there for half an hour, his cute face smiling and his gaze fixed on the movement, while I contemplate everything that has happened in the last couple of weeks. My thoughts bounce all over the place, mostly around the polarity of Rick and Luka's actions.

Dark days are slowly taking over. I can't even remember the last time we had a good streak.

Why not leave?

Sonny's question flashes, but I shoo it away.

I made vows, a promise to one man to stand by him, love him, and stay through the good and the bad. Besides, I have no job, no income, no means to support the two of us. As much as those thoughts pain me, I know I am bound to this life, and I am determined to make the most out of it. Still, I can't control my mind, or all that spirals over daily.

I want to matter, to be wanted, not needed in the sense of doing everything for everybody else. I already have a son depending on me; I don't need a grown-up in that mix, and somehow my heart is beating for one.

Tired, I am so damn tired of it all…

Of thinking, dreaming, enduring…

Everything turns into a big blob, an inextricable web of suppressed thoughts and feelings I have no intention of untangling, not anymore.

Somewhere down the line, I think I just gave up the moment my eyes couldn't produce any more tears. I read once that you get a specific number of tears per person, so maybe Rick's run out. I look at my boy, at that smile on his face that is the only reason for my existence. It's the breath of life, the only answer I'll ever need. My sole purpose, the reason I was put on this earth, was to be his mother. Nothing else matters.

Sometimes, I have heated discussions with the universe. I wonder why I was put in charge of this task. I feel like I'm not fit for it, and that he deserves better. Both of them do… It's the same thought that keeps me up at night.

Not being enough…

It's written in invisible ink over my heart, like a scarlet letter, my cross to bear, and mine alone, not seen by any other, as intended. And as if the universe wanted to give me some feedback, the sky opens, and rain starts pouring, washing every negative notion away. I take Dec's other hand, and we start spinning… We don't stop until we get so dizzy we both fall on the ground, bursting into laughter. Dec lies down, and I follow, lying on the wet concrete, inviting the droplets to drum over my skin. I graze my fingers through his damp hair, feeling the warmth. As we both welcome the shower, a new sensation rushes through me, and for the first time in forever, I tell myself, "You can do this." The only problem is that I don't know what I mean by it.

85

Enough

From the start, I was told I didn't belong
From the start, I learned I wasn't strong
Truth be told, I knew it all along
There was no way of proving them wrong

Dreams were shattered
Life was altered
Like nothing ever mattered

My worst fear comes to life.
Your words cut deeper than a knife.
I thought that I was strong, that I was tough
But you made me believe I would never be enough

From the start, right then, I knew
Everything got lost in a darkened blur
Your cuts run deep, words flew
Making every insecurity appear, they grew

Dreams were shattered,
Life was altered
All the things I thought that mattered
Got replaced and got splattered

Chapter 13

Luka

I'm staring at the ceiling, a canvas for my regrets. I'm lying flat on my back, one arm under my head, the other resting on the mattress like it's waiting for someone who'll never arrive. I gave up on sleep an hour ago.

I can hear my heart beating to the rhythm of her name.

Nora—Nora—Nora

Everything about her is so vivid. The way her smile creeps up slowly, like it knows it shouldn't be happening. The way she tucks her hair behind her ear and plays with her necklace when she is nervous-all the stuff I've noticed after watching her too long, too often. The memory of her laugh still echoes in my head, the light sound that makes my chest tighten and stomach twist.

I close my eyes and roll onto my side, but she follows me.

I am trying. I am trying my best to think of anything else, but it keeps circling back to her, the way her glances carry more weight than they should.

Her wedding ring flashes, like a warning. That alone should be enough... But the world has shut down, no one is watching, and the guilt doesn't have to hide. So, I give up, indulge it. I'm going to hell for it, but I'm ok with that.

As long as I get to see her face when I cross over.

I snort at myself, running a hand through my hair. Turning

again, I press my face into the pillow in hopes it will smother the want.

Hazel eyes are staring at me, making the simple act of breathing nearly impossible.

"Hi, you two," she steps aside, "come in." Ryan goes in first, and I follow.

The pitter-patter of little feet echoes as Declan runs toward Ryan and jumps into his arms. He lifts him and tosses him into the air; the kid laughs so hard I think my heart will burst at the sound. When Ryan lets him down, the boy comes in front of me. I take a knee, getting on his eye level when he surprises me by lifting his hand, palm wide open. A rush of air escapes me as I lift mine and clasp it with his. After receiving a high five, he waves his hand and starts jumping up and down, smiling from ear to ear. I turn to Nora only to find her bewildered, her watery eyes fixed on me, one hand covering her chest and the other playing with the pendant around her neck. Standing up, I turn to Ryan, his eyes wide, mouth open in disbelief. Something about their reaction makes me think Declan's gesture is special.

I want to say something, but words fail me. Ryan clears his throat, and I take that as my cue to follow him outside. When the door slides shut, I turn to find my best friend staring at me, as if he's seeing me for the first time. "He never does that. He's more comfortable around women. It took him a long time to accept me."

I can't read too much into it. It will only cause another turmoil that I am not ready to face. So I bark out, "Let's get to work."

In the middle of securing the joints, I hear the door sliding. I turn to find Nora in the frame, two coffees in hand. She places them on a small table in the corner that wasn't there yesterday. She must've put it there just for us.

"Today's supposed to be hot, so if it gets too much, let me know, and I'll bring out a ventilator. I'll also make you some lemonade, or do you guys want a beer?"

"No drinking on the job in front of the boss, El," Ryan titters as he nervously bites his inner cheek.

"Oh, come on, he's not a typical boss," Nora counters.

Ryan gives her a pointed look I can't quite decipher. "How would you know?"

"Just look at him, he's a total softy."

And there goes my sanity.

"We could share a beer when we finish, if you join us," I chime in.

"Oh, you don't want me with alcohol."

I want you—period.

Where did that come from? That thought goes straight into the forbidden zone.

"You really don't," Ryan drags, pointing his thumb at her with a chuckle. "A lightweight is an understatement when it comes to our El."

"No need to exaggerate, but yeah. Alcohol and I don't mesh well," she mutters.

"Now I have to see that."

"Not gonna happen, TB," she chortles, and I raise my brows.

"TB?"

"Think about it."

It takes me a minute, but when it comes to me, I burst into laughter, belly and all. Yup, I'm back to being screwed.

"Did you eat breakfast? I can make you something."

There she goes, thinking of others. I don't know if I should hate her for it or like her that much more. We all know it's the latter.

"We ate on the way, but thanks anyway," Ryan answers, and I bob my head to confirm.

She lingers there for a bit longer before she waves and slides the door shut, leaving my mind to wander.

I focus on the job at hand, fixating on the beams, trying not to share any thoughts with the guy working next to me. That's one place I can't go, not with him being her best friend, not to mention family. I need to find a new person to vent to. Sabrina comes to mind. I can always count on her harsh honesty, so I know she'll do her best to set my mind straight.

The door slides open again, and I can smell her scent as she leans on the frame. "I'm gonna take Dec to the park. If you need to use the toilet in the next thirty minutes, please use the upstairs bathroom. I put the cleaning tab in this one." She points to the door of the downstairs toilet.

"No problem," both Ryan and I note, waving them goodbye.

As soon as I hear the front door click shut, I check the time. A safe amount of minutes later, five to be exact, I lay down my tools and leave Ryan to go to the bathroom.

I walk up the stairs, but have to stop at each step. Framed photos cover both stairwell walls.   I take my sweet time checking each one out, laughing when I find Declan as a baby, dressed in a ladybug costume. He's on Nora's lap. She's wearing a headband with antennas, her nose is black, and she has black dots all over her face. The photo itself is cute as hell, but it's the smile on both their faces that gets me. I don't know how, but I feel their beam all the way to the center of my chest.

I continue on my way to the bathroom, where I relieve myself and then wash my hands. On my way back downstairs, I stop in front of a large bookcase hugging the wall between two rooms. I skim the contents of the shelves, my smile growing bigger with each title I read. If I could create a perfect woman, somewhere on top of the list would be that she has to be a book lover.

I come from a family where reading is mandatory, essential for survival, and understanding. Our mother created a book club when we were young boys, just starting to discover the world. She introduced us to different universes and the inner thoughts of all kinds of people. Reading made us understand things better and even helped heal some broken parts. So for me, the love of books in a woman is a must, if not even a deal-breaker.

The morning light spills through the blinds, casting long shadows across the spines. I pause, spotting something familiar out of the corner of my eye. I pull the leather binder free, one just like Mateo's from MIT. The hinges creak a little as I open it.

The first thing I see is McGill University's red coat of arms. Her full name, in script, ink slightly faded: *Eleonora Grace Baker*. And under it, proudly states in bold: **Doctor of Music (D.Mus.): Performance Studies and Composition.**

I blink.

What the actual fuck? She's a doctor of music. Full disclosure, I didn't even know it was a thing. I trace my fingers over the letters, feeling a sense of awe. When I turn it over, a couple of photos fall out, and I quickly pick them up for inspection. A slightly younger version of Nora lights up a spark inside me—a different instrument in hand in each photo, and the biggest smile on her face. From the pictures, she seemed to play the violin, piano, and guitar. In the last photo, she's sitting in front of a spreadsheet stand, writing something in a notebook placed on her lap.

Composing?

She can compose music as well as play it. How is this woman real? I see some words scribbled on the picture when I turn it over; they are all smudged, unreadable. I smile at myself, close it gently, and slide it back where I found it. I might never learn her entire story, but now that I know a little bit more, it makes all this worse.

Chapter 14

"What does Nora do for work?" I blurt as soon as I step outside. Ryan answers with a smirk, turning to face me, hammer in hand.

"She's a stay-at-home mom." He raises his brows, giving me the *duh* look.

"You said she went to college, right?" I play ignorant, hiding my recent discovery.

"Yeah. Graduated with honors," he boasts, like a proud big brother. And I would know, being in the role myself on multiple occasions.

I can also read between the lines, a clear reason for her diploma collecting dust on a shelf.

Ryan straightens his posture, letting me know he is turning serious.

"Look, it's a sensitive topic in our family. El turned her life upside down, pouring herself into that boy and making him her only priority. Sure, she drew the short end of the stick, but she's the one who chose it. We gave up on that long ago."

"On what exactly?"

He draws in a breath, dropping the tool.

"El is as selfless as they come, Luka. We tried, we all did, even our in-laws begged her not to give up on her life, but she never listens. By putting everyone first, she lost herself on the way."

So to sum it all up, she sacrificed her whole life for a prick who can't even bother to help his wife with some heavy lifting. Makes me think about all the different weights Nora pulls on with her own two hands. My fists clench, angry at her burdens.

"We're back!"

I startle at the sound of Nora's voice, so lost in thought I didn't hear the patio door sliding open.

"You guys need anything?"

"We're good," both Ryan and I murmur, pretending we were working, eyes glued on the beams connecting on the ground.

"Ok, I will put Dec down for his nap and work on lunch. Do you have any preferences?"

"You don't have to make us lunch," I turn to face her, but Ryan's retort stops me. "Don't bother, no point in arguing with her."

She scoffs, and I growl.

"You do know I am bigger than both of you, right?"

"You don't scare me," she taunts, crossing her arms over her chest.

And there go the butterflies.

I shake my head, eying her delicate fingers playing with the pendant on her necklace. Her hair is pulled up in a high ponytail, revealing her shoulders. It's then that I see that most of her skin is covered with small dots.

"Also, Poutine with a side of breaded stakes, it is."

"What the fuck is a Poutine?"

"Home, my friend, it's home." Ryan pats my shoulder with

sparkling eyes, and then Nora mumbles something in French, making Ryan laugh. Isn't it a popular opinion among women that the French accent sounds sexy in a man? But have they ever heard Nora speak it? My dick sure has. And now I have to hide the sporting tent, like I am some horny teenager. What is this woman doing to me?

"That's not fair. And how weird is it that this is the first time I heard you speak French?" I point my gaze at Ryan, though the question is directed at both of them.

"If you wanted me to speak French to you, all you had to do was ask." Ryan bats his lashes and wiggles his brows. I frown with a distinguished "yuck."

"She, on the other hand, can speak it all the time." My eyes slide over Nora's body, from her bare feet to her eyes.

"You sure about that? I could cuss, commanding your doom or something?"

Cuss? This woman couldn't say a swear word if her life depended on it.

"Considering I've never heard you curse before, I highly doubt it."

Ryan snickers. Immediately, I know there's a story there, so I avoid Nora's death glare and prob, "What?"

You have to know something about my best friend. He likes to talk, too much for my liking, but we'll bypass it for the time being.

"Oh, Luka…" he shakes his head, his tone mocking, as he gives Nora a pointed look, one I can read with ease. He's about to spill.

Nora doesn't get a chance to protest; Ryan is too fast, taking a deep breath in preparation for the babble. "This one used to have the biggest trucker mouth on her."

I'm having a hard time picturing it. Nora screams innocence and kindness. Then again, he's known her longer, better. That ping of jealousy hits, but I brush it off quickly.

"I once dared her to last five minutes without a swear word. She lasted ten seconds. We even tried with a swear jar—easiest fifty bucks of my life."

"Fifty?"

"One hour's work," he adds.

I lift a brow, then turn to Nora. Her cheeks are blushing, but I have a feeling it isn't out of embarrassment. No, it's something else I can't quite figure out.

"Anyway," she deflects, "I had to tame it when Dec turned into a parrot." She finishes with a shrug, her cheeks still red.

With my mouth dry and an empty bottle, I go inside with the sole purpose of filling said bottle in the downstairs toilet. Weird sounds coming from the kitchen stop me in my tracks, pulling me in the other direction.

The closer I get to the kitchen, the more distinctive the male voice becomes, but the words are not what I focus on. It's the sobs, though quiet, speaking volumes. I come behind her and look at her shoulders, motioning up and down at full speed, and all I want is to wrap her in my arms. The alarm sounds in my head, and I take a step back, knowing I am not allowed to touch someone who belongs to another. Still, the need to comfort her is stronger, so without realizing it, my mouth opens. "Are you ok?"

"Osti," she jumps with a quick turn, mumbling gibberish. "You scared me." Cheeks red, eyes swollen, her hand moves from her chest to her phone on the countertop, pausing the voice.

"Sorry, uhm… It's this stupid book," she mutters, shaking her head, "just a heart-wrenching scene, and I'm a crier." She finishes with a hand wave across the air, like she's shooing away a fly.

"A crier?"

"Yeah, I cry over everything, overemotional and all that."

I don't know what it is about that statement that makes her so adorable, but here we are. Stealthily, carefully, so as not to be noticeable, I take a small step forward.

"Right. So, you're crying over a book?"

"Only way to read 'em. Technically listen. I don't have time to sit and read all the time, and I do like multitasking, hence…" She sniffles, pointing at her phone. "Audio books are my jam," she singsongs with a slight curve of her lips, her eyes still watery.

"Your jam?"

"You gonna keep on doing that?"

"What?"

"Repeating the last thing I said in the form of a question?"

"Sorry, I didn't realize," I admit, my shoulders plummeting. It's as if I lost all my knowledge of holding a conversation. The kitchen is small, her presence all I can feel in it, her scent so strong, even with the mixture of spices trying to muffle it.

"You do know how to talk, right?"

I crack a smile at the twinkle that appears in her eyes; it's impossible not to.

"There you are," she whispers loud enough for me to hear. Her smile widens, and I turn around, expecting to find someone standing behind me, but there's no one. I turn back to her, furrowed brows and all, only to be met by her gorgeous, beaming face.

"I can't believe Teddy Hamilton made me cry," she perplexes, dropping her shoulders for the full disappointed effect.

"Who the hell is Teddy Hamilton?"

"He's a narrator. One that usually has a different effect on m—" she swallows the rest. Her cheeks turn red, and she drops her head. I don't try to coax the mentioned effect; I've already rounded up my own conclusions, one that causes a new kind of sensation to form. I don't like it one bit.

"God, I'm a sob fest." She wipes her tears with more effort than necessary. "But what the hell was I supposed to do when Colt point-blank asked Beckett..." she trails off, her voice shaky. And even though she forces herself to stop talking, the forehead scratching tells me she wants the opposite. Naturally, every fiber of my body needs to indulge her, so I carry on with it.

"Sure. *The Last letter* would do that to you."

"What?" she gasps, eyes locked on mine.

"That *is* what you're reading," I point out, not asking. There's only one book with those characters as far as I know.

"How do you know that?" She tilts her head to the side,

the action making her ponytail swing a bit.

"I read it last year," I divulge, leaning my hip on the counter and crossing my ankles. It was the first book I wanted to act like Joey over and stuff it in the freezer. I was in a long reading slump after finishing it, or rather after it finished me, but I'm not gonna tell her that.

"No, you didn't."

I can't help but chuckle at her attempt at debate. She shakes her head, waving her hands, as if the action would somehow make it untrue.

"I did," I boast, cocking a brow.

Normally, this kind of reaction (which is way too common from the opposite sex whenever any of my family members mentions that we're in an actual book club and that we like reading, including romance novels) would irritate me, but Nora is not being judgmental, nor prejudiced. She's simply refusing to believe that we might have something in common.

"No," she shrieks this time, and I cross my arms over my chest, trying my best to get all serious.

"YES!"

"NO!"

A devilish smirk appears on her face, and I know the intent behind it. So, before she has a chance to open her mouth fully, I answer in advance, "Chaos."

That one word is enough to prove my point, since it's the main character's pseudonym after all. Her jaw drops, but her eyes start glowing, making goosebumps erupt all over my flesh.

"I am officially impressed."

Grabbing the large set of tweezers from the counter, she

turns to the stove and flips over what I presume are breaded steaks. The sound of sizzling oil intensifies, and she leans on the counter, challenge in her gaze.

"Lose a bet or something, or was it a girl who got you into it?"

"Something like it," I keep it vague, fishing for a hint of jealousy. She doesn't even flinch, and I have to hide my disappointment.

"Not sharing?"

"Contemplating it?"

"What can I do to change your mind?"

I tap a finger to my lips, putting on a show in my thinking, down with the humming sound.

"Answer me this: what book made you cry the most?"

"Uh, that's a hard one, cuz obviously sooo many."

"You can choose more than one."

"Uhm… *Reminders of him*, any Chloe Walsh book, *A Thousand Boy Kisses* was gut-wrenching, and then there's *A Doll's Ho*—" Her eyes widen before she finishes, but I know the last three letters she ate. Regret covers her features, and she averts her gaze to the floor. At first, I don't recognize why her hands are shaking, or why that title in particular got her to react this way. And then it all hits me at once—the couch, the pain in her eyes, the beams. My heart breaks for her, making me feel so damn helpless. I want to burn whatever is building up inside her.

"Nora?" I take a step closer, and she takes two back, lifting her hand between us with the universal stop sign. I watch a single tear drop to the floor, leaving a small stain on the laminate between her feet.

"I need to check on Dec," she whispers, passing me by before she disappears.

Chapter 15

Nora

How do people do this?

How does someone cope with the constant reminders and the accompanying regret?

I am falling apart, breaking at the seams on my bathroom floor—over nothing.

He probably didn't realize.

Fudge!

And why am I thinking about what is going through Luka's mind?

Why do I care?

Because you don't want anyone to know.

Because you're ashamed.

Because you don't want to admit you're a failure.

"Can you do anything right?"

"You're too soft on him, you'll turn him into a wimp."

"Why is the floor dirty? It's not like you have better things to do."

"You talk too loudly."

"Can you not sing?"

"You're always tired. At least think of a better excuse."

God, I want to scream.

Wanna know something funny? My mother named me

after the protagonist of the book that's practically a script of my life, though a bit more contemporary.

Oh, the irony.

How pathetic, right?

Pull yourself together, Nora.

Manifesting my inner Elsa, I repeat the phrase in my head until I become numb.

Conceal, don't feel.

Conceal, don't feel.

Taking another deep breath, I stand up to look at myself in the mirror. There I am—the perfect representation of f-up. At least my ponytail is still standing, so there's that. I wash my face, letting the cold water do its work, dropping the temperature of my skin, when it hits me.

Fudge!

I forgot about lunch.

Oh fudge, oh shoot!

I sprint downstairs expecting to find the kitchen in flames. I blink once, twice, five times before I gasp in disbelief. Stakes are done, resting on the hot plate. The potatoes I've laid out earlier are peeled and ready for the next step.

I blink again. Have I lost my mind?

I did have a full-on meltdown in the middle of cooking, right?

Luka.

The only logical explanation hits me like a smack in the face. I don't have much time till Dec wakes up, so I cut the potatoes into perfect stripes while the oil heats up in the fryer. As I do all that, I cry like I've never cried before. And for the life of me, I don't even know why. Plus, I want to laugh hysterically for some reason. It's like my own tears can't decide which direction to feel in the overflow of emotions.

I am trying to wrap my mind around it. For a practical stranger to waltz in, take the reins, and hold the fort makes me want to scream. At Luka for being the person I don't deserve… At Rick for being the same.

Luka's action, though insignificant to some, makes me see the bigger picture more clearly. If he can step in for someone he barely knows, why can't Rick do the same for someone he loves?

Just last week, when I was in the middle of ironing, Dec had a meltdown. I had to stop mid-steam to do damage control because Rick was too busy playing on his phone. When Declan finally calmed down, I returned to the board and found my shirt ruined. Thankfully, our iron has a safety feature that turns itself off, but it didn't act before leaving a large brown mark.

The worst part? I didn't even have the strength to yell at Rick for not turning it off himself, let alone jump in and iron a shirt or two.

God, I hate how Luka affects me. I need it all to stop.

Getting my mind out of the gutter, I set the table just as Dec rushes to me. I pick him up, kiss his chubby cheek, and call the guys.

We eat in silence, my legs shaking under the table while I try my best not to let it show. The inner turmoil is trying to eat me alive, and as soon as Dec is finished, I jump to my feet, bursting out a squeakish "Laundry awaits."

I take Dec with me without looking, but I can feel both men's gazes on me. I must look like a crazy person, fleeing like that, except I don't care. Escape is what I need right now.

In the laundry room, I place Dec on the dryer, and we sing the ABC song while I fold. In the middle of the load, a knock interrupts the harmony, and Ryan's voice rips through the barrier. "El, we're finished." The door cracks open, and my best friend's head peeks through the small opening.

"What's wrong?" He swings the door fully, scanning my face.

"Nothing," I mumble, folding another towel to keep my mind busy.

"Don't! Not with me."

He knows me too well; there's no point in lying.

"Luka thinks I have problems with Rick," I confess under my breath, and even though I haven't admitted the actual problem at hand, it doesn't stop my shoulder from feeling just a bit lighter.

His left eyebrow skyrockets, and he scoffs, "So?"

"I don't want him thinking anything bad about Rick," I admit, "or me."

"Why does it matter what Luka thinks?"

Ain't that the question of the day!? I've been having trouble with that one myself. And not even the question itself, but with the feelings the mere thought causes.

"It doesn't," I lie, picking up the hamper before I place it on top of the washing machine.

"Right," he drags it out, pointing out how unconvincing my statement is.

"Just forget it," I brush it off, shaking my head.

"What is going on between the two of you?" Ryan leans back against the wall, hands tangled on his chest.

I wish I could answer that. Most of all, I wish I could figure me out. This constant baffling is finally taking its toll, and I am too dang tired to fight it.

"Nothing," I croak, "what do you mean?"

"Yeah, like that tone is gonna persuade me."

"It's not like that."

"You are playing with fire, El."

And I am trying my best to put it out.

"It's not like that, and you know it. I would never do that. You know me."

Yes, being around Luka is confusing, but there's nothing beyond a possible friendship. I love Rick and would never do anything to hurt him. My best friend knows that. At least, I hope he does.

"You know you can tell me anything, El?"

Not really.

Though my inner self wants to get it out, the suppressed part wants it so badly. Alas, the stupid part prevails. "Yeah."

He wouldn't understand. No one can. Not even I do.

A beat passes, and I know he's struggling, trying his best not to cross the line and speak his mind. He fights it, just like I do time and time again.

So he sighs, and, like the best friend he is, pulls me in for a hug. And it's that Disneyland hug, you know the one where the person waits for you to be ready to let go. His hands wrap around me in a tight grip that has the power to shut down the world—almost.

Finally ready to return to reality, my hands relax by my sides, and I give Ryan a reassuring smile. It's a talent, a gift—actually... how easy it is to plaster a mask on and repress everything.

Behind closed doors, it's a different story.

I shake it off, grab Dec's hand, and follow Ryan downstairs, where Luka is waiting in the hallway.

Composing myself, I turn all business. "How much do I owe you?"

"Your money's no good here," Luka says in a flat tone, trying to hide what I can only assume is pity. I can't stand it.

"That's not how this works. I want a receipt and the full price. No objections," I huff, crossing my arms over my chest for emphasis.

"You made us coffee and lunch, we're even," he barks back, trying to look all tough. It's his eyes that give him away—soft, warm.

"Luka, please, I don't function like that."

"Too bad 'cuz I do."

"I will feel like I owe you guys and won't be able to sleep. Please, for the sake of my eye and body recuperation, just let this one go and let me pay." I raise my hands in prayer to my chest.

"Guilt-tripping me into it?"

"You want puppy eyes to go with that?" I coax, turning my mouth into a pout.

"No need, I couldn't take it." His lips twitch, but don't turn into a smile.

He scribbles something on a piece of paper and hands it over to me. When I read out the 100% discount, I laugh and rip the paper in front of him. "Try again."

"You're a stubborn one."

"You have no idea," Ryan jumps in before I can.

Luka takes out a receipt book, stamps over his signature, and turns it to me for inspection. I glance at the number and nod in approval. He leaves the bill on the shoe cabinet, then extends his hand to mark the completion of our business. I hesitate for a breath, not fully understanding why. Swallowing, I give him my hand and shake it without either of us uttering a single word. A strange current flows through my blood vessels, sending strong impulses to my skin at the contact. Our eyes stay locked for what seems to be an eternity before I release his hand. I expected relief at the withdrawal, but instead, there's this dread taking over. Like my hand knows this is the last time it will feel his. My heart grows heavy, and I hold back the tears.

It's when Ryan hugs me that I almost crack. Why do I have this need to cry? I step back, watching Declan tug on Luka's shirt. The man kneels in front of him, giving my boy all of his attention. Both simultaneously pull their palms up in the air and high-five each other, my soul melting at the sight. Luka's face changes into something close to elation. The way his smile grows, revealing those dimples, the ones that have the power to flatline any heart.

I watch them get into the pick-up and wave. The second I shut the door behind me, I crumble at the loss. With the door acting like a shield behind me, I collapse on the floor, pulling my knees to my chest, and fall apart.

Behind closed doors

Nobody sees
Nobody knows
All my fears won't be exposed
It's just how it goes

In the dark, without the light
I lost my will to fight
The sum doesn't go with the math
I should've chosen a different path

Behind the smiles, behind the eyes
Behind it all, there are no more lies
Behind closed doors, behind the frames
Behind the facade, nothing remains

If my eyes could speak
If someone wanted to seek
They would reveal
The secrets that lie within

In the dark, I don't see the light
I don't even want to fight
I want to do the math
The divide ending our path

Behind the smiles, behind the eyes
Behind it all, there are no more lies
Behind closed doors, behind the frames
Behind the facade, nothing remains

Chapter 16

Luka

Escaping the heated argument going on in the living room, I beeline for the kitchen. My physical and emotional state is drained, so my mood isn't up for discussing whether Mak is prettier than Tristan. I hear footsteps following, and I know to whom they belong. Sabrina's mind-reading isn't part of the agenda, either.

She comes by my side, but I don't acknowledge her, pouring myself a glass of water. I chug it down, desperate to avoid whatever can of worms she wants to open. Naturally, my mission fails.

"Luka." Her soft voice calls to me, but I refuse to greet it. Sabrina is as stubborn as they come, so she turns up the volume. "Don't you dare ignore me!"

I can feel her death glare all the way to my stomach, and I know she has her hands on her hips, the ultimate commanding stance, like the boss woman she is.

Sabrina became a part of our lives three years ago when Mateo fell head over heels. I had my reservations about her at first, and can now admit the error of my ways. I judged her for her appearance, not realizing how innocent and kind she truly was. Is. She changed my mind and my heart, becoming one of my closest friends and most trusted confidants.

"Look at me. NOW!" That tone does it, the determinant

one with a kick to it that only Sabrina can produce. Grabbing my hand, she drags me outside, safe from prowling eyes and ears. The fresh air hits like a cold drink on a hot day, easing me a fraction. We take a seat on the bench overlooking the backyard. It's so quiet, the only sound coming from the swaying trees in the breeze.

One quick breath. That's all it takes for her to read me like an open book because she sputters a bit too enthusiastically, if I might add. "You met a woman!"

It's not a question, but I nod anyway.

"I thought I saw a new kind of smile last weekend, but didn't want to prowl."

"You didn't want to prowl?" My tone matches my thought because if there's one thing I know about Sabrina, it's her meddling character.

"I was trying to be respectful, full house and all."

That earns her a chuckle, and she takes out a cigarette, lighting it up before a cloud of smoke gets between us.

"What's the problem?" She crosses one leg over the other, taking a long drag.

"She's married."

"Oh."

"And has a kid."

A kid whose smile is so deeply imprinted in my psyche that it causes my own to form. I love kids, but Declan has taken a special place in my heart from the start. Never have I felt such a connection with a kid as I have with him. My mind goes back to all the pictures covering the wall. A glimpse into Nora's life was enough for the heaviness of it to press onto my chest. When they left for therapy this afternoon, I took my chance to snoop, guilt-free—so no judging. Every wall is a shrine to the boy who's the center of her universe—a timeline of his life in framed photos, from the day he was born to the present.

"Oh, Luka." Sabrina's gentle voice feels like a comforting hug; her presence alone works wonders, calming me. She scoots over and places her head on my shoulder.

"I don't know what to do," I say, my voice trembling with uncertainty and a hint of vulnerability. Resting my chin on her head, I try to make sense of my tangled feelings.

"What do you mean?"

"Something feels off with her husband," I whisper, and I know she's heard it, cuz her body goes stiff.

"Have you met him?"

"No."

Frankly, I don't want to see his face. If I do, I might lose control and do something I'll regret, like punch him. The idea of him sleeping through Nora's suffering fills me with a mix of anger and helplessness I can't shake. And then, there's that whole scene in the kitchen, when she had that little slip thinking I hadn't caught it. Sure, I had to brush up on my Ibsen classic, having read it back in high school, but it didn't take long for my mind to put it all together, making me wonder if Nora is truly happy in her marriage.

"She has this look in her eyes, there's so much pain and emptiness there that it breaks my heart every time I see her. All I want to do is fix it," I falter, "I don't know how to fix it."

That's what I do. I am a fixer. It's my purpose. It's who I am.

"I know you don't want to look at me right now, and I am

going to respect it. That said, I hate to break it to you, but that is not your job. You don't know the story, her reasons, and it is not fair of you to make assumptions. Be her friend. I'm sure she could use one as great as you."

That's what I'm talking about. That's Sabrina for you—heart of gold with a tough exterior, same as yours truly.

I take a long breath, but it comes out shaky. My lungs are obviously trying to tell me something. It's Sabrina who verbalizes it. "You know you can't go there, right? Whether it's a happy marriage or not, it's still wrong."

"Going there was never my intention, not since I became aware of the ring on her finger."

"Good, keep it that way, for both your sakes," she concludes. "What is it with all of you Harts falling for women with baggage?"

"You tell me, you were the first member of the club."

Sabrina waltzed into our family with a heavy load of her own: parents who didn't love her, emotionally abused her, and had done disgusting things not only to her but also to others. Her father, who was a state judge at the time, had wronged the system, and Sabrina took it upon herself to bring his wrongdoings to light. Doing so, she lost everything, her family, her inheritance, all her possessions... she found a new family at the end, with my brother's push. At first, she refused his love, and it took a fair amount of convincing, but eventually she found her way to him, and the rest is history.

"Hey, I am a ray of sunshine and the best thing that ever happened to your brother."

The ray of sunshine is debatable, but the other part, now that one is an understatement. Mateo has never been happier, and that's all thanks to her.

"And to us," I add, tightening my grip around her to show how thankful I am for her blowing into our lives. She squeezes herself into me in understanding.

Sabrina pushes away and lifts her head, captivating my eyes with one of her famous scans.

"She already broke your heart, didn't she?"

I acknowledge the admission by dropping my head. She broke my heart the second I learned her name and felt the metal that represents a promise she made to someone else.

Chapter 17

Nora

I hear the key in the lock and freeze halfway through peeling the onion. The rest of the ingredients sit untouched on the counter, the rice still unopened.

The door clicks shut.

"You're just starting now?" His voice comes from behind me, not even a hello to start with.

Not turning around, I say through gritted teeth, "It's Wednesday."

So?

My mind enjoys playing the guessing game of his retorts.

"So?"

Score.

So, you can't even memorize a simple weekly schedule.

One that hasn't changed in over a year.

One that says: Wednesday, therapy 04:30-05:30 PM.

"We just got home."

He steps into the kitchen, drops his keys on the counter with a clatter that feels like a deliberate punctuation mark. "You were home all day."

I keep my eyes on the cutting board. The onion is already stinging, but it's not the reason why my eyes fill with water. Most days, I make lunch while Dec naps, but sometimes I don't get a chance because of other housework.

Not accepting my silence for an answer, he tsks. "I'm not asking for much, Nor. Just dinner when I get home."

I set the knife down carefully. At the moment, it looks way too much like a weapon. The edge scrapes the board louder than intended.

Wow.

Just—wow.

God bless my body for multitasking all the restraints… Not letting my tears fall, not allowing my hand to break something, and keeping my tongue at bay.

"Give me half an hour and dinner will be ready."

He folds his arms. "It's not about the food. It's about effort."

Oh no, he didn't.

"Effort?" I turn now, facing him fully.

The nerve of him.

You mean like me holding my tongue every time you toss your socks on the living room floor? Or me staying quiet when you play on your phone during dinner? Or how my body refuses to flinch at all your disparages… and let's not mention how I bite my tongue while you enter me without any preparation, while I am completely dry…

Though the last part hasn't happened in far too long, not that I'm complaining.

Be that as it may, I don't verbalize any of it out loud. What's the use?

His jaw clenches as he exhales.

Here we go.

The veins on his neck are popping out, which tells me

he's yelling, but I don't hear his insults. They don't get to me, ricocheting. It's moments like these when I don't feel like a person, a wife, a mother. I am nothing. I'm floating away, a shell.

"Whatever. I'll make a sandwich."

I stand there, heart thudding. Anger—gone, hurt—gone. Just… tired. So utterly tired. I watch him open a fridge, then I turn back to the onion, contemplating tossing it.

Maybe I'll still make dinner, just not for him.

Cozied up in my corner on the couch, I roll my eyes at another one of Rick's remarks on how the heartfelt scene annoys him. Finding something we can watch together is another of my many challenges. It takes a couple of episodes for Rick to find a character who starts getting on his nerves. That usually makes us stop watching mid-show. His tolerance limit has reached a new low, barely making it through one entire episode. So when I stumbled across a detective show with excellent ratings, I was more than excited.

With Declan tucked in, we are miraculously reaching the second season finale. After giving me the silent treatment, Rick sat down, tossed the remote, and acted as if nothing had happened.

Something I am very much au fait with.

There I am, bawling my eyes out as Will Trent has a

conversation with his mother's ghost, reflecting on his past. The more Will confesses to the guilt he feels, the more Rick scoffs. Something in me snaps. "Why do feelings bother you so much? Don't you understand that these things are crucial for humanizing a character, not to mention for their development?"

It's funny, really, how I've found the strength to fight, and not for me, but rather for a fictional character.

"What's up your ass?" he seethes, not bothering to look at me.

"It worries me, the fact that you get so negative over everything. You weren't like this before," I avow.

"Life didn't kick me in the ass on the daily before." It comes out in a growl, and I can't say the words don't sting. I pause the TV, grabbing his attention.

"Is your life, *our* life, so bad?"

I regret the question instantly, fear taking over at the thought of his possible answer.

He remains stoic, his expression that of a robot devoid of emotion.

"That's not what I meant."

"I'm not sure anymore." I drop my head, playing with my fingers on my lap. I let out a long sigh, nerves taking over as I let my thoughts linger at the tip of my tongue.

"What's that supposed to mean?"

"It means you're not happy."

I'm rewarded with indifference. How sad is it that I want him to yell, shout, do anything other than just sit there?

The baby monitor decides it's time to start emitting static. I take that as a sign.

With a mental push, I spout, "I think we should try couples therapy. I found one in the autistic help center, they would take care of Declan during our session."

This has been on the back burner for quite some time. I've done my part, writing it over with Sunny and surfing the internet to find someone suitable to hear our story. I never confronted Rick about it, too scared of what he might say.

"I don't need that shit," he blusters, unbothered as ever.

Even knowing what he was gonna say, his words still managed to weigh on my chest, pressing, and pressing, leaving no room for air. I should know better, but this was a Hail Mary, my last resort before I go all coo-coo.

"Well, I do. I can't keep going on like this," I assert, all my energy going into keeping my voice firm and determined.

"Like what?" For the first time, I see a glimpse of concern that sparks a glimmer of hope.

"The back and forth. I tell you I miss you, that I need something to change, and you do it for two days, only to go back to the way things were. We keep going in circles, and I can't stand it anymore."

I wonder if he can hear the tremor in my voice.

"What are you saying? You want out?" His abrasive tone sends the wrong kind of shivers down my spine, so I stand up, pulling on my hair, averting the pain into a physical one.

"Why can't you ever listen to what I am saying for fudge's sake? I am telling you that I want to work on this, us, our life. The life you seem not to be so happy about. We both know something is wrong. I begged you, time and again, to tell me what I could do. I did my part; I spread my legs more often, and I asked you for one thing, one thing, Rick. Guess what?

You failed; you didn't deliver on your promise. Now it's time to bring someone else in to help find common ground, because I want to make this work. I want you to be happy with me." By the end, I sound miserable, giving my all into my delivery.

"I *am* happy."

His voice begs to differ.

I've gotten so used to the pain in my chest that I surprise myself by pushing back.

"Well, I'm not," I break down, not able to contain the waterfalls. I guess I was wrong; I hadn't shed all the tears meant for Rick, not by a long shot.

"Nor? Fuck." He stands up and wraps his long arms around me, and I lean into him, pressing my cheek against his chest.

"Please, Rick, I miss you, I can't take it any longer, it hurts so much," I sob, choking on the words. He stays silent, his grip tight. I want it to be tighter. I need it, if only for some much-needed reassurance.

"Fine, but don't expect any miracles."

His words shouldn't relax me, nor should relief wash over whatever's been building inside of me, and yet it happens. It's a crumb, a mere pinch of effort, but I take it anyway. It's my signature move after all.

He kisses the top of my head. It's a quick peck, but it's enough to pull me in.

He's still there... The guy who rode a bike for twelve miles because the bus didn't run during the night, and he couldn't wait to see me. The guy who went to eight different record stores to get me the newest Britney album.

He's still there, and God, how I've missed him.

"I love you more than you can even imagine. Thank you," I mumble into his shirt.

Hope flies around us as I stay there, all warmed up by his body. I know we have a long way to go, but I am willing to do anything and everything to keep on building our life.

Don't

Days go by
Weeks pass
Now it's years away
From the time I knew you would stay

I'm slowly breaking
Begging, holding tight to the past
I'm slowly breaking
Knowing I have to loosen my ties

Please don't stop loving me
My heart begs for you to stay
Not to leave, so please don't go
Don't abandon me or our love

Days go by
Weeks pass
Now, it's years away
And I still put you first

I'm slowly breaking
Begging, holding tight to the past
I'm slowly breaking
Knowing I have to loosen my ties

Please don't stop loving me.
My heart begs for you to stay
Not to leave, so please don't go
Don't abandon me or your love

Chapter 18

Luka

Finally, the weekend. It comes like an answered prayer, since it's been a hell of a week. Work was hectic, but at least we passed the safety inspection, and everything is up to date. So that's a huge load off my shoulders.

"Morning," Mama sings as I step into the kitchen.

"Morning," I parrot, going straight for the coffee pot. Footsteps thunder over the steps, and yes, I can distinguish whose they belong to. First comes Tristan, followed by Mak. Tyler is last to descend, his steps always slow. He's not a morning person, same as me, so he mostly drags himself. He's on his summer break, so we are blessed with his presence, as he put it, the moment I picked him up at the train station.

We say our greetings, and each fills our mugs with the wake-up juice before taking our seats at the table. We all look at the empty chair and chuckle. As if summoning him, the door swings open and in walks Mateo.

Mama's smile reaches her eyes, and she jumps to her feet to embrace him. We all join in that big family hug, lingering longer than necessary. Or maybe it is necessary. We're getting older. Mateo moved out to live with his wife, and Tyler is living his best college life in New York. Tristan will be doing the same in a couple of months. Things are changing. We're still close, and we try to keep it that way over Zoom calls and visits whenever we can, but I can't help but feel a bit resentful. Is it wrong? I know it is.

Everyone is moving on. Mateo and Sabrina are conquering the world. Tyler is in a happy relationship with Maddison. Tristan is making a name for himself in football. Mak is busy becoming a doctor. And here I am, stuck.

That brings out the question… When will it be my turn? Is it even in the cards for me? Something real? That feeling when you meet someone and it just clicks? The kind of connection that makes you forget about how fucked up the world is. When it feels like finally someone sees you, and for a split second, you think, maybe this is what I've been waiting for…

You felt it, though.

My mind reminds me of that zing. Hazel eyes flash by, freckled skin, full lips pulled in a smile… Instantly, the flutter in my stomach grows bigger, restless.

It's wrong, I think to myself.

"Where's the wife?" Tristan mocks our brother, wiggling his brows. Yes, when they first started dating, Tristan had a huge crush on Sabrina, but I think it was more of him trying to mess with Mateo than anything else.

"Working on a case, she'll come by later for the book club."

Tristan nods and turns to Ty. "MJ knows the time?"

She's in Chicago, spending the summer with her mom. They've been estranged, so to speak, and it took them a while to get close again, especially after everything Maddison has been through. To say I am proud of that firecracker would be an understatement.

"Yup," Tyler answers, popping the P.

It was a no-brainer to add the girls to our club. Though it was awkward for them at first, especially when discussing romance books, they eventually relaxed into it.

Mateo comes to my side, "How are you doing?"

"I'm good," I answer, leaving out the fact that I am missing someone like crazy and can't do a fucking thing about it.

"You know you can talk to us. You're always there for others, let us be here for you," it's Mak who jumps in, coming to my other side. I cross my arms over my chest, locking my hands under my armpits.

I feel wrong talking about it," I falter. As if uttering my feelings out loud would send me straight to hell, especially since I'm already one foot in just having them in silence.

"Why?" Tristan cuts in. Guess this is turning into a family discussion.

"Because she's married, and talking about it is admitting it."

"Am I hearing this right? A married woman, Luka?" Mama shouts, pushing through my brothers to come in front of me. Our mother is a petite woman, her nose in line with the middle of my chest. But don't let that fool you. That woman is scary. Almost as much as Sabrina. No, scratch that, worse than Sabrina.

"It's nothing, Mama. It's just a friendship. Not even that," I try to downplay it, but it's useless. Yes, we only had a couple of interactions, but I feel like I know her. Like she knows me. Better than anyone, and that's saying something. That's saying a lot.

"But you like her?"

"It's impossible not to," I shudder.

"Oh, Luka," she sighs, bringing her hand up to cup my cheek. I lean into her touch, allowing the warmth to spread.

"Don't worry. I'm keeping my distance. Though it's gonna be hard since she's Ryan's best friend and the co-godparent to his daughter."

"What?" every member of the family screams at me. Yeah, I haven't really revealed that information yet.

"Yeah, turns out she's Auntie El."

The shock on their faces is almost laughable. Like me, they heard all the stories about the woman in question. Tristan once debated whether she was a figment of the kids' imagination, since we never got to meet her, calling her "too good to be true."

"I thought you said her name is Nora," Mateo jumps in, surprising me. I don't remember ever mentioning her name. One person comes to mind: Sabrina. How on earth she got that information is beyond me, but I will get it out of her eventually.

"Long story short. Her full name is Eleonora, but only the kids call her El. She introduced herself to me as Nora. Hence, why I didn't connect the dots," I state, trying my best not to smile while saying her name.

"Wow," Tyler gasps, "what are the odds?"

My brothers bob their heads in perfect sync, but my eyes are on Mama.

One loud clearing of her throat is all it takes for my brothers to skedaddle so fast that both Tristan and Mak stumble on their way upstairs.

"What can I do?" she offers in her soft voice, taking a seat on the couch and patting the spot next to her. I take it, dropping my head into my palms.

That's Eva Hart for you. Always putting others first. If you thought she'd yell at me, tell me how stupid I am, you're wrong. That's not who she is. She has the purest of hearts and the ability to read people with 100% accuracy.

"Tell me what to do here," I agonizingly lament, placing my head on her lap. Her hand flies to my hair, fingers gently brushing through as if to let me know she understands.

"Tell me something, is the reason you're keeping your distance for your benefit or hers?"

I don't hesitate when I say, "Hers."

After spending some time with her, and all the stories I've heard over the years, one thing's for sure. Nora is loyal. And not just that, she cares too much. So, my making a move would only result in her feeling guilty, and that is something I don't dare allow.

"I raised you right," Mama boasts, her voice screaming with pride. And that settles the nerves, making my mind at ease. This woman gave me a life, a purpose, and her undivided love when she took me in all those years ago. And despite my reservations, no matter how many times I pushed her away at the beginning, she never gave up on me, winning me over in the end. Sure, trust issues are still a big part of me, and who can blame me? I spent the first five years of my childhood fearing for my life. Literally. I was one hit away from serious brain damage, courtesy of my parents, before I was taken from the house of terror. Then Eva came along, with her gentle voice, touch, and eyes that screamed kindness. She was patient, never raised her voice at me, and did everything in her power to keep me. She held my hand as I watched my birth father get taken away, his hands cuffed behind him, with people shouting 'Murderer' around us. He got a life sentence, not enough of a punishment, in my opinion.

"You'll find the one, my sweet boy, just you wait," she declares, and I sigh.

What if I already found her?

Chapter 19

Luka

"Luka, my man," Ryan shouts as he steps out of the truck. I wave at the guys and walk to meet them.

It's a hot day today, and the humidity is getting on my last nerves. I'm not even halfway through my day, and I am already soaked in sweat.

"Thank you for coming. We need all hands on deck," I salute my appreciation, using my hand to shield my eyes from the burning sun.

One of the electricians struck a pipe, flooding the site. Thankfully, it was only the ground floor, so the damage wasn't as severe. Now I need as many workers as I can get to help move things along. I called in a favor and brought five large dehumidifiers. They are already set up, with some air movers (big fans) to speed up the process. This will put us behind by at least two days, but as long as it stays at that number, it will be okay.

"No problem," Leo, Ryan's boss, says, extending his hand. I shake it, and they follow me inside. After a quick rundown, I take my best friend into my office. They've arrived just in time for the lunch break, so I figure it'd be best if we hide out and enjoy some peace and quiet.

It doesn't last long, because as soon as I take a first bite of my pastrami, Ryan's phone starts to ring. He turns the screen to me, showing Nora's name flashing. I'm on my feet and take the seat next to him before he answers.

"El, is everything okay?" I hate that he's started the conversation like that. It makes me think it's the only reason why she'd call him in the first place.

I don't hear what she's saying, but I do see Ryan go pale, and I feel a pang of worry. I place my hand on his shoulder, and he puts the phone on speaker.

"What happened? Where's Rick?" he asks.

She clears her throat.

"You know there's no service."

I know Rick works in the mines, but that is no excuse. There has to be some emergency contact. I can't even think straight.

"It's fine. I just fell and hit my head. It doesn't hurt, but just in case..." she hesitates for a beat before adding, "Declan." When she says his name, I can hear the panic in her voice.

"We're on our way," I say, standing up. Ryan follows, and we are in my pickup and on the road so fast that my heartbeat is all over the place. I can feel the loud thumping, the thing trying to jump out of my chest. I am speeding, but I don't care. It's Nora for fuck's sake.

She fell.

In her driveway, I leave the truck running, and Ryan uses his key to rush us inside. Nora is on the floor, Declan next to her, playing with wooden blocks.

"You didn't have to come," she looks up at us, but something is off.

I get on my knees in front of her, coming face to face. Her left eye isn't looking at me. More panic strikes, and I pick her up without a word.

"You stay with Declan; he knows you better, and I'll take her to the hospital," I tell Ryan, and he nods, plastering her ass on the floor next to his nephew.

"It's not necessary. I'm fine," she mutters.

Her being difficult right now only adds to the fuming. What? She'd just sleep it off if it weren't for us? Not on my watch.

"This is nonnegotiable," I snap, carrying her to my truck. I help her get settled and buckle her seatbelt, then round the car, trying not to slam the door. Her head must be throbbing, and no matter how enraged I am, I don't want to add to the headache.

"I am so angry at you right now," I admit, my voice cracking. I get out my phone and dial my brother as I back out of the driveway. He answers on the second ring.

Skipping the salutations, I blurt, "Nora fell, hit her head, her left eye is out of focus. I'm taking her to Mass General."

"It's probably just a minor concussion," Mak says in a steady voice, "I'll wait for you at the entrance. And Luka?"

"Yeah?"

"Breathe," he defuses, and I listen, taking a deep breath.

He knows me too well. I tend to go into a state of panic when the people I care about are hurt. And he knows Nora is on that list of people. She needs me to be there for her, and I need to keep my mind sharp, at least until I get her to him.

As we pull up at the emergency entrance, I see Mak in his scrubs, a nurse at his side, holding onto a wheelchair. I get out of my truck and round it to open the door for Nora. She tries to get out on her own, but I don't allow it; I pick her up instead.

"I can walk just fine, Luk," she groans. I don't have time to delve into how the shortened name slipped past her lips, too busy carrying her to my brother. He gives me a nod, and I watch him take her behind the sliding doors. Knowing she's not alone gives me a small sense of relief.

My hands fly to the back of my neck, fingers intertwining, keeping me from punching a wall.

"She'll be okay," I tell myself.

She has to be ok.

Declan needs her.

I need her.

Fuck.

I take out my phone and call Ryan on my way to move my truck. It doesn't even ring before his worried voice reverberates through the line. "Is she ok?"

As much as I am freaking out here, I need him calm for that kid's sake. So I take a breath, shaking off the tremble.

"Mak has her," I disclose, "How's Declan?"

I find an empty parking spot nearby and back up into it.

"He's ok. He's watching Bluey."

I get out of my truck and take long strides to the waiting room. Feeling helpless and overwhelmed, I start pacing. Every second feels like an eternity, and I can't shake the dread that's settling in.

"She'll be ok. El is a tough one."

It does fuck all to calm the nerves; they're all over the place. I take in my surroundings, all the people sharing the same expression I must be sporting.

"I know," I falter. "Ryan?"

"Hm?"

My free hand makes a fist, my body's attempt to suppress the rage.

"Rick…" I hesitate, "I can't get past this. How can he be unavailable? He's got a wife and a kid, for crying out loud."

There is no way on earth I would ever make myself unreachable to my family. No chance in hell.

"I know, and I am right there with you. It's how it is with them. I don't understand it, but El asked me to respect it, and I am doing my best to do so."

That's not good enough. Not in the slightest. Releasing my clenched fist, I stretch out my fingers, stopping the spasm from happening.

"Well, I didn't make such promises," I hiss, eyeing my shaking hand.

"Don't meddle. It will only make it worse. Trust me." There's a plea in his voice that I can't ignore. So I leave it at that, letting him know I will call with any updates before I hang up.

The door opens, and out comes my brother. I meet him halfway.

"Minor concussion, no damage to the optic nerve. She shouldn't take any medication just in case. If you want, I can leave her here for the night."

"No, she wouldn't want that. She wouldn't want to leave Declan."

He nods.

"She has to take it easy, rest for at least two days."

I snicker on the inside, knowing Nora, that won't be happening.

"I'll take her to the ophthalmologist for a check and get back to you right after," my brother adds.

God, how lucky I am to have a doctor in the family. I don't know what I would've done if it weren't for him. Just knowing he's there by her side eases the helplessness I feel.

"Thank you," I sigh, pinching the bridge of my nose. A headache is coming. I can feel it.

"Are you ok?"

"No," I admit, my voice cracking. "I've never been so scared in my life."

"Not even…" he swallows.

"No, not even when I thought my father was going to kill me," I finish for him.

"Shit," he mumbles, pushing up his glasses.

"I know. I am so fucked up."

"Luka, you can't do this to yourself. It's not your fault that you fell for someone who isn't available."

"It's eating me alive anyway," I wail, and he opens his arms.

"Come here."

A nervous laugh escapes me. Mak is half my size, despite being two years older than me, yet he's the one who wants to embrace me? I take it anyway, relaxing in his hold, knowing damn well that we must look silly.

I hear my name being called from behind me, and I see the rest of my brothers rushing in, followed by our mama. Mak must've called them.

"We're here, brother."

And with that, I fall apart, lucky to be a part of this family, this support system we created together.

However, I hate that a part of me wants to add two more members.

135

Chapter 20

Nora

I feel like a five-year-old again, hiding in my room while the adults are at each other's throats downstairs. My parents didn't fight much, but when they did, it was brutal. Back then, my go-to was to run. I can't do that now. I have a kid to think about. Plus, Tessa is giving me a weird look. I can't believe Ryan called her, as if she doesn't have enough on her plate with three kids and a baby stuck to her boob.

Luka drove me home from the hospital, things between us awkward. He barely looked at me, and we didn't exchange a single word. None. I know he's angry with me. He said so himself. And there's nothing I can say to that.

Anyway, when I got home, the tension could've been cut with a knife. Ryan sent daggers at my husband through his glare, and Rick couldn't be bothered. Tessa hugged Luka. Rick ignored him completely. Ryan, my soon-to-be ex-best friend, picked me up like a baby and carried me upstairs, where he tucked me in with a kiss to the forehead. "Don't you dare move," is what he said—demanded, actually. Soon after, Tessa came, my baby boy in hand, and took a seat on the bed next to me. Dec went to his favorite corner on the floor and flipped through his book. And that's when all hell broke loose. They were loud, but not loud enough for us to understand a single word. The sound of the front door slamming shut echoed, followed by an engine roaring to life.

With two voices left, I count each tear as Ryan and Rick continue with their stupid altercation. I don't want a repeat of last year. I bring my knees to my chest at the mere thought. About a year ago, Ryan decided to tell Rick off. It turned into a heated argument and ended with them on non-speaking terms. We missed every single family gathering from then on.

"I'm sorry," I snivel, using my T-shirt as a handkerchief.

"What are you sorry for?"

"You should be with your kids, not here. I can take care of myself," I say, proud at how firmly I sound.

"Yeah, El, we got that," Tessa scoffs, and I narrow my eyes.

"What is that supposed to mean?"

"You should rest," she insists, deflecting my question. "I'll get Dec to bed. If you need anything, call me."

"Tess?" I say her name like I am begging for something, except I don't know what it is I'm begging for. Her understanding, maybe…

"It's ok, El. I get it," she falters, and I drop my head. Dec goes with her, and as soon as the door closes behind them, I crumble.

I wake up with the biggest headache I've ever endured. I check the time—five AM. I get up and go to Dec's room to check on him. I creak the door open and watch him through the crack, sound asleep. I linger for a moment, thankful to Tessa for tucking him in, then head downstairs to get a glass of water. Mak, Luka's brother, told me I shouldn't take any medications, so I am honestly hoping that a cold glass of water will help with the pounding in my head. I reach the couch, where Rick has his leg sprained over the armrest. Honestly, I don't even understand how he can sleep on that thing. I find it uncomfortable. That's when I see a figure in the corner. Ryan. He stayed the night? Shoot. I hate this. And he's all scrunched up in the armchair. I walk to him and tap his shoulder gently. He flinches and jumps to his feet. "What?" His head is turning in every direction until it settles on me. "Are you ok?"

"I'm good, go to my bed. I'll sleep in Dec's room."

His bed has a pull-out bed underneath. Ryan knows that, and he still chose the stupid chair. He doesn't protest, dragging himself behind me. Over my shoulder, I whisper, "Thank you, Ry."

"Anything for you. You know that."

I do. We've been thick as thieves since the age of five. Inseparable. He knows me to my core. So when I tuck him in this time, his words surprise me: "I hate him."

Ryan is not a hateful person. There was never animosity toward anyone, not the bullies in school, not his parents, no one. So, for him to say it out loud comes as a shock. I know he's referring to Rick, and for the first time, I don't have the urge to defend him. I give my best friend a peck on the cheek and whisper, "Me too." The words linger in the air, a heavy secret for us to share.

I get downstairs again, hoping this time there'll be no distractions in my attempt to soothe the headache, only to find my husband on his feet. He's angry, and by the look he's sending my way, I am the reason. He doesn't look me over, doesn't ask if I'm ok, or to tell him what happened. No, Rick doesn't care for that.

"You allowed him to take you to the hospital?"

I should be stunned, disgusted even. Yet, I am none of those things. With my breath steady, heart rate at the perfect pace, I walk past him, grab a glass of water, and head back to Dec's room.

When I reach the first step, so does his scrutiny. "Wow, the silent treatment. Really, Nor?"

"I learned from the best," I reply over my shoulder without giving him a single glance.

Chapter 21

Nora

Me: *I need some of your wisdom*

Sunny: *I'm all eyes*

I chuckle. Typing away. I have my laptop open on the kitchen table; Dec is in the middle of his nap, so I have enough time to pour my heart out.

Me: *So… you know how I have a best friend who is a guy, and no one ever questions our relationship because it's overplatonic?*

Sunny: *Yes?*

Me: *Well, I met a new friend, except this friendship feels different*

Sunny: *Different how?*

Me: *I don't know how to explain it. He makes me rethink my entire relationship with Rick. Like every interaction or action has a side effect called reflection.*

Sunny: *Can you give me an example?*

Me: *It's the small, stupid things I never paid much attention to, like picking up a plate and putting it in the sink. Rick has never done that, even after I begged and begged. To Luka, it's second nature.*

Sunny: *Who is this Luka guy? You never mentioned him.*

Me: *He's Hulk*

Sunny: Interesting *monocle face emoji.

Me: *He did the sidewalk thing*

Sunny: *Oh, snap*

You must be wondering why that's a big deal. It is, trust me. Especially when you're a mother. I always walk on the curb side; it's like an instinct. Rick has never done that. He's always the furthest one away. And then there's Luka. When we went for ice cream, he was the one walking along the edge, no matter which side of the road we were on, like it was part of his DNA.

Me: *How terrible a person am I?*

Sunny: *You're human, Nor. But I am curious about this Luka character. Can you maybe give me a picturesque* *description?*

Me: *Imagine the new Jack Reacher, only with dark hair.*

Sunny: **drooling emoji*
Sunny: *So you have eyes, big whoop. Is there anything more to it?*

Me: *No! I would never*

Sunny: *I know you wouldn't, but are there feelings involved?*

Are there? I love Rick, that's all I know. I don't want anyone else. I never have. But around Luka, I can tell that I'm more open, relaxed, almost like I can breathe. I don't have to pick my words or think before I speak. It's confusing. I don't understand what these feelings mean or if they are just a fleeting distraction.

Me: *I don't know*

Sunny: *Want my professional opinion or a woman-to-woman?*

Me: *Door number two, please.*

Sunny: *There is nothing wrong with getting close to someone else, especially when you're not feeling appreciated in your own home. As long as you don't cross the line, which I* *know you would never do.*

Me: *Not in a million years. On that note, Rick agreed to therapy. We have an appointment on Wednesday.*

Sunny: *That's great. Bring the letters with you.*

Me: *Why?*

Sunny: *Professionally speaking, even though you refuse to accept it, Rick has narcissistic tendencies, and there is a possibility he will charm the therapist, which will result in you forgetting every bad thing he's done. Having the letters with you will be a physical reminder.*

I stare at the screen, dumfounded by her message. When I don't reply, Sunny throws a word bomb at me.

Sunny: *I am gonna say something I am not supposed to. Abuse is not always physical. It's not always loud. Most of it is silent, to punish you. It's smart, making you feel guilty for things you didn't do, and you end up questioning yourself. It alters your perception, confuses you to the point where you begin to doubt everything. It erodes your self-worth until you don't know what's real anymore. The longer it goes on, the more it damages your brain. And you think if you stay a little longer, if you try a bit harder, that things will work out, but the longer you wait, the more it's gonna break you.*

I don't believe what I'm reading. Abuse? I mull over what

she's getting at. Is it so far-fetched? No. I refuse to believe it, focusing on the last thing she wrote.

Me: *Leaving is not an option*

Sunny: *Do me a favor. Imagine being loved the way you love. Just for a minute, indulge me on this. Don't think too much, just picture it. To be loved without wondering if you're too much or not enough. To have someone who chooses you, loudly, wholly, without needing a reminder. If that's Rick, great. But if it's not… then you need to prioritize your happiness and finally speak up.*

I blink, reading her words over and over again, letting them sink in. Growing up, I was taught that keeping quiet keeps the peace. I lived by that notion my entire life. But now I wonder… whose peace was it keeping?

Without thinking, I open a new tab and type the word 'narcissist' in the bar. I read over the definition. At first, I don't see the connection to Rick's personality. But the more I scroll, the more my stomach twists. Going over the characteristics and behaviors, I linger on gaslighting. And I remember all the times I ended up on the bathroom floor, rethinking whether I'd gotten it all wrong, doubting my own memory.

I find an article that discusses the impact that narcissistic behavior has on the partner: emotional exhaustion, loss of self-esteem, isolation, anxiety, and confusion. The words are mocking me as I stare at them in disbelief.

I think about the person I was before we moved to Boston. I had so many friends, a future… I was somebody.

Who am I now?

With that, I close the tabs and open a file on the desktop. The albums are neatly separated by eras. I click on my college years. The first one that pops up is of me, center stage, a violin on my shoulders. My eyes are closed, and I know that I am in the middle of performing. I always played with my eyes closed so that I could feel the music. I go to the next one; it's the entire music orchestra. I am the first chair, next to Tina, my roommate and best friend at the time. She also played the violin. I can't even recall the last time I saw her, probably at my wedding. Tears start to fall, and I can feel my heart sinking with each new photo. Where is this woman? Have I repressed her so much that I can't even remember her anymore? I skim through the pictures a little faster, stopping when I see words scribbled on the screen. There are music notes above each word.

If you dream, it will happen
If you want it, you have to take it
No one does you better than you do
So why not be the best you can
Reach for the stars, but make sure yours is the brightest
You are your own light, don't need another to shine it
The world is yours, all you gotta do is take it
Live it
Love it
Be it

I close the laptop with a smack.   There's a fire burning inside of me, anger taking over. How did I let this happen?

Worse of all, I didn't even see it. I see it now. And I am ready to fight. For me. For Declan.

Chapter 22

Nora

I check the clock for the umpteenth time: 5:20.

He's not coming.

I pretend my phone is buzzing, bringing the screen to life.

"It's Rick. Says he got caught up at work and can't make it," I lie, hiding my embarrassment. Dr. Neven gives me a slight nod, pressing her lips together. She doesn't buy it. I can see it in her eyes, the pity.

"How does that make you feel?"

I wonder how many times a day she says that line.

We've been quiet so far, waiting for my husband to join the session. A part of me knew he wouldn't, the other part, the delusional one, still hoped.

"It's fine," I blurt out my usual line, camouflaging the fact that I feel hollow.

"Ok. Let's talk about your son." She checks her notes, or whatever it is she's holding in her hand. "Says here he's five?"

"Yeah, just turned a couple of months ago."

We took him to Disneyland, despite Rick's protests. Money was tight, but I made do, for him. The smile on that kid's face when he saw the *Dumbo* ride will forever be imprinted in my brain cells. It was a perfect day, until it wasn't.

Rick got bored, we left early, and that was that. Luckily, Dec got through all his favorites, so it wasn't a total bust.

Clearing her throat, Dr. Neven nods. She seems like a nice lady. Very polished, polite, back straight, not a single hair out of place in her tight bun hairdo. Her nails are glossy, oval-shaped, and perfectly manicured. Wearing a beige pencil skirt and a white button-down, the woman looks like the poster model for her profession. The only thing missing is the glasses, but we'll bypass it.

"So tell me about him," she encourages, and I wiggle on the two-seater, straightening up a bit. Declan happens to be my favorite subject in the world.

"He's an early bird, loves water, and the playground. He's smart, extremely so. At the age of three, he got into the alphabet, and could name at least five words for each letter," I yap, taking quick breaths between sentences. "He's starting to read, and he loves books, mostly Disney. Right now, he's in his *Bambi* phase. We have the whole shebang: toys, books, bedding..." I trail off, toning down the proud mama bear.

"Tell me about your typical day, a quick round-up."

At least I don't have to think about how or what to answer, since most of my days are pretty much the same.

"I get up, box up Rick's lunch so he can take it to work. At six, Dec wakes up, and we get dressed, have breakfast, and play a bit. It's mostly just me watching him play, but that's beside the point. We take a walk, go to the playground, and walk back home. Then he has his nap, during which I make lunch and clean up around the house. When he wakes up, we eat, play, go to therapy, and then take another long walk.

When we get back home, I give Dec a bath, make dinner, we eat it, then go through our bedtime routine before I put him to bed."

That's it. That's my life for ya.

"And you do all that by yourself." It's not a question, and there's a slight tone in her statement that she tried to hide. I heard it. I always do. Judgment.

"I am the one home with him while Rick works," I get on the defensive, my eyes locked on hers. She tilts her head, reading me. I hope she doesn't see the fear, but I have a feeling she's seeing a lot more than I give away.

"When he's home, does he help in any way?"

My silence answers for me.

"How about on the weekends?"

Internally, I am scoffing; on the outside, I play dumb. "What about them?"

"Do the three of you do anything together? Do Declan and Rick do something alone?"

I play with the pendant around my neck, brushing it between my fingers, focusing on the cold metal. I need to get out of this conversation before I say something I'm going to regret.

"I don't see the point of these kinds of questions; we're here to talk about my marriage, not my parenting."

I know what I'm doing. And the look on her face tells me it's working.

"I am just trying to get the bigger picture here. I didn't mean to offend you."

She doesn't deserve my outburst; she's only doing her job, and she's good at it. That is the problem. I thought I was ready. I thought I had it all figured out. Boy, was I wrong.

"You didn't. I am a good mother. I'm doing the best I can," I lash out, getting to my feet.

"Eleonora…" She doesn't get to finish; I am already out the door, storming out like a spoiled little brat who just heard the word 'no' for the first time. God, what is wrong with me?

Why can't I talk about shit? Why can't I admit out loud that I am miserable? That I spend every night in my bed in silence? Centrifuge of thoughts. Questions without answers. The one that hurts the most: *What if I don't want to do this anymore?* And the truth is, I don't even know what *this* is, what it means. All I know is that I am tired. Tired of fighting, of trying, of pretending. I am tired of this version of myself. A version built on proving, repressing, forgetting, insecurity, silence, acting, fear, *shame*…

I wipe the tears that I didn't even register were falling down my cheek in my outburst, and continue walking to the child care area. I take three breaths, compose myself, and open the door. Dec is in the corner, building a tower with blocks in various colors. Sometimes I think it's best he doesn't notice the world around him, especially in times like these, when I am one tear away from completely breaking. I wave at the woman at the counter, and she calls out his name.

Nothing.

Dec doesn't even flinch—one of many things that come with having autism. When he was two, we had to do a hearing test to check whether that was why he never reacted to his name being called. Nope. Perfect hearing.

The nice lady, with long, black hair, sets down her pen and walks over to him, stroking his back gently before he turns to face her. Then he sees me and jumps to his feet, flapping his hands. I tell him to tidy up his toys, and like the good boy he is, he does what he's told. I wait, sharing a smile with the caretaker.

Every toy back in its place, he runs to me, and I wrap him in my arms. It's weird. We've been separated for barely half an hour, and I've missed him every single second. This parenthood thing is so crazy… You want, need, some alone time away from your kid, only to end up missing them.

We take a stroll around the building, a planned diversion on my part. You see, right across the building is The Charles, and that is one route we can not take, or else I'll end up with pneumonia. How, you ask? Well, since Dec loves water so much, he'll want to jump in it, even though he still can't swim (and he doesn't understand danger), meaning I'll have to stop him. So that is a scenario I am trying to avoid.

We take the bus back, and I watch Dec gaze out the window at the trees we pass. We have three more stops to go when the wheels in my head start working. It's a nice day out, and I'm not ready to face reality just yet, so I pull Dec to his feet. He doesn't protest; in fact, his hand is flapping in excitement. We say goodbye to the driver, hop off, and take the longer route to the right.

Slowing our pace, I try my best not to overthink. I'm dreading going home, not knowing what's waiting for me. Birds chirp around us, and Dec tries and fails to mimic the sounds, getting aggravated by the second. I purse my lips into a circle, adjust my tongue, and let out a mild whistle. Dec laughs and pulls my hand—his sign to do it again. I oblige, desperate for the distraction.

When our house comes into view, the heaviness on my chest intensifies, each step forward getting harder.

My guard in place, I put the key in the hole and turn. The door swings open, and my stomach lurches. I am not even angry. How sad is that?

Dec and I go straight upstairs. I see Rick from the corner of my eye, sitting on the couch, but I don't acknowledge him. What's the point anyway? He doesn't listen to me. No, actually, he does listen. But it's not to understand, it's so that he can reply with his point, undermining mine.

My little Bug goes straight for his bookcase and gets out his dinosaur book. I sit on the floor, and he takes his place in my lap, opening the first page. I read the facts about the Aardonyx aloud, feigning fascination, having read them a hundred times before. I never even knew there were so many dinosaurs in the first place. Fun fact: the accurate number doesn't even exist.

We get to the middle when I hear Dec's stomach growling.

Shoot.

I hate myself.

I was so busy avoiding my husband that I forgot to feed my son.

I drop my head in my hands, and bite the sob trying its best to escape.

Guess it's time to face the music.

Chapter 23

Nora

The drive is silent, save for the radio acting as background noise. The tension, now that can be cut with a knife. After Rick skipped the therapy session, we've been more distant than ever. He hasn't apologized, I haven't brought it up, and that's that on the subject. We barely talked over the past month, back to roommate territory.

Familiar opening notes reach my ears, and my hand itches to turn it up. I recoil, recollecting all the times Rick has shut my singing down. I used to belt my lungs out on our road trips, until one day he just told me to stop. It was more in the lines of 'Can you not?', add to it the annoyance in his voice, and puff, another part of me gone.

With that, I turn back to the window, watching life pass by. We're on our way to their family cottage. It was Tessa's idea to celebrate the baptism—a weekend extravaganza, as she put it. I was so honored when she asked me to be the baby's godmother that I almost choked on my own happy tears.

As we approach the property, my stomach flutters with excitement. I haven't been here in far too long, and honestly, I've missed this place.

We're the first to arrive, evident by the empty driveway.

Rick parks the car, and I step out, taking a deep breath. The air is so different here. Not only fresh, but almost unblemished, pure.

I open the back door, and Dec jumps right out. I grab his bag and hold his hand on our way to the water.

It's exactly as I remember it. Breathtaking. Located on its own peninsula, the cottage is all wood, surrounded by nature. A vast yard surrounds the property, with a dock, a patio around a fire pit, and a small private beach area. It's our own little piece of heaven.

I do a quick rundown of all the safety hazards and death traps outside, then beeline to full-on concur the inside, leaving Rick and Dec to fend for themselves a bit. As soon as I step in, the smell of nostalgia hits, reminding me exactly why I love this place so much.

The interior is all wooden-paneled rooms, with a large living area and an unnecessary fireplace. The stunning water views are visible from almost every window, and all the furniture is leather-meets-wood. This cottage was a gift from my in-laws, one we share with the Martins (aka Ryan and Tessa). Sadly, Rick and I haven't been here in… I can't even remember.

I open a couple of windows to air out the space, then bring our stuff up to our room. It's just as I left it.

Downstairs, I step out onto the porch, enjoying the sun's reflection on the water, a kaleidoscope of colors flying across the horizon, making it biblical. I turn my gaze to my little menace running around the grass. The serenity is taking over, so I close my eyes for a moment to take a deep breath, inhaling the scent of pines and water.

Although the inside is great, the outside is where the real magic is, the genuine peace and serenity making this place so enjoyable.

The private beach allows me to relax while Dec does what he does best: own water. Plus, the property is secluded, not to mention gated, so no way for Dec to run out.

Car doors slam in the distance, and I smile.

They're here.

I sprint out back in record time.

You'd think that I'd get greeted, maybe hugged, or something in that direction. But nope. As soon as I step next to the SUV, my arms are overfilled with bags and boxes. So, like the donkey my best friends see me as, I carry it all inside. By my third load, my in-laws park their car next to Ryan's. Elizabeth, or Lizzy, my oldest niece, is the first one to step out of the back seat, sprinting toward me, yelling out my name. I open my arms, and she jumps into my embrace.

"Kid, what are you eating? You've grown so much." I place my hand on top of her head, playing with it as if it's a measuring tape.

I love Rick's family more than I ever thought possible. Being an only child had its perks, but also many downsides. Loneliness being the biggest one. So when I got a brother and a sister with one slip of a ring, I couldn't be happier. I proved myself wrong when Lizzy was born. That was a whole new kind of love that just kept growing with each new member, making me the proudest and happiest of aunts.

"Auntie El!" Ethan and Elijah trap me in a sandwich hug, squeezing the breath out of me.

"Give Auntie El some air, we want her to live,

remember?" Tessa mocks, but they listen, freeing me from their little grips. I give both Tessa and my newest little bundle of joy a hug and a smooching kiss, then turn my attention to Bianca, my mother-in-law, who takes both my hands and scans me from head to toe.

"You're not taking care of yourself enough," she points out.

Fun fact: she always says that.

"Don't worry about me. I'm good," I deadpan, hugging her before turning to Jack. My father-in-law is pure warmth and love, not to mention he gives the softest hugs, one I am now fully taking advantage of.

"How are you, Nor? We've missed you the most," he whispers in my ear so only I can hear.

I hide my snort, lingering a beat longer before I let go.

"I missed you, too. And I'm good, you know me. How are the two of you?"

"Same old, same old. Emphasis on the old," Bianca chirps, adding a wink.

"I can relate, my back turned sixty this morning." We all chuckle and head toward the house.

"Now, Nor, what did I say about being funny?" Jack gives me a nudge with his elbow. He's not Rick and Tessa's biological father, but he has been a true father figure to them ever since Bianca left her ex-husband. She was in an abusive marriage, and when Rick was about three years old, she took the kids and left, never looking back. Jack came soon after, changing their world for the better. He even took Bianca's maiden name, so now they all share it.

"Don't do it, you're already perfect as is," I reiterate his catchphrase for me.

"Damn straight." He gives me an approving nod, followed by a once-over. "You look tired?"

Don't I always? At this point, the bags under my eyes are etched into my skin.

"I only had one coffee," I lie. I had three this morning, but we'll keep that between us.

"Let's remedy that." He drapes an arm over my shoulder, guiding me the rest of the way.

Settled around the sun deck, we do a quick recap of all the action missed since we last saw each other. Jack goes on about his new house project, making Bianca's eyes roll. At this rate, they'll end up stuck with all the exaggeration. She does it with love, though, and it's hard not to giggle at them. Sure, they're in their sixties, but the way they tease each other, feeding off of it, it's hard to take them seriously sometimes. And yes, I envy them daily.

The kids are running through the house, checking whether everything is as they left it. My eyes land on Declan, splashing the water with his little feet, laughing out loud. Somehow, my ear isolates all the noise, anticipating any new sounds that might arrive.

Chapter 24

Luka

Sturbridge is about an hour's drive away. With Tyler in training camp and Mak on call, it's just me, Tristan, and Mama in my truck. Mateo and Sabrina said they'd be popping up later. There's so much excitement and anticipation in knowing my mom will meet Nora and Declan. She's a great judge of character, and her approval means a great deal to me. Last to arrive, I park my pickup behind Ryan's SUV. Tristan had a game this morning, and we drove straight after the big win.

Getting out of my truck, I take in the fresh air and smile. I love this place, been here a couple of times, mostly fishing with Ryan during the fall.

With Tristan's help, I get the stuff out of the bed, and we head to the front of the house. The first thing I do is scan the property, my nerves getting the better of me. I smile at the people filling the sun deck, no sign of Nora or Declan.

"There's the man of the hour," Jack hollers, standing up to greet me. He looks good, too good if I may add. The man could easily pass for a forty-year-old.

"Hardly. This weekend is all about your newest granddaughter," I point out, stopping right in front of him. He taps my shoulder, chuckling just as Bianca opens her arms.

I wrap her in my embrace, muffling her voice. "How are

you, big guy?"

"Good as always, and yourself?"

"Can't complain."

Ryan's in-laws are like an extended family. Growing up, I didn't have the best track record with adult men. Jack changed that perspective with his kindness. They live in Canada, but make sure to visit as much as they can. It's been more frequent since their retirement.

After everyone shares hugs and kisses, I approach Rick. Last time, more accurately, the first time I saw him was after I brought Nora from the hospital. That interaction didn't go all too well. I may have raised my voice, telling him off before I stormed out.

He doesn't bother standing up, so I take that as a challenge by plastering on my best fake smile and extending my hand. He stares at my offering but eventually takes it, finally getting on his feet. I squash the impulse to puff out my chest at the height difference and mumble my name, holding off on the pleasantries.

We shake hands, and he finally speaks, "Rick."

That's it. It's official. I hate the guy. I really, really hate him. Even his voice irks me, and don't get me started on the smug look on his face, like he's better than me.

While my mother and brother make their introductions, I take a chance to check my surroundings once again in hopes of finding two people I've had trouble keeping out of my head.

One whole month. That's how long it's been since that last high five I can still feel on my palm.

"Where's Tessa?" I ask Ryan, who's sprawled on the porch lounger.

"Inside feeding Elle."

Yes. Tessa named my goddaughter after the amazing aunt I'll be sharing my new role with.

"Uncle Hulk!" I hear two little voices echoing, and I turn around to find my favorite boys running right at me. I squat, opening my arms, and they collide into my chest, gushing the wind out of me. "What are you two sluggers up to?" I ask, picking them up.

"We're making sandcastles, wanna join us?" Ethan beams, and I give him an enthusiastic nod. Over my shoulder, I shout, "Be right back," and carry them out back to where the big sand pit I built with my own two hands is.

One distinguished laugh, one that has been playing like a song on repeat in my head, tingles my ears as we approach the pit. The moment I close in on the sound echoing around Cedar Lake, every part of me lights up. With one single breath, I inhale life at the sight of Nora and Declan rolling in the sand. As if sensing me, she stops to lift her head, showing me what I've been missing too damn much. Maybe it's my mind playing tricks on me, but I swear there's a spark in her eyes when they meet mine.

God, how I've missed those hazels.

"Hi, stranger."

The word stings, but it doesn't last long, thanks to the curve of her lips that reaches her freckles. It's impossible to feel anything but bliss at the sight of her.

"Hi, beautiful," I blurt out before I can think better of it. Her cheeks blush at my slip, and I have to fight this craving to pull her into my arms.

While I am contemplating whether I should say sorry for

my inappropriate greeting, Declan's little voice yells, "Crane!" His finger is pointing right at me, turning me into a puddle. That's what he does to me. Sure, it's not my name, but he remembers me, and that's enough—more than enough.

"No, honey. Luka," Nora corrects, taking his hand and mouthing my name in his ear a couple of times. Ok, it was five. I know, because it's caused goosebumps to rise all over my skin. I want to make the sound of her saying my name into a freakin' ringtone.

"I need coffee, so I'm gonna head back. My mother and my youngest brother came with me, if you want to meet them," I say without blinking, not wanting to lose sight of her, them.

"Of course I do!" she exclaims, dusting off the sand. There's eagerness in her voice, and that alone gets me all the more excited.

She takes Declan's hand and comes to my side.

"Are your other brothers coming? You have four, right?"

I nod, taking slow steps to match their pace. "Mateo will come later with his wife. Tyler is in camp for the week, and Mak has to work."

"I'm sorry to pry, but Ryan mentioned you were adopted."

"Is there a question hidden somewhere in there?"

She nudges me with her elbow, the act letting the butterflies inside of me loose.

"We were all fostered," I correct, "Four brothers and one big old me make five."

"What's that like?"

I can't help but notice the playfulness in her voice, the skip in her step, and the smile on her face. She seems different somehow, yet not at all. It's hard to explain. One thing's for sure—I like it.

"As perfect as it is chaotic."

Our family is loud, messy, crazy even, but all wrapped in love. It took us a while to get there, but in truth, it's only made us stronger.

"Don't tell him I said it, but Ryan's kinda jealous of your family," she whispers as if he could hear us. He can't; we're still way too far from the rest of the bunch.

"What?" I chuckle through the word.

"He doesn't have any siblings, and he didn't have a good relationship with his parents; it was the thing that brought us together. We were both running away from home," she reveals.

I'm stunned. This is new information, and I'm not sure why Ryan left that part out.

"He never told me that."

"Really? It's his favorite story," she mumbles, her smile growing wider.

"He told me you met at an old, abandoned playground."

Declan bends down to pick something up, so we stop for a minute before we continue walking to the house. It's a nice day, warm enough for me to start sweating, but not so hot to jump in the lake.

"Yeah, I was building a fort for me to sleep in, and he found me in the middle of fixing up my impromptu roof. He was so impressed that he begged to be my roommate." Her eyes sparkle at the memory.

In my head, I'm rewinding all the conversations shared with Ryan until I get to the information I need.

"Wait, weren't you like five?"

"Yeah," she brushes it with a laugh.

"And you both ran away?"

"Mm-hmm," she hums. "His parents fought a lot, and he couldn't stand the yelling."

"And you?"

"I was more of a drama queen. I wanted attention, so I thought that by running away, my parents would give me the time of day." She tries to hide her frown, but it's all I can see. My heart breaks for her once more—a recurrence at this point.

"That must've been tough," is all I can think to say.

She shrugs. "I had a roof over my head, food on the table, the newest trendy clothes, and all the best toys. It all comes down to me being ungrateful." The sadness in her voice is undeniable, even though she tries to pass it off as sarcasm.

"I don't buy it."

"Whatever, it's no big deal. Not comparable to you anyway."

"What makes you say that?"

She swallows, and I know she's thinking about whether or not to say what's on her mind. I'm about to encourage her to share her thoughts, but she does it all by herself.

"I don't know your story, but there's a reason you were adopted, so my guess is something bad happened."

I press my hand on my chest, pointing out, "Fostered."

It's a technicality, one my family likes shedding light on, because despite not being able to get adopted, we chose each other anyway. For us, it means more than anything else.

The fact that my brothers and I legally took our mama's last name when we turned eighteen speaks louder than any adoption paper ever could. She's our mother through and through, no stamp of approval from the state required.

"Right, sorry, I just thought since you've been living in the same home since…" she trails off, pressing her lips together, probably coming to the same conclusion as me; she was five when she ran away from home, and I was five when I was taken from mine.

"They didn't relinquish my father's parental rights," I spill, preparing myself for what's to come.

"And your mom?"

"Died when I was five."

She gulps, looking ahead.

I can see it on her face, the need to know more, and she tells me as much.

"Sorry, I'm a nosy person, and I don't want to step out of line. You know you don't have to tell me anything."

Except I do. I want to give her every part of me, down to the worst.

"My father is in prison," I say matter-of-factly.

She doesn't react, just patiently waits for me to finish.

"For killing my mother," I add, my voice flat. Truth be told, my mother's death is the only reason I'm here today, alive. Someone must've heard her screams, and before my father could finish the job with me, the police barged in. I wasn't only one hit away from serious brain damage; I was one hit away from meeting the big guy upstairs.

Taking another step, the front porch comes into view, but I stop my movements when I don't feel Nora by my side anymore.

When I turn around, I find her feet glued to the ground, her chest heaving hard, her hand tightly holding onto Declan's little one. In slow motion, I trace the tear that slowly slides down her cheek. Another one follows.

I rush to her, shielding her with my body so that the others won't see.

"Don't cry over me. I got the better end of the deal. The best woman took me in and gave me a whole new family, one that I belong in."

"I can't imagine. And you were so young, you probably didn't even understand it. Oh, God... I'm so sorry." Another sob escapes her.

"What are you apologizing for?"

"Everything that happened. For you telling me and me acting like this, making it worse. I am so not worthy of your story."

I can't say I wasn't warned. Ryan said she's as selfless as they come, but witnessing it—fuck if it doesn't hit right to the center of my chest. I want to hug her even though I know I can't, shouldn't.

"My story is just that—a story. A part of the past that got me into the present, but won't be a part of my future."

"Smart much?" She laughs through a sob, wiping her tears.

"I dabble," I muse, desperate to drag her from the dark place she's keen to crawl into.

"I don't think I've ever met anyone like you."

"Like what exactly?"

She doesn't even take a beat to think, like she's had the

whole thing at the ready.

"Rough on the outside, yet soft on the inside. Smart, not just intelligent - more life smart. There's so much kindness in you, and I know for a fact you're big on family. You're a boss, but also a friend, and the best part of you is your understanding."

"Okay, you lost me there," I mumble, a bit confused.

"If someone needs a push, you'll do the nudging... If someone needs time, you'll give it. You would fight when necessary and step down just the same."

Well, color me stunned. My Mama might have some competition regarding her famous ability.

"You got all of that from five feet away?" I joke, quickly glancing at Declan. He's smiling, twirling the little twig he picked up before.

"You read situations, I read people," she shrugs.

"Is that so?"

"No," she spills, "it was a total bluff."

"I knew it," I chuckle, not believing it for a second. We both know she's been reading right through me from the start.

Chapter 25

Nora

A tall, rugged teenage boy comes rushing toward me with open arms. "I'm Tristan, Luka's brother," he chirps before he pulls me into a soft hug.

"I'm Nora, nice to meet you," I mumble, lingering in his arms. Pulling away, I take a better look at him. He's tall, athletic, with piercing greenish eyes. His face is covered with zits, yet somehow they look good on him—a classic popular jock. "How did the game go?"

"We won?"

"Congratulations."

"Thanks," he beams, making a clicking sound and pointing his index fingers into guns. Somehow, the kid pulls it off, and I am sure he has a line of girls drooling over him.

"Any touchdowns?"

I have zero knowledge of the sport, except the one word, one I don't know the meaning of it. Oops.

"Just two," he shrugs.

"Oh, just?"

"I'm being humble here."

"Don't let him fool you, he doesn't have a humble bone in his body." I turn to the woman who's causing Tristan's eye roll, extending my hand. It gets brushed away.

"We're huggers, honey."

God, even her voice is like a warm blanket.

"Good, cuz so am I," I cackle, spreading my arms wide.

She's a bit shorter, but the fit is perfect. "It's nice to meet you finally, Ms. Hart."

"Oh no, you don't. It's Eva, and don't you forget it."

"Yes, ma'am."

Eva is a gorgeous woman, with dark gray hair pulled back into a tight bun, her skin wrinkled but still soft. She has a fair share of beauty marks on her face, and her gray eyes define her kindness. The lashes around her eyes are so light they almost seem nonexistent, and I have to say I envy those eyebrows, long and arched.

"I need more coffee. Any takers?" I call to everyone.

"Count us out, we need our senior nap," Bianca shouts back, her hand looped around her husband as they wave and retreat inside.

I count the hands in the air and beeline to the kitchen to make good on their orders. While the coffee machine does its job, I prep some snacks and slice the pie I made last night. I am not much of a baker; it takes too much time and concentration, except for a simple apple pie. Now that's my specialty.

Outside, I spread the offerings on the large table while glancing around. Lizzy is on her phone, comfortable in the steamer chair. The boys are playing hide-and-seek while Luka is tying up a hammock between two trees. Tessa is rocking Elle with Ryan next to her, his eyes sparkling with so much love. Rick is on the far end, lying on the lounger, nose in his phone. I zoom in on Dec, sitting in the shallow water, splashing it. Somehow, I feel Luka keeping an eye on him, and it does something to me, spreading warmth throughout my bloodstream.

"Order up," I holler, and watch how quickly everyone gathers around the table.

Being a mother 24/7, relaxation is a foreign concept most of the time. Mom life is my life, and I wouldn't have it any other way. At this moment, I love it a bit more. As selfish as it may sound, being around people without worrying so much is just what the doctor ordered. Knowing Dec is happy and safe makes my shoulders lighter and my mind unchained.

Now it's the middle of the day, and all the guys are gathered around the grill, making steaks and burgers. Us ladies are sitting on the sun porch soaking in the rays. Eva is beside me, and we're engaged in a polite conversation that flows surprisingly easily. I smile when I look at Dec, attempting to catch a fish with his bare hands.

"He's something," she speaks out, her gaze following mine.

"Yeah, he really is. We love it here, he has more freedom, and I don't have to yell the word 'No' every other minute." We both laugh, and she gives me a sympathetic nod.

"How did you do it with five kids?" I swallow the *all alone* part that's almost slipped out.

"I got lucky. All they wanted was love, and I had an abundance of it."

"I have no words, truly. The strength it took."

I don't even know the woman, and I am in awe of her. If Luka is any indication, she raised her sons right, compassionate, kind... I wonder how I would've turned out if I had a fraction of her love growing up… the love I can easily see radiating out of her.

"I was scared at first. I've fostered before, mostly just as a stepping stone between adoptions, and then Tyler and Mateo came along. I couldn't allow them to get separated. And soon after, I got a call about a boy struggling in a group home. I didn't even blink."

She places a hand on her chest, her eyes firmly locked on Luka, who's deep into a conversation with Ryan next to the grill.

"He wouldn't speak at first and refused to eat anything other than plain bread," she recalls, chuckling. "The first time he spoke, he quoted Plato."

I don't know how or why, but I can picture it so clearly.

"He was six," she adds, and I can't help it; I shake my head.

"That totally sounds like him."

To my words, she smiles, that hopeful kind of smile, causing my heart to crack for some reason.

The splashing sound makes us both turn to the beach, where Dec is creating a vortex with all the spinning he's doing.

"He's obsessed with water. He's teaching himself to swim," I beam with pride.

I can see her frown beside me, and my enthusiasm skyrockets, my tone following suit when I exclaim, "No, really! He's been cautious, staying in the shallow water where he can touch the bottom with his hands." I mimic the movement as I explain, "He moves like that, and every now and then he lets go and takes one or two strokes."

"That's amazing."

"Yeah," I pause, realizing my blabbing. "I'm sorry, I'm fluent in everything Declan-related, so it's most of my conversational topics. That and smutty romance novels."

"Did someone say smut?" A woman's voice comes from behind me, right before she takes a seat next to me. When I face her, I am blindsided.

"Oh wow, I think I'm in love," I gush at her, untamed.

Somehow, I morph into a teenage boy with his first hard-on, not able to take my eyes off the most beautiful woman I have ever seen, though oddly familiar. After further inspection, it clicks, and my mouth opens. "Do you know that your eyes look exactly like they belong to that model who was plastered on a building on Main Street?"

"That's what you remember? The eyes?" she marvels at that.

"Yeah, it's the first thing I notice, frankly, and yours are just wow. I have no words."

They are so green, so clear, alive. I think I actually might be drooling.

"Ok, you are officially my favorite," she squeals, wrapping her arms around me tightly.

"Sweetie, you might want to introduce yourself first," Eva chimes, and the woman pulls away.

"Right… Sorry, I'm Sabrina," she reveals, smiling widely. I can't stop staring at her eyes, though.

"I'm Nora, nice to meet you."

"Oh, I know, and I've been dying to meet you." She adds a wink.

"What?" I gasp, not quite sure why I want to know about her statement.

"Hi." A tall, mocha-skinned man cuts in, breaking me out of my thoughts as he sets down two bike helmets next to Sabrina's feet.

"Oh. You must be Mateo." Used to it by now, I don't even bother to outstretch my arm, opening both for an incoming hug.

"It's nice to meet you, Nora." His voice is deep, gentle, and friendly.

"Coffee or beer?" I look at both of them.

"Beer is fine," Mateo says with a smile.

"Me too," Sabrina adds, and I grab two bottles from the cooler under my chair and hand them over.

"I'm surprised Luka left you in charge of the cooler. It's usually his thing," Mateo puzzles, and I raise an eyebrow in question. "It's my cooler," I point out, my tone a bit defensive.

Sabrina and Mateo share a look, a conversation happening without words. I envy the exchange, but my thoughts get cut off when Luka comes over. They all pull in a hug, and I stare unblinkingly at their closeness, the connection. It reminds me of Ryan and me. Luka pulls Mateo away, and Sabrina takes off her bike jacket before taking a seat.

I take the now-empty cooler and go inside to restock

when I find Lizzy wandering around.

"You bored, kid?"

"Extremely," she exasperates.

"How bout we do your hair?"

That perks her up. "Really?"

"Yeah, get the stuff, and I'll meet you outside."

She jumps, clapping and squealing, before she skedaddles.

Chapter 26

Nora

Entirely focused on French braiding her long, blonde hair, I start to hum, forgetting about where I am. Lizzy turns around so quickly that it almost ruins my whole progress.

"What?" I ask at the weird look she's giving me, a mixture of confusion and surprise in her ocean eyes, the same as her mama's.

"I haven't heard that in so long."

I tilt my head to the side, holding on to the braid for dear life so it won't untangle. "Heard what?"

"The humming."

I draw back, wincing at her words.

"Really?"

"Yeah, you haven't been singing either."

That's impossible.

I mull it over. Singing is second nature to me, or it was. I used to do it all the time and told people it was in my DNA. I am one of those people who sings in their sleep, for crying out loud.

So when did I stop? When was the last time I wrote something?

"Keep going, please," my niece pleads, turning toward the water. She positions herself so I can continue my braiding.

Deep in the twists and turns, my mind goes numb with comprehension. How could I let this happen? Let go of something I lived for, and without even realizing it?

That empty feeling intensifies.

That's when everything rushes all at once, like a destructive flood mixed with a tornado. I've forgone my entire life, my friends, my music, even my personality, and it's all my fault. How could I have been so blind, so oblivious? Or was it my way of coping? The reality of it is too much for me to delve into, especially now. We're here for a reason, and I don't want my mood to ruin this happy occasion, so I shake it off and plaster on a smile.

My hand trembles as I twist the last chunk of hair.

"All done." I release the tied-up braid, proud of the job well done, and Lizzy takes out her mirror to inspect it. With a tight hug and the biggest smile, she rewards me with a loud shriek, "Thank you! Thank you!"

"You're welcome. I love you."

"Love you too… I'll go look in the big mirror."

"You do that."

She scurries inside, and I cross my legs just as the best smell in the world finds my senses, and I swear my heart starts jumping like it's on a trampoline. I narrow my eyes, finding the source, spread on a tray Tessa is carrying. When she walks by, I steal a bread roll from the top, still hot. I am a sucker for any pastry. I can live on anything made from flour, even sourdough itself. After some heavy blowing, I finally get it warm enough to take a big bite, and oh. My. God. My mouth goes straight to heaven with all the fluffiness. In the middle of devouring the roll, Luka appears in front of me—shirtless. I almost choke, but thankfully, no one notices. I can't help it, a deer caught in the headlights of all the ink. He wasn't kidding; his chest is covered in various tattoos, and I want to see them under a microscope. One in particular draws me in, like a strong magnet; it pulls me to my feet.

"Is that?" I ask no one as my feet continue walking to a bare-chested Luka.

"Stand still, turn your head," I point to his right, "and don't move!"

"What are you doing?"

"Shhhhhh."

I lift my finger and read, over and over again, unable to contain my smile.

Right there, over his heart, is a tattoo of a music sheet filled with the lyrics of a forgotten song.

What compels my fingers to trace over the letters is beyond me, but I regret it as soon as I feel it. My smile turns to a full-on panic mixed with so much sorrow that my breath hitches. Behind the ink, not so easily to spot, there are scars... So, so many of them, and what look like cigarette burns.

"Nora?" he cracks.

"Turn around," I say through a shaky breath, body weak, my legs barely holding me upright.

"Nora." My name is like a plea, his voice soft, making mine more determined.

"Turn around," I demand through gritted teeth. He obliges, giving me the full view of his back. There, a large lion envelops his entire right shoulder blade, and I graze my fingers over the uneven skin, feeling every damaged tissue.

The scars have healed, but there is no doubt that they run deep. Most resemble knife cuts, but a few larger ones may be from a belt or something similar.

I think I actually hear my heart break into a million pieces.

"Nora?"

I ignore him, trying hard to keep afloat, tears already welling.

"Who did this to you?"

No answer.

"Tell me," I beg, yet he stays silent.

My feet bolt, fists clenched so tightly that my nonexistent nails dig into my palms, a surge of helplessness and fury threatening to overwhelm me.

"Why?" I scream when I pull to a stop in front of Eva, my vision blurry. Mateo steps in between, shielding his mother.

"Did you do that to him? Or was it one of you?" My eyes shift from Eva to Mateo to Tristan. I see it on their faces, the same pain I feel. I can't think straight. I want to burn the whole world, to chase away the demons, to save him…

Why did no one save him?

My chest tightens. I can't breathe. I think I might be suffocating.

"Oh, sweetie." Eva tries to take my hand, but I escape her attempt, unable to look her in the eyes.

Why? Why *him*?

Sobbing, I watch my tears soak the ground before me, and hug myself, hearing muffled voices around me. It's all blurred out, my mind isolating them to heighten my inside scream. Every part of me hurts, my entire body shaking. It stops when I feel a hand on my shoulder. I smell his scent, cedar and wood; feel his breath in my ear, and my heart starts beating again.

Chapter 27

Luka

"Nora, please," I beg, and she finally turns to face me, but she won't look at me. She's visibly shaking, and I need her to stop before the sight ruins me. I put on a shirt and drag her away from prowling eyes. Only when we get behind the cottage do her eyes lift to mine, arms wrapped around, holding herself at bay.

"Who did that to you?" She airs out.

"My birth parents?" I answer in a single breath, like ripping off a band-aid. It's like a blow to the chest, her chest, by the way she reacts to my words. She's struggling to understand, and I want nothing more than to touch her, to let my touch speak for me, to reassure her it's all right.

I came to terms with my past a long time ago, worked through all my self-doubts about my worth, and rose above it all with the help of my family. Eva chose me and worked with me to silence all the nightmares that haunted me, never leaving my side. Only a few people know about what happened to me when I was a kid, and those who learned the truth didn't react the way Nora did. In her state, it's hard to get a read on her.

"I don't understand. You said you were five when..." She doesn't finish, and frankly, neither can I, so I nod.

"That means that they did that when you were... No... Oh

God, no…"

She turns around, grabbing the back of her neck, releasing a muffled cry. Then I see her lose her footing, her body crumbling. I fly, catching her before she hits the ground, not giving a single fuck about the consequences. In the middle of her meltdown, she still manages to speak the words that will forever haunt me.

"I'm in awe of you."

Dumbfounded, I open my mouth to speak, but nothing comes out.

"I don't know how you do it."

"Do what?"

"Have such a big heart after everything you've been through. I'm sorry, Luka, I am so sorry," she sobs, clenching the fabric of my t-shirt, holding on for dear life to me, almost as if by letting me go, she'd explode. Me? I am at the point of self-destruction as everything around me crumbles. It's been twenty-six years since I gained my last scar. I buried all of it so deep, covered them up with shame, never allowing them to truly heal.

It takes her five minutes to stop shaking, another three to settle her breathing.

"What are you doing?" I blurt out when she starts to lift my shirt.

Her fingers hover, a mere inch away from my exposed skin, and she sniffles, "I don't know, but I need to… just, please, let me."

I allow it, lifting my arms so she can take it off.

The earth stops spinning; time stands still as she traces every anomaly on my arms and chest before she turns to my back. With my eyes shut, I feel every touch, every light, shaky stroke of her fingers.

"Can you pretend my fingertips are an eraser, just for a moment?" she whispers from behind me, and I answer with silence, unable to find the right words. Little does she know that in my mind, I am already doing it, replacing every bad memory with the shiver her touch causes. She continues to mend every broken part of me, and I welcome the resurfacing pain, the agony… With each brush, I let a part of it go, freeing myself.

Tiers appear out of nowhere, and I release a breath I didn't even know I've been holding for most of my life. I thought I had healed, I thought I left the past where it belongs, but this woman's brought everything back, only to free me of it. Some of the weight off my shoulder lifts, doubts get smashed, and a sense of safety takes over. Letting it go, it feels like a breath of life is forced into me. I welcome it with open lungs. Never could I have imagined such peace. With one simple act, she's created a sanctuary for my broken soul and remedied my wounded heart.

"Thank you," I murmur after an eternity of silence.

I turn around, finding her back to me, her shoulders shaking, her hands nowhere in sight.

It's not my place, I think to myself. I know it, and yet I press my chest to her spine and enfold her in my arms. Before I can lock them, she turns, leaning her cheek over my heart like she needs the proof that it's beating.

Not trying to be overdramatic, but this woman is breaking every wall I've ever built. Closing my eyes, I take in her signature scent, letting it consume me. I shouldn't want her, but I do. And it's killing me, eating me up from the inside.

The moment she pulls away, separation anxiety hits. Her expression turns into shock, like she just thought of something. She grabs my arm and gasps, "I yelled at your mother."

"You did," I chuckle, and her fist collides with my chest.

"Oh God," she smacks her forehead, "and your brothers."

Why is it cute?

"Yup," I pop the P, beaming at her.

"They hate me," she gulps, shutting her eyes.

"No, they probably love you more."

As do I.

She stood up for me without a second's thought, and even though it was pointed at the wrong people, she bared her teeth. For me.

"But I yelled."

Oh, she didn't just yell; she screamed at them, and it took everything in me not to kiss her right there in front of everybody.

"Because you care."

"I'm sorry."

"No reason to be."

"I just wish…"

I grab her shoulders to gain her attention in order for her to understand it. I want the words I am about to say to sink in, for both our sakes.

"If it didn't happen, I would've never met Eva or gained four brothers that I couldn't even imagine not being a part of my life." I swallow, "I never would've met you."

All the pain I endured, every threat, every swing of that

stupid brown leather belt was worth it just for this. They got me here, next to the woman who, without even trying, brought my heart to life.

"We can't have that; that would be a tragedy," she teases, and the sight of her mouth curving upward does something to me.

"Glad we agree."

That's Nora's superpower—turning a mood around with one simple smile. And there I go again, feeling the stupid butterflies.

As if my body wants to prove a point, I giggle. I fucking giggle.

"I was joking," she mutters, wiping her beautiful face.

"Well, I'm not. I'm glad I met you, happy to call you a friend." The word tastes as heavy as my heart does when it sinks.

"Can I ask you something?"

She starts standing up, and I follow. We're close, standing face to face, her head lifted, and mine dipped for the full effect. My heart is trying to jump out of my chest, my hands fighting the urge to cup her face.

"Anything."

"What does this one mean?" Her fingers travel over my upper arm, where one of my favorites is displayed.

"I get the arrow for power, just not this part. What is it?"

So she has some knowledge of tattoo meanings. Makes sense, since she's mentioned having five herself.

"It's an Unalome, a symbol for the journey to enlightenment." I put my finger at the bottom where the line twirls upward. "This represents the chaos." I move the finger up to the swirling part, "This represents the transition, the lessons learned." Next, over the straight line. "This is nirvana." I look down as she looks up. "The dot is the goal, the enlightenment." I take a deep breath, letting her scent hit that sweet spot. "Life is messy, filled with suffering and chaos, missteps and lessons learned. There's no right or perfect way, nor is there a straight line to wherever you need to go."

"I love that," she chokes on her words, and I choke—period.

And I think I could love you!

I shouldn't, though, but I'm helpless to it, powerless to the pull she has over me. She snuck in, no warning, and planted herself like a seed that's been growing with each shared look, desperate for more.

Chapter 28

Nora

When we get back to the front porch, all eyes snap to us while mine search for Declan. Before I start panicking, Tessa tells me she put him down for his nap. When she asks if I'm ok, I don't know how to answer. Sabrina jumps into Luka's arms, whispering something that makes him nod. I watch as he exchanges a look with Eva, a silent conversation unfolding. Then the woman saunters toward me. My mouth opens, but before the first syllable escapes me, she takes my hand and pulls me away. Wordlessly, I follow.

After a short walk, she sits on a rock beneath a large willow and taps the spot beside her. One pointed look is all it takes for me to plaster my ass on the cold surface, a bit frightened for whatever is coming.

"I am so sorry," I blurt out, knowing damn well it won't cut it. I yelled at the woman, too angry for any logical thinking.

"Oh, no, honey. This is going to be a long monologue, so I'm gonna need you to listen very carefully." She places her warm hand on my knee, which I only now realize has been bouncing. Sweat consumes my body, even in places that aren't supposed to be sweating.

"I don't play favorites when it comes to my children, and each is special in their own way. With that said, Luka…" She pauses, taking a breath, and I join with a deep one of my own.

"Oh, that boy was so lost for so long…"

Unsure why she's telling me this, or why it's relevant, I mute my thoughts, wipe my palm, and cover her hand with it.

"He's been through so much; it took a long time for him to open up, to let anyone in. He was too proud for therapy, so I kept trying to find new ways to help him. Then one night I caught him reading." Her eyes are getting all teary, and I fight the urge to hug her.

"He hadn't even started school, and he chose Moby Dick."

My imagination starts working wonders, picturing a kid-sized Luka finding comfort between pages. Warmth spreads through me at the thought.

"The day after, I went and bought every book in the domestic violence section."

She goes on saying how those books ended up in flames. So she introduced him to different realms, worlds, and places filled with magic.

"Somehow, *The Hobbit* did the trick," she marvels, recalling how excited he was when she took him to the library to get the other books in the series.

"He took the role of a big brother with ease, reading to Mateo and Tyler every night."

I can't help my smile, knowing he was made to care. And I can see it in the way he carries himself around his brothers, how protective he is of them.

Her voice cracks when she shares about his school days, the bullies, the authoritative teachers who brought back the nightmares. She finally laughs when she mentions being called in by the school principal.

"Imagine walking into that school, Tristan in hand, finding four boys, each sporting a black eye," she bubbles, and I shake my head, unable to contain my amusement.

"What happened?" I ask, causing her to smirk.

"They joined forces and confronted the infamous school bully."

"No," I gasp.

"You are not to repeat this…" she warns, lifting a finger for emphasis. I zip my mouth shut and mimic tossing the key.

"I was so proud of them."

The way her whole face lights up only feeds my curiosity. "What did you do?"

"What any good mother would have—" a dramatic pause "—I took them for ice cream."

I full-on guffaw.

"That day, they formed a strong bond, even started calling themselves The Lost Boys."

"Oh my God," I snort out a laugh, covering my forehead with my shaky hand.

The dangling branches above us begin to sway when a gust of wind brushes past, creating a rhythmic sound. The rustling leaves almost sound like a murmur, telling a story as the wind carries them to their next destination.

"Anyway, I swear I had a point going," she says dismissively.

"No, please, keep going."

Tell me everything—I want to shout, but I don't want to scare the woman away. In fact, I want her to like me.

She takes my hand in hers, and our gazes meet; her gray eyes pierce through me.

"I want to thank you."

"What?" I gasp in disbelief. I yelled at the woman, accused her of something she had no part in, and she's… thanking me?

"Whatever you did, thank you," she repeats, not making any sense.

"I don't understand."

At all.

"Maybe you don't, but I do, because I saw something in my son's eyes I haven't seen in a very long time."

"What?"

"Hope."

And there goes my heart.

"You need to know that even though he smiles now, it didn't come easily. It was carved from sorrow, taught out of fear, and shaped by loud nights. It wasn't gifted; he fought for it. And he reserves the biggest smiles for special people."

I blink, letting it sink in.

Life is the ultimate enigma. Some people pass through your life without leaving a mark, while others pave a way into parts of you, opening doors you never knew were locked. Luka is the latter for me, opening me like a can of worms, except my worms were my repressed emotions. Not so repressed as they were nonexistent. The worst part of it is that I know it's wrong. As much as I thought it was against my nature to have any feelings other than for my husband, the one person I promised my whole heart to, there's no escaping the truth. Feelings have erupted in every fiber of my being.

One thing is certain—my head has seniority over my heart, and it has a lot of years of experience behind it. So I know what I have to do—let it do what it does best—silence my heart once again.

Chapter 29

Nora

After my heart-to-heart with Eva, we returned just in time for lunch. Ethan and Elijah started fighting over who'd get the biggest burger, while Sabrina and Jack got into a heated argument over some political bullshoot no one seemed to understand.

I was surprised the whole thing didn't end up in a food fight.

Now, I'm hiding in the kitchen under the pretense of washing the dishes.

"El, you do know there's a perfectly functioning dishwasher, right?" Tessa's voice comes from behind me.

This takes longer, and I am avoiding everyone.

I shrug, giving the sink my undivided attention.

"What's going on?"

My entire life is imploding.

Before I start digging my own grave, I deadpan, "Nothing."

There, that's better. Denial.

"El, don't lie to me."

I have to, or I'll lose everything. I'm falling already, diving deep into something very much unknown, and it's swallowing me whole. I'm afraid of my own thoughts.

"It's nothing, I just want to be alone and clear my head."

"So you chose dishes?"

"What can I say, I'm a sucker for dish soap. I mean, look at all these bubbles," I tease, lifting my foamy hands. When I turn to look at her, she has her arms crossed over her chest, one foot tapping in annoyance. Her sandy-blonde hair is up in a messy bun, giving a perfect view of her serious face. I envy the makeup, subtle, natural-looking. I envy her even more for having the time to do her makeup.

"Is Dec behaving?" I steer the best way I know how.

"Yeah, Mom has him, don't worry."

I sigh in relief and finish scrubbing the last plate. I rinse the dishes and stack them perfectly on the drying rack.

"Just let it out," I cave, just like she knew I would.

"You know I love you, right?"

I met Tessa when I was seventeen, working in a small diner in our hometown. She came every day for a breakfast pick-up. It didn't take us long to become best friends. Then I introduced her to Ryan, and it was love at first sight. It was different with Rick and me. At first, we couldn't stand each other, but we grew to tolerate one another over time. The toleration turned into comfort, and that comfort turned into love.

"Well, you better," I retort.

"And you know I have to love Rick, him being my brother and all?"

"Tessa," I warn.

She doesn't give a shit about my little hint, cuz she keeps going, "But I also love Luka."

"What does he have to do with anything?"

"Oh, don't play dumb with me."

I have to. It's my only way to keep my sanity and pivot the conversation.

How would that even go?

Hey, remember your brother, who is also my husband? Well, lately we haven't been doing so well. Truth be told, we haven't been good for over five years, but who's counting? Oh, and yeah, I'm maybe, kinda, perhaps, developing some feelings toward your husband's best friend.

Yeah, those thoughts need to stay buried.

And just like that, it is made clear my goddaughter is going to be my favorite, because she's chosen that moment to save me and wakes up with a soft cry. Tessa turns off the baby monitor, and I jump in, "Let me get her."

Her hands fall to her sides, her face screaming dissatisfaction. Grinning, I run upstairs, tiptoeing to the crib where little Elle smiles right at me. I love how Tessa and Ryan named all their kids starting with the same letter. It made it easier for me when I got my tattoo, one letter to mark them all.

"I guess we won't be talking about it?" Tessa snarls when I emerge back in the kitchen with her baby girl cradled in my arms. I don't bother answering, having no care in the world. Not while holding one.

"I need some quality time with this one," I beam, "I'm in withdrawal from the baby smell, and I need my fix."

I look down at my blue-eyed girl, hoping they will stay this shade forever. The door slides open, and Sabrina enters, hands full of empty bottles.

"Sorry to interrupt, I was summoned for refreshments."

"Here," Tessa says, the bottles clanking when she frees Sabrina's hands. "I'll take care of it."

"Thanks," the supermodel-turned-lawyer chirps. During lunch, she gave me the bullet points of her story, and what a story it is, intriguing enough to be made into a movie, that's for dang sure.

"So, is this the reason we've all gathered here?"

Sabrina comes to my side, taking in every detail of the little bundle.

"Yeah, this is little Elle," I say proudly.

Then, in what I can only assume to be Sabrina's fashion, she utters, "Thinking about another one?"

I know she meant well, and it's not like she's aware it's a sore subject.

I watch through the window at the happiest kid alive as he jumps hard in the water, splashing it all around, and I smile away the tears.

"I always wanted more kids, being an only child myself…" I trail off, not wanting to admit the truth. Between us, another kid is out of the question. I am already in over my head doing it all on my own, so I can't bear to take on another responsibility, no matter how much I want Declan to have a sibling.

"I get it," she says, saving me from another web of lies.

Tessa reemerges, dusting off her hands. "There, everyone is refreshed. Do you want something else to drink?" She points that question at the newcomer.

"Beer is fine."

Tessa hands her a cold brew straight from the fridge, and Sabrina tips it to us before she leaves, closing the door behind her quietly. I want to yell, *'Don't go, don't leave me alone with her,'* but it's pointless. There's no avoiding Tessa.

"So, I overheard," Tessa drags it out.

"Of course you did," I scoff, and she hauls, turning on her serious BFF face, pushing the sister-in-law aside. Trust me, I can tell the difference.

"If you're having any doubts, then you know your answer. For me, it was an easy decision. Ry has my back, and I know that I will never be alone in it. That said, I know Rick, and it pains me that his behavior is the reason you're having doubts."

I'm a bit of a green-eyed monster right now, and I know what you're thinking. How dare I? You have to understand that I had a front seat, watching those two build their family, happy for them while feeling sorry for myself.

When we were kids, Ryan and I always talked about having a full house. He wanted five kids, and I wanted at least three. He's on the right track to fulfilling his dream, and I'm at a standstill.

"Can I ask you something?" Tessa's voice startles me, but I quickly recover.

"Like me saying no is gonna stop you."

She grins at that, proud of herself. I want to pinch her, but I know better. We've entered serious territory, so I have to act accordingly, even though I really don't want to.

"Why do you always put everyone else before yourself?"

"I don't," I counter way too quickly.

"Yes, you do, but do *you* know why?"

"I don't get it," I whisper.

"I think it's because it's easier for you."

That took a turn. Where is she going with this?

"What do you mean?"

She takes in a deep breath, grabbing her phone from the counter.

"I think it's easier to focus on someone else than to face your own pain. That's why you offer your hand instead of reaching out for someone to take yours."

Suddenly, I feel so small, my chest tightening. I can't even look her in the eyes.

"You give and give, hoping that no one will see what you hide while simultaneously wishing for the opposite."

"Tessa," I warn again, every fiber of my body begging her to stop.

"What? I told you, I am biased."

"It's unnecessary, because this is taboo."

"I love that game," she marvels, and I retort. "Don't play with me. I mean it. This is not the conversation we are ever going to have."

"Fine," she finally drops it, shaking her head. I can feel her disappointment all the way to my core.

"Thank you. Now let me get a head start with spoiling this one." I switch my focus to the most perfect little girl. In the background, slow notes start to fill the room. I turn to find Tessa's phone on the island. I smile and start rocking little Elle, hearing the door slide shut. With the two of us finally alone, I hum to the beat, swaying a bit.

It's when I focus on the lyrics that a tear slides down my face, another one following right after.

I thought I could hurt forever if it kept you happy

'Cause there were days I thought we'd be alright

Chapter 30

The post-sunset hush is interrupted by music blasting from a small speaker, making everyone snap their attention to the deck.

Everything around me blurs out with one thing in full focus. Nora is dancing with her niece, belting out the lyrics with a smile, one I have never seen pointed at anything other than her son. They jump to the side, hands zigzagging in between them, with their heads bobbing in every direction. The music is loud, so I can't hear Nora's voice, but I do see her mouth moving.

I shift my focus to Lizzy, who looks at her aunt with admiration.

I get it, kid.

They do a crisscross move, and I hear Ryan laughing next to me.

"Look how happy she is," I say, staring at the infatuated kid.

"I thought we lost her," he says under his breath, like it wasn't meant to be heard.

"Lizzy?"

"El," he clarifies.

"Oh."

What do I say to that? I want an elaboration. The need to

know everything is strong. Thankfully, Ryan doesn't need my push.

"Do you know how hard it is to watch the best person in the world dim her light?"

I look at him, really look at him, the pain screaming out of him. Tears cover the corners of his eyes as he watches his friend spin around.

"Don't get me wrong, I love my wife and her family, I really do," he takes a breath. "But her brother…" he pauses, probably debating whether to share further. Before I open my mouth to reassure him, he continues, "El has been there for almost my entire life. She was always a force of nature that one, and somewhere along the way, I lost her; we all did." His voice cracks. "Rick broke her spirit."

I never knew that one sentence could hold so much power over someone, and yet here I am, heartbroken over one.

Rick broke her spirit.

"You know, she was the one who supported them back in Canada. She worked while attending school. Paid her own rent and fed him. Now she depends on *him*, and I think that's the biggest reason why…" he trails off, shaking his head, gaze pointed at the spot his fingers are working to scratch off the label of the beer bottle, and sighs. We both look at Nora as another song starts to play, and she grabs Lizzy's hands, pulling them both into a spinning frenzy.

"See that woman right there," he points at Nora, "that's El. That's my best friend. And I just stood by while she slowly dissipated."

The more he shares, the more it hurts him, me… I can't

imagine. I only wish to fix it, make this version of hers stick.

"She gave up so much. Before she even graduated, she got first chair in the Montreal orchestra and turned it down to move here after Rick got a job offer."

My fists clench, and I want him to stop talking and keep going at the same time.

"Back in Canada, he couldn't find a job, and she had so many offers. She was the one with so many opportunities, yet she gave up on her whole future for him."

I stand there, shocked by his confession, even though he is the one who told me Rick is a forbidden subject.

"After Declan was born, she was still playing and making music. She wrote him a lullaby; she did for my kids, too. When he turned three, she pawned her guitar for the diagnosis test, and she sold her piano so they could pay for a trip to Disneyland for Declan's fifth birthday."

He takes a moment, turning his gaze to his wife, who is sitting on the porch in a rocking chair with little Elle cradled in her arms.

He goes on telling me how they tried to talk some sense into her, but she wouldn't allow it. He even went on about how he and Rick got into a fight last year after he tried to reason with him.

"It took us a long time to be able to be under the same roof, let alone in the same room."

"Is that why I never met them before?"

Kid's birthday parties, barbecues, their anniversary. I was there for it all, and Auntie El was nowhere to be found, a ghost.

"Yeah. I would invite her, but she had this notion that it

would be wrong since Rick is actual family. She's never believed any of us when we tell her we love her more than we do him, and that she's more of our family than he ever could be. Even Tessa resents her brother and would toss him to the curb without a doubt."

I've had my own judgments regarding Rick, but hearing Ryan say that, I honestly think that I've been downplaying this entire thing.

"Fuck, that's just messed up."

"You have no idea," he falters, then clears his throat. "Look, I don't know what this thing between the two of you is, and frankly, I don't care. All I know is that you seem good for her."

That gets me to backtrack. When I don't say a thing, Ryan rails, "Ever since you two met, she's been more open, more like her old self."

I can't take credit for that. I didn't do a goddamn thing except pine for her in silence.

"What was she like? You know, before…"

He smiles at that and straightens his shoulders. I know that face. He just got an idea.

"Let me demonstrate." He holds up his hand in the '*wait here*' kind, and I oblige while he disappears from my sight just as the loud music fades out. Tessa calls everyone to move over to the fire pit, but I choose to remain at my spot, nervously waiting for Ryan to reappear. Sabrina takes a seat in her favorite chair—Mateo's lap while the kids run around the fire under Bianca's careful eye. Jack is sitting next to her, a hand draped over her shoulder. Nora takes a chair across from him, clenching onto the baby monitor while losing herself in the flames. She already put Declan down for the night after dinner, and Rick soon followed. I wanted to ask why he couldn't just go with his son since he was turning in anyway, but thought better of it.

Ryan rushes out, acoustic guitar in hand, and all eyes snap to him, all except Nora's. He gets in front of her, waving the guitar in her face. Her palms fly out, her head shaking in the universal no. My feet move on their own accord, getting closer so I can hear their so-called argument, a pointless one at that. Ryan has his '*I mean business*' stance. Nora's only defense—her red cheeks.

Mama and Tristan walk over, taking the empty wooden two-seater next to Mateo and Sabrina. My focus is on Nora, her hands rubbing over her thighs while Ryan taps his foot, waiting. Her fingers tremble, but eventually she takes the instrument, seething at him, "I hate you, I hope you're aware of that."

She inspects the guitar and strums it once. The sound makes her face cringe, so she starts tuning it—by ear. Ryan comes to my side again, handing me a fresh beer.

"I can't believe you still have this," Nora gushes, looking up at her best friend, then shakes her head before returning her focus to the strings. She turns the pegs and plays each string, tilting her head with each move of her fingers. When she's satisfied with the tweaking, she strums once, then twice for good measure, revealing a Duchenne smile. Lifting her head, she scans the crowd and raises her voice, "Any requests?"

Ethan is the one who shouts, "Play us the one you did before bedtime." Lizzy chimes in, "Yeah. Your favorite, remember?"

"Of course," she smirks, turning to me, holding my gaze as she adds, "how could I forget?"

I cock a brown, frozen in place, unprepared for whatever is coming.

When she starts playing the first few chords, I feel the shift, and my eyes snap to my mother's watery eyes. She recognizes it, too, and Nora hasn't even started singing. And then, without warning, her mouth opens, releasing the most beautiful symphony created from the depths of her lungs.

When I stumbled upon her diploma, I thought she played an instrument or two, but her singing never even crossed my mind.

'I'll be' by Edwin McCain, performed by Nora, starts slow, her voice hushed, easing her into it. Or maybe, she's easing us into it. My stare goes between my mother and Nora as I try my best to comprehend what's happening. My mother gives me a nod, and I turn my eyes to the woman pouring her soul, her eyes closed shut while she loses herself in the music. As the song progresses, her voice grows louder, her gentle hands strumming harder. Everything in me sparks to life as she sings her favorite song, the same song my mama sang to me every night to fight away the nightmare, one etched over my heart—*my favorite song.*

Chapter 31

Nora

Music is a language of its own. There are hidden words in the melody and the notes behind the actual lyrics. One simple hum has so many different meanings. No two people can interpret a song in the same way, nor can it be covered exactly. To put it as simply as possible… Music is what feelings sound like!

For me, music used to be an escape from the world, silencing all the outside forces—the most potent kind of magic that sheds light on the soul.

My hands have found the rhythm so easily, spreading fire through my veins with each strum.

Oh, how I've missed you!

When I finally open my eyes, I find everyone staring at me, speechless and stunned.

"That awful?" I snicker, and Sabrina cries out, "Are you kidding me? What the hell was that?"

"Sorry?" I gawk at her, unease settling over me.

It's been a while, so losing my touch is a definite probability. My nerves get the best of me, and I bite my inner cheek, hoping she'll go easy on me.

"My God, Nora, that was magnificent, you were transformed and…" she clasps her palms to her chest, pointing the tips at me, "you had me at smut, but this, I can't even…"

I release the breath I've been holding, eating up her words.

You still got it!

"Smut, you say?" Luka's left eyebrow rises, and the sight sends fire to my cheeks.

"Oh, look, she's blushing again. Isn't it cute?" Sabrina quips, and I hide my face behind the guitar.

"Sab, don't tease." Mateo jumps in with his rescue, and I decide he is my favorite Hart.

"I can't help it… a grown woman holds a record for blushing."

Well, she has me there.

Luka takes a seat next to me and leans enough for me to hear him whisper, "Why didn't you say anything?" I slowly turn to face him, placing the guitar back on my lap. The moon reflects in his eyes, hypnotizing me for a beat. I've almost forgotten how beautiful they are.

I look at him pointedly, reminding him that something interrupted the moment when I was tracing over his chest tattoo. It felt like kismet, him having my favorite song sprawled over his heart. He nods in understanding, so I decide to give him another piece of me.

"When they handed Declan to me for the first time," I gasp, the memory taking over, "when I had him in my arms finally after nine months of imagining him… All I wanted to do from that moment on was to love him and protect him. Of all the songs in the world, that one popped into my head, so I sang it to him, and I swear to God—he smiled."

The image rushes through like a gust of wind, and I simper, continuing, "I just kept on singing it every time he cried, every time he smiled. It became a part of me, and I can't believe I haven't sung it in so long."

Too long.

"Why?"

Thinking it over, I realize it got hard at some point—the notion that I'll never get to share it, wouldn't live it as I had planned many moons ago. Music in every capacity has been my vent, my way out, my very own canvas. For me, where words failed, music took over, speaking for me.

Growing up, I never kept a diary, but I had this pink notebook in which I scribbled words. Over time, they began to complement each other, eventually becoming lyrics. The first pages were filled with songs about ladybugs and flowers, and somewhere in the middle, they transformed into songs about running away, begging for attention, for love. By the end, it was all about lost dreams and not being enough, which might be why I buried it. So now, after just one interaction, I want to dig it all back up and dive into the world long lost. I need my music back, the feeling I used to get when creating something.

I want *me* back.

Desperate to change the subject, I turn to a grinning Ryan, "I can't believe you kept it!" I look over the old guitar, covered with faded stickers and doodles, down to my name written in bold. It's the only thing that hasn't faded, and I find it oddly satisfying.

"Yeah, I couldn't get rid of it, now could I?" He winks at me, giving me a look I unfortunately know very well. He's about to embarrass me.

"Growing up, she used to sneak out and go to this hidden music store. They had a grand piano there. It was old and ugly, but she loved that thing. The salesman took pity on her and allowed her to play whenever she wanted. She would spend hours there, dabbling around, creating different melodies." Ryan's face is filled with pride, the sight of it like a warm hug. The burn in my cheeks intensifies when I notice everyone immersed in the story.

"Ok, can we not?" I shake my head, trying not to turn to mush.

"Why?" Ryan jolts, and Luka follows. "Yeah, why?"

Great, now they're joining forces.

"I don't like the topic," I admit.

"Well, too bad 'cuz he sure does," Tessa speaks up, nodding her head in Ryan's direction, no sarcasm in her tone.

Sabrina stares at Tessa with the look she's very familiar with, especially when the three of us are together, and she reads right through it.

"You know, people always ask me if I'm jealous of the way he praises her, and I never understand it. I love their story, and I love how much he loves sharing it." Tessa wraps an arm around Ryan's waist, while her other hand rolls the stroller back and forth. She looks up at her husband, then rises on her tiptoes and gives him a small but significant peck on the lips.

"Trust me, I'm El's second biggest fan, and the love they have for each other is one of a kind. They called themselves 'The Renegades' when they were kids, for crying out loud."

"How original," Luka smirks.

"Oh, bite me, Lost Boy," I blurt, then feel the sudden drop of my jaw when realization strikes. My eyes widen and snap to Eva.

"Mama," Luka whines, to which she chuckles.

I mouth a sorry, and she surprises me by winking.

What the melon does that mean?

Just as I am about to enter overthinking mode, Tessa carries on. "Anyway, we have to do this thing every once in a while because this one," she points her finger at me, "tends to forget how awesome she is."

"Well, I want to know more. So, you play the guitar and the piano?" Sabrina takes a sip of her beer and gives me her full attention.

"Also, the violin, and I dabble with drums."

And when I say I dabble, I mean I own them. It was by far the hardest instrument to learn, but I got there eventually.

"Wow, could you be any more impressive?" Sabrina is staring at me like she's actually in awe of me.

"Oh, I got you covered there. El, my friends, is a walking, talking jukebox."

"Ryan, stop!" I yell at him, covering my face to hide another blush creeping in.

"Hell no… You can't control this," Tessa chimes in, giving Ryan the floor.

"And it's not that she can just name a song or something; it's that she can sing it and play it on any instrument."

"Seriously?" Sabrina shrieks, taking another sip while her free hand plays with Mateo's hair.

"Yeah, any song ever," Ryan confirms.

"Prove it," Tristan, who's moved to sit on the ground by

the pit, dares.

"Oh, how I wanted you to say that… so for her college application…"

"Ryan," I warn, "we don't need to dump them with too much information."

"If you don't wanna listen, cover your ears. But I would rather you tell the story."

Why my eyes go straight to Luka's is beyond me. The way he looks at me, curiously, makes it hard not to give in.

"Fine."

So I tell them all about my audition, where I had to compose a piece, perform it, and cover both classical and modern styles. The problem was that I couldn't decide what to pick for the modern portion.

Ryan hands me a beer, reading my mind like always. I take a sip, then another one before I continue my praises…

"So I asked the panel to choose any song in English or French for me to play."

Sabrina's jaw drops, Mateo's face goes blank, and I can't even look at Luka.

"Naturally, they took it as a challenge."

"So what did you play?"

I laugh at the memory, the scene playing out before me with such clarity.

"This posh guy, a bit older with glasses, asked for James Arthur's version of 'Impossible' on the piano."

"Wait? They got to pick the instrument, too?" Mateo gets a bit befuddled there. I nod when Sabrina sputters, "How is that even possible?"

"I told you," Ryan raves.

"Please continue." Luka's voice sends shivers up my spine. And I hate it. Hate myself.

"On the violin, I played Celine Dion's 'Pour que tu m'aimes encore'."

Sabrina squirms in Mateo's lap, fanning her face. "Say that again."

"Down, girl. Married, remember," her husband reminds her, pointing at his wedding band. She performs one of the best puppy dog faces I've ever seen. "But, French. She just spoke French. I'm sorry, Babe, I think I'm switching teams."

Mateo pinches her side, and she screams. It soon turns into laughter before she clears her throat and gives me a pointed look. "Please, keep going."

I puff out a breath, "Next was 'Seasons of Love' from Rent on the piano. What else?" I pause to think it over when Ryan reminds me, "Uh, 'Californication'—RHCP."

"Right, and 'Smells Like Teen Spirit' both on the guitar," I conclude.

"So you played all the songs just like that, without music sheets?"

I nod at Tristan, leaving out the fact that I changed the key to accommodate my range, and all that, without a cheat sheet.

"Marry me?" Sabrina proposes, one knee on the ground, making me giggle.

"Sorry, you're not my type," I tease, and she places her hand on her chest, playing all wounded.

"Prove it," Luka dares, his arms over his chest, hands hidden under his armpits. I might kill him. I don't know how, since he's so big, but I will find a way.

Despite my eye roll, I can't help but feel electrified. Something is thrilling about the challenge, and I want to prove myself, allow them to see me, the real me.

"Fine. Pick a song."

Sabrina turns to Mateo and says, "Ruin my life" without so much as a blink.

My guitar resting on my lap, I strum a couple of chords until I get to where I need to be. I sing the first verse and stop when all I can see is Sabrina and Mateo in a full-on lip lock.

"Long story, don't ask." Luka shakes his head.

"Wasn't gonna," I deadpan, going back to the song, entering a trance. I feel Luka's gaze on me; my skin feels it too, because it's burning up. The last chord fades, and I settle the guitar on the ground next to me when I see the devilish look on Ryan's stupid, punchable face.

"Nope," I snap, trying to nip it in the bud.

"Well, tough luck because I'm on my fifth beer and you know what that means."

"Oh no, Ryan, please," I beg, hands clasped in front of my chest.

"What?" he pretends to be ignorant.

"I hate you!"

"You love me, and you know it… Come on now, tick tock," he sings, tapping on his watch. I stand up and start walking toward the water. On my way, I make sure he fully sees my death stare.

"What is happening?" I hear Luka's voice behind me, but I don't hear the rest.

Chapter 32

Luka

Nora walks to the tree beside the pear and climbs up. A moment later, a tire swings down from the branch, and Nora jumps on it. She shouts, "I hate you," in our direction, but we all know it's meant for Ryan. He gawks, and I join his stare as Nora clings to the tire and swings over the water, screaming "Cannonbaaaall," before she lets go and dives in, fully clothed.

"I made a bet that I would get her to play; this was her payment, making this the first bet I ever won over her." Ryan crosses his arms over his chest, and I tap his back.

"I'm proud of you, man."

"Yeah, me too."

The kids all shriek, rushing past us toward the water, and jump up and down, clapping their hands as Nora emerges from the water in slow motion. The now very wet dress hangs to her body, revealing her curves, and the sight of her glory sends impulses somewhere it's definitely not supposed to. Strategically placing the cold beer bottle to my growing crotch, I start naming all the different types of wood in my head to get rid of the one pulsing in my pants. Sabrina whistles from behind me because, of course, she'd do that, and Nora's face blushes at the noise. If she only knew the effect she has over me, her entire skin would be turning crimson.

Continuing her torture, she slips down her dress, leaving her body covered in nothing but a two-piece swimsuit, making my mouth water. Ryan nudges me with his elbow, and I shake my head, snapping out of it. I give him a thankful nod, not even denying anything. Smirking through a *"fuck it,"* I stride to the tire, and before I know it, I'm flying into the deep, cold water.

In mere minutes, everyone follows. Mama waves us goodnight from the porch, as we all stay in the water, splashing it around. Nora comes back in and lifts Elijah onto her shoulder. I take Ethan and place him over mine, just as Ryan does the same with Lizzy. Some heavy tugging and pushing is happening, and the sound of Nora's laughter echoes into the night, filling me with warmth.

No matter how hard I try to deny it, Nora came into my life tied to another man. Despite it, I'm glad I've gotten to know her, even if it could never be anything more than this. If the only reason I'm part of her life is to give her these passing moments, it has to be enough.

"I won," Ethan yells when both Lizzy and Elijah fall backward with a loud splash.

"Of course you did; you had *The Hulk* holding you up—so not fair," Nora mocks.

I send a daggered stare in Nora's direction, and she chortles, "What?"

"You don't get to call me that!"

"Why not?"

"I don't like it coming from you."

"Ok, Teddy Bear," she gibes, smirking.

"That won't work either."

"Then what do you want me to call you?"

I repress the truth, biting away the one word I want her to say more than anything.

Mine.

"I think I'll go with Luk," she shrugs, then looks past me, and I see her cheeks blushing, but it has nothing to do with me. The reason becomes obvious when I turn in the direction of her stare, where Sabrina and Mateo are deep in their PDA. While she stares, I take the opportunity to gaze over the rest of her tattoos. This morning, I saw the one around her ankle, an anklet with pendants of the letters D and E. I quickly glance at the one under her breast while trying not to think about it. It's a treble clef in the shape of a heart. I frown when I see the one down her side is in French.

A clearing of a throat makes my eyes snap up. I'm met with raised eyebrows and a scowl. "It's from *Le Petit Prince:* Toutes les grandes personnes ont d'abord été des enfants. Mais peu d'entre elles s'en souviennent," she quotes with a lilt that sends shivers up my spine.

"All grown-ups were once children, but only a few of them remember it," I guess. The tilt of her head and the curve of her lips let me know I'm right.

Before I open my mouth to ask, she turns her back, lifting her hair to reveal the sign of the Deathly Hollows inked on her nape.

I want to trace over it, suck on her neck, and press her to me. Just as my thoughts peak, so does every hair on her body, covering every inch with goosebumps.

It's the cold water. I think to myself.

Tessa yells, her hands around her mouth, to reach us all: "Kids, bedtime!"

With a simultaneous groan, the kids get out of the water and follow their parents inside. I dry myself with the large towel, all the while keeping my eye on Nora, doing the same. I reach the pit and toss in another log to keep the fire going. Mateo and Sabrina join me as we stare at the flames in silence. Nora emerges later, placing a cooler next to her chair. She slumps in her seat and opens the lid, taking out three beers and handing one to each of us. Mumbling a thank you, I watch her lift her head toward the sky. It's so clear, you can see all the stars lighting up the night.

Ryan takes a seat next to me, and Tessa takes his lap, clasping her hands together. "So, Poker, Taboo, or Pictionary?"

Everyone shares a look, and Ryan and I burst into laughter, knowing that a game night is the worst idea. Nora puts our thoughts into words. "No way, you're the sourest of losers."

"Come on, I'm free for the next two hours, and I need some fun."

Half an hour later, we are deep into an intense game of Taboo, Tessa's favorite. Ryan gets another one wrong, and she smacks him over the head, cursing him with love. Nora and I are on the same team, and it's our turn to play. I am the clue giver. Shifting in my seat, I lock eyes with Nora, giving her a pointed stare, letting her know we've got this. She nods in confirmation.

Tessa turns the hourglass, and we're on.

I pull out the first card and smirk. This is way too easy. I also see it as a sign.

"Arrow."

Nora doesn't even blink before saying, "Power?"

I flip the next card, and my smile widens. For the first time, the cards are in my favor. I saw the book on her shelf, so I am sure she'll get it.

"Pflight before Christmas."

She hums to herself, then quickly yells, "Gravity?"

I nod and take another card. We're obviously on the same wavelength here. And it's a funny thing, how such a connection forms, unintentionally but somehow naturally, like it was meant to happen.

Thinking over the hints, it hits me. It's so obvious.

"Lady Gaga, Oscar, here."

Her stare hits deep when she mumbles, "Shallow?"

"Yes!" I pump my fist and take out a new card. Looking at the hourglass, I note we're halfway through. I can't help but marvel at how well we work together with ease.

By the time the last grain sets, we're seven points ahead. As expected, Tessa starts protesting.

"That's not fair. How did you get all of that?"

"Luka knew where to hit," Nora tells her, as if it were plain and simple.

Tessa takes out the cards and starts her deliberation.

"Explain this one," she demands, showing the one saying Gravity.

Mateo jumps in, "It's the family motto from the book title he mentioned."

"Okay," Tessa doesn't falter, "How about this?" It's the power card.

"His tattoo, the arrow. It represents power." Nora explains. And I'm here, thinking about how she looked at me while I explained the meaning; the intensity, intrigue in her eyes, sucking me in.

"Damn," Ryan smirks.

"Ok, on this one you cheated; I'm sure of it." She picks up the one stating Friday.

"That one is way too easy," Sabrina speaks up, winking at me. Tessa furrows her brows without even trying to put two and two together.

"Emily Gilmore? Friday night dinners? Ring any bells?" Nora ribs, looking straight at me, a full smile on her face, melting my heart.

"It's like you two share a brain," Mateo titters, swinging an arm around my shoulders. We all laugh. Well, all except a very mad, pouty Tessa.

Settling back in my chair, I try and fail to keep my feelings at bay. My heart is beating so strongly, and it's doing so for one person. Okay, two.

We play some more, and the overall score, if you must know: Nora and I wiped the floor with the rest of them. Enough said.

Chapter 33

Nora

There are days in a person's life that mark crucial moments, shaping character. My days are a mixture of challenging and happy ones. Today is no different. Sure, some heavy stuff went down, but it ended on a high note.

When we finally resolved to turn in, I was too buzzed to go to sleep.

I make my way to the backyard, far from the bedroom windows, so that no one can hear me. I've gotten reacquainted with music today, and I don't want to lose the momentum.

The night is quiet, save for the crickets making their presence known. The moon shines brightly, and the stars around it illuminate the sky. Everything about it feels poetic.

I place the guitar on my lap and strum away, finding a new melody. Words rush, pouring out of me with ease, a story unfolding.

I hum the bridge, the feeling of Luka's skin lingering at the tip of my fingers. I switch to a lower chord, matching the sound of my heart beating. The melody is both sad and hopeful. I take my phone out to write down the words, Dec's face as my background lighting up. I smile at my favorite picture of his, tracing my fingers over his bright eyes, a moment of pure happiness captured with a click.

I open a note app and type until the sound of a branch cracking stops me. Mateo reveals himself with a wave.

"Hi," I whisper, and he takes a seat next to me. "Couldn't sleep?"

"Just wanted to smoke one in peace before I turned in," he mumbles, taking one cigarette from a pack and flicking open his Zippo. He lights the tip with the flame and draws in a long breath. "I don't like smoking in front of Luka."

That's a true Hart right there, considerate. I am glad Luka has him. Them.

"I'll leave, give you your space," I start getting up, but he stops me by grabbing my wrist and pulling me back down.

"That's not where I was going," he swallows. "Ever since he told us what happened to him, I feel guilty for smoking. I started way too young, but he wouldn't hear it. He just told me to see it for what it is, a coping mechanism."

"He's a real smartass, isn't he?"

"You have no idea," he chuckles.

My brain wheels start working, then I gawk at him. "Wait, how old were you when he told you?"

After what Eva shared, I'm pretty sure Luka took his time filling his brothers in, and that only pains me, knowing he went through it alone. His scars tell a story he tried to conceal, hide from everyone around him, that he is a survivor.

"I was fifteen. Growing up, he always wore a shirt, even when we went swimming, so we never noticed. On his sixteenth birthday, Mama signed a waiver so he could cover all the scars with tattoos. He thought he was doing it to make other people more comfortable, but in all honesty, he did it for himself. He was ashamed of them and never could admit it."

My eyes well up, and I have to turn away to stop myself from breaking down.

"He sat us all down, told the story once, and never repeated it."

I wish I could've been there, holding Luka's hand. No, scratch that. I wish I could have been there to stop it from happening when he was just a hopeless little boy.

"I can't even imagine…" I trail off, thinking about how they must've felt, how Luka dealt with it.

"Whatever you did before, thank you."

What is it with this family thanking me? First Eva, now him. I don't get it. In fact, I find it ridiculous.

"I didn't do anything."

He scoffs, like what I've just said is redundant.

"You know what Sabrina told me earlier?"

"What?"

"That she didn't know Luka had dimples."

I stare at him in shock, his mother's words echoing through my head.

He reserves the biggest smile for special people.

"We've been together for over three years now, and she has never seen that side of my brother. I'm ashamed to say I forgot it existed."

I find that hard to believe, especially since Luka's been so open with me. Come to think of it, I think I've been different around him as well, like the old me.

My hand takes his without my say-so, but Mateo doesn't pull away, allowing this connection to form. The moment stretches, my wheels spinning. I may have to oil them up a little to make them run more smoothly, because they've been working overtime for lord knows how long.

"I don't know what to say," I sputter, my voice trembling.

He drags another long puff, blowing out smoke before adding, "He's different with you."

So many things are happening inside me, from the tight grip on my chest, heart, and throat, to a throbbing ache somewhere far too deep.

Luka's been my dilemma ever since I first saw him, possibly even before, having heard all the stories about him. He's infiltrated my mind, and no matter how hard I've tried, I can't get him out of my head. And not only that, he's slowly been taking over another part of me. And regarding it, I'm acting delusional with a whole lot of refusal.

Mateo takes one last drag, flicks the cigar to the ground, and stubs the butt with his boot.

"You're good people, Nora," he asserts, making it hard to ignore.

I'm far from it, but I'll let it slide. He doesn't need me to go all wrecked woman on him. I won't be spilling my guts out to Luka's brother. Not gonna happen.

"So are you. All of you. I am happy I got to meet you, and I hope to meet the rest of the Harts," I gush, wondering if I'll ever get a chance to.

"Oh, trust me, you met the most important one." He adds a wink to his snicker.

God, what's with this family? It's so easy with them, natural. It feels fated somehow, and that... I don't think I can handle it.

Scars

Every wrong stroke, every deep cut
The look of it went straight to my gut
The pain, the misery
Confronted all of my agony

You tried to hide it, but failed
You tried to bury the path they paved
The canvas of you was stained
You believed it was engraved

With my own two hands hell will raise
My fingers will make it disappear, erase the past
The scars that mark you will heal
Those scars are the reason your power is real

The deepest of wounds have enough space
For new memories, you could easily embrace
Oh, how I want to make them with you
To walk by your side around and through

You tried to hide it, but failed
You wanted it all to simply fade
Nowhere to hide, not from me
I see you, see it all, oh so clear

With my own two hands hell will raise
My fingers will make it disappear, erase the past
The scars that mark you will heal
Those scars are the reason my love is real

Chapter 34

Luka

The alarm's sound jolts me upright.

I'm surprised that I managed to fall asleep. I spent the night staring at the ceiling. Again. Every time I closed my eyes, I saw her smile. The guilt consumed me, the core of it all wrong, and it pained me. She's married, and yet, I couldn't help it.

Every possible distraction I tried was a bust.

Reading? I imagined her as the FMC…

Listening to music? I heard her voice…

A cold shower? Let's pretend that I didn't picture her naked under the stream.

Officially, the worst person on the planet right here.

Dreading the day ahead, I go straight to the bathroom and relieve myself before brushing my teeth. I shave my five o'clock shadow, then take another shower. The water cascades on my face as my mind swirls. We'll be next to each other during the ceremony. I'm going to be exposed to her scent all the while fighting away the urge to fully take it in. Turning the water off, I sigh and step out. Using a large towel, I dry myself and take another look in the mirror. The bags under my eyes are a reminder of another night spent in a bed alone, thinking about the one person I shouldn't be thinking of.

I need coffee, and I don't want to stain my suit, so I put on my shorts and head downstairs. The kitchen is empty, thank fuck. I notice the pot is full and still warm, and something tells me it's Nora's doing. I fill a large mug and take it with me back to my room. I reach to turn the knob when I hear yelling. I freeze. I know that voice, and I hear the pain behind it from over here. I lean in, focusing my ear better.

"I don't understand the problem."

"It's wrinkled right here, can't you see it?"

"Rick, you saw me ironing." Her voice is cracking, and so is my heart. Fucking again.

"Well, do it again, and do it better."

I can't just ignore this, right? I clench my fist, restraining the urge to storm in there and do what? Punch him? Kill him? It'll only end up hurting Nora. And Declan.

Fuck.

Something comes over me. Realization. Why isn't she fighting back? Why is she allowing him to treat her like this?

Ryan's words flash.

She was the one who supported them back in Canada.

Now she depends on him.

Rick broke her spirit.

My heart increases the speed of its pounding the more I think it over. The pain in her smile the first time I saw her, all the times she had trouble letting go of Declan, the patio… she does it all alone. From what I learned about her, she's always relied on one person—herself. Nora is self-sufficient, independent, strong, and self-made. She just lost sight of it. I can make her see. I can help her get there, even if it means I lose her forever…

No way is this much beauty possible...

A vision in a blue dress, as conservative as revealing, is making me question my sanity. Her locks make her hair look shinier. The gold and green in her eyes are popping, framed by the outline of her makeup. Her lips are plush in a lighter shade of purple, and her cheeks are flushed with her natural blush. And then the high heels, bare legs. The dress she's wearing is a weapon of my personal torment, clinging to her body, hourglass-ing it (yup, I made up a word).

Did my heart skip a beat the moment my eyes landed on her? No doubt.

Did I forget how to breathe when she looked at me? Damn straight.

Have I been staring at her the whole time the minister has been praying? Guilty as charged.

We're in the middle of the Renunciation of Sin and the Profession of Faith when her scent invades my nostrils. That familiar mix of vanilla and orchid (something I discovered after spending half an hour in the perfume aisle) activates all of my senses and heightens the illuminating desire.

How terrible a person am I for having unholy thoughts in front of the altar?

Did I mention I am in the middle of Ella's baptism?

Did I mention Tessa named her daughter after the favorite aunt, torturing me without even knowing it?

Did I mention I am crazy about Nora?

She radiates by Tessa's side, tightly holding Ella as if she's the most precious thing in the world. St. Anne St. Patrick is a five-minute drive from their cottage. It's peaceful inside, serene. Before we started, one of the pastors gave us a walk-through of the place. We were all mesmerized by the crutches, canes, and braces lining the walls, testifying to past miracles.

The minister hands me a white candle wrapped in lace, and I light it up with the fire from the Paschal candle standing on the right side of the altar. A white garment is placed over Ella's chest. I watch without drawing a breath as one single tear slides down Nora's cheek, colliding with the curve of her lips.

Fuck, she is breathtaking!

When it comes to Nora, it's hard not to take notice of every little thing. Like how she shuts her eyes to keep the tears away, or how she keeps looking at Tessa and Ryan now and then, smiling at their happy expressions. How her eyes glisten as she takes in every detail of the little bundle in her arms. How she turns over her shoulder every thirty seconds to check on Declan.

He's in his stroller, book in hand and headphones covering his ears, his grandmother rolling him back and forth.

I try to be inconspicuous while scanning the crowd, though there's not much of one. Tessa and Ryan invited their immediate family and closest friends to share this special moment. My eyes snap in Rick's direction, and I regret it immediately. There's this stupid expression on his face, unbothered, mixed with anger.

Did they make up?

Did he apologize for being a prick?

Does he know his name rhymes with the word?

And why the hell is he angry, anyway? His mother is taking care of *his* son, while he sits there, not even looking at his wife. Maybe I should introduce him to my fist. How can he not be infatuated with his woman? I can't unglue my eyes from her, and she's not even mine. It's wrong, I know, but how did that motherfucker even get so lucky to snatch someone as pure-hearted as Nora? And then there's Declan. Does he even know how blessed he is to have a son like him? I mean, just look at the little guy, hands stimming (yes, I did some research), a wide smile on his cute little face. He's adorable, with those squeezable, chubby cheeks. Another thing questioning my sanity. It's not enough that I'm infatuated with the woman, no… add to that an obsession with her kid.

I spent a fair share of hours reading every book I could find about autism, some articles online as well, just trying to understand him better. I want to make an effort for a deeper connection, using what I've learned, and I hope I'll get the chance.

The ceremony concludes with everyone congratulating one another, and we head to a restaurant for a celebratory lunch. My eyes stay on Nora as she approaches her husband and frees Declan from the stroller. The three of them go to their car, and I watch as Rick takes his seat behind the wheel, waiting while Nora straps her son into his car seat, places the stroller in the trunk, and gets inside.

Can someone explain to me why that whole scene bothers me so much?

It makes every part of me ache for her. Nora's the kind of person who wipes her own tears before anyone sees them fall. The kind who breaks down in the shower, then steps out as if nothing happened… laughs loudly, talks fast, plasters a smile that never reaches her eyes. She hides it so well that you'd never guess her world is quietly crumbling beneath that facade. But I do. Her family does. Her husband is blind to it, and I'm sure he uses it to his advantage. Maybe someone should shed some light. I'll happily volunteer as tribute.

Chapter 35

Nora

Taking another bite of my salmon, I bob my head at something Tessa is telling me, or trying to at least. I'm zoned out, still thinking about this morning.

For my role as a godmother, I wanted to put some effort into my appearance, so I curled my hair and applied some makeup after watching a YouTube tutorial. The result brought a smile to my face, reflected in the bathroom mirror. When I got out, I was fully expecting a gasp, a hand over the chest, and the words '*wow*', maybe even '*you look beautiful*'. Disappointment hit deep when Rick glanced over me and shrewdly said, "It's too much makeup."

The fact that I barely had any on, save for my eyes and mouth, made the statement even worse. I dressed Dec in a blue button-up shirt and dark jeans, matching his father's look. When my handsome little man came to my side, he smiled and said, "Mama, princess," making my day with that one. I immediately turned to Rick and snapped, "See, the kid knows how to compliment a woman."

"What's to complement? You don't look like yourself."

And we left it at that.

To think I used to find it endearing that Rick wasn't a fan of makeup. Boy, how my confidence took a toll when it turned from sweet to controlling. And he was good at it, too, making it sound like a question for my best interests and whatnot, masking it in compliments and concern. And I was dumb enough to take it, to listen, to change. Still am.

We haven't even had decent eye contact in the past month, and now, sitting across from him, I'm desperate for it. Imagine my surprise when I realize the severity of its penance.

"You should try this dip," Rick says, looking at me with a smile, acting like nothing happened. Per usual. It's so easy for him to flip the switch.

Ryan's face turns red as he eyes the small bowl Rick is passing to me across the table. I see the color too, know dang well what my husband is offering.

"Are you fucking kidding me?" my best friend roars, making Rick flinch.

"What?"

Is he really that oblivious, or does he not care?

The latter, Nora. It's always the latter.

My legs start to shake under the table, head spinning with memories of his wrongdoings... I'm nothing to him. I realize it now. I truly don't matter, not even a little bit.

"It's corn dip."

My heart plummets.

Ten years!

We've been married for ten fudging years...

How is this happening?

A boulder comes down on my chest, pressing all the weight.

"So?" he dares to feign indifference.

My blood boils. I didn't know a heart could break so many times, but once again, Rick proves me wrong.

"She's allergic," Luka snaps at him, standing up abruptly, causing the chair to fall back with a thwack. That catches everyone's attention, including mine. Eva squeezes his hand, and his body relaxes at her touch. Then his eyes meet mine. Time stops, everything around me ceases to exist, and all I want to do is jump into Luka's protective arms. I know I'd be safe there. But those strong hands aren't made to hold me. Someone else will have that privilege, and somehow that hurts more than this entire situation.

"Oh, right," I hear my husband brush it off with a smirk.

Just like that, another part of me dies.

Back at the cottage, the kids run toward the bouncy house. Tessa has outdone herself with pull-out tables decorated in pink and so many balloons that the ones from 'Up' can be put to shame. A familiar scent invades my senses like a gust of wind breathing much-needed air into life, and I find Luka by my side. For the last thirty or so days, he has been the constant thought invading my mind's personal space. After yesterday, it only got worse. He occupies my thoughts and most of my dreams. As much as I tried to fight it, to cancel him altogether, I failed miserably. I don't know what it is about him that makes me so weak, so helpless against the craving that only keeps growing.

His presence is all-consuming, and something else I can't say out loud.

Real.

I sense his eyes on me, roaming all over. My skin feels the admiration, so does every fiber of my body, seconds from combusting.

"You're beautiful." The words come out in a whisper, but I hear them, loud and clear; so do my toes—the epicenter of the earth-shattering before me.

And why do those words coming from him make me feel appreciated? Alive?

"Thank you," I mutter, keeping my eyes on the ground. I can't look at him, or I'll lose myself in his ambers.

Because no matter what, I won't do that to my husband.

"Auntie El," Ethan and Elijah's screams makes me turn. They charge toward me, knocking me to the ground. I wrap them in a hug, bursting out in a belly laugh, and plaster so many kisses all over their heads. When I look up, I find Luka frowning, hand over his heart, head shaking. "What am I? Chopped liver?"

I giggle, and the boys snap up at him, jumping into a sloth-like grab. He manages to lift each over one shoulder, and the sight does something unimaginable. My ovaries react in a way they definitely shouldn't, for obvious reasons. My eyes stay glued on the trio as they spin like a vortex. It's nice to see them interact after hearing how much my nephews love The Hulk. Their little hands are locked around his massive neck, and I might vomit at the speed they're spinning around.

Dec gets into view, snapping his hands and jumping in place at the sight of them running in circles, doing his all-time favorite motion. Their laughter makes my day, turning it around.

There's no warning, no indication of any possibility that my heart might burst. Somehow, simultaneously, a combustion happens, accompanied by a whole new set of feelings I've never experienced before, so I don't bother trying to define them. I forget how to breathe when Luka squats, freeing my nephews of his hold, only for it to be filled with the only thing that matters most to me. He picks Declan up, and they both fly away, or at least it seems that way in my mind. The sounds of the high-pitched scream/laugh coming from the depths of Declan's lungs gets a lump stuck in the middle of my throat.

Dec's laugh shouldn't feel this dangerous.

My whole body trembles, and someone needs to call the doctor because I am pretty sure I am having a heart attack. My Bug crashes into me, hugging my leg, and I don't have the strength to smile. I take his hand and walk him to Rick.

"Can you please watch him? I forgot something in the car," I lie; he nods, and I bolt.

Chapter 36

Nora

Deep breaths, Nora. Deep breaths!

It's hard to steady the chaos of my out-of-balance core, to find some common ground with this ripping-apart thing that's going on somewhere in the middle of my conflicted self.

Torn, I am so damn torn between the two pulls that have no right to even be there. Something is very wrong, and I am so lost in it all that I can't see any way out. Tears keep pouring from every direction, not caring about the makeup it took me four tries to perfect.

You're a terrible person!

That's an understatement.

I deserve whatever is coming my way because I am, hands down, the worst person in the world. How did I let this happen? How did I manage to develop feelings toward someone else while loving my husband? Worst of all, I am starting to doubt the love I feel for Rick. It's a short thought, barely a second long, but it's there, ruining me.

In the car, I insert the key and turn to ACC, needing something to fill the silence. I turn the radio up enough to muffle my thoughts. Next thing, I take out my phone and start typing.

Me: *You there?*

Sunny: *What's wrong?*

You see, that's a true friend right there. We've never met in person, only exchanged typed-out words, and yet she knows me so well.

Me: *Everything*

My fingers hover over the screen. Am I really going to do this? I already hate myself, so what's one more pin to it!?

Me: *I don't know if I can do this anymore, and the mere thought is tearing me apart.*

Sunny: *First, I am so proud of you for admitting it; second, he did this. You understand that? This is all his doing. You're lucky I was scrolling through TikTok just now, 'cause I came across a quote: "Love needs action, trust needs proof, and sorry needs change!" You got none of that. He never gave you any of it. You fought for it, Nora, I know, because we've been at this for over a year now—you refusing to see the truth, that you're not happy in this marriage.*

Me: *I am not happy*

Wow. I just wrote that, didn't I?
And it feels… Scary. Liberating.

Sunny: *Good for you! Now do something about it!*

She's right. I think it's time for the last resort—ultimatum. I hate those. Frankly, as much as it hurts to admit, I left myself no choice. I let it go on for far too long, pouring everything into a person who gave away his love in grams, while I gave out tons. Maybe my conception of love is all wrong.

Think about it… Your own parents didn't love you.

Twist the knife, why don't you, mind!

I mull it over for a minute.

In my own home, all I've ever been is needed.

I felt needed.

Never wanted.

Never loved.

My mother and I didn't have a normal relationship, especially since both of us were power-willed, hardheaded women. Our arguments were heated, mostly because neither of us could hear the other. At some point, I gave up on trying. Thinking about it now, I scoff at myself. How many nights did I cry, feeling guilty? And for what? She was the grown-up; she was supposed to be the voice of reason.

Alas, my heart doesn't hold grudges, and it never loves halfway. Nope. My most vital organ gives it its all, and then some, all the while exposing itself to get shredded into pieces. Can I patch it up? Or has it had enough?

I type a quick thank-you, wipe my tears, and fix my makeup, giving myself a stern look in the mirror.

"You're going to get whatever strength you have left in you for one last fight!"

This is it. Ready or not, things are about to change.

I give myself another deep breath, and then I'm out of the safety of my car, determination full throttle, getting firmer with each new step. I have my words ready, at the tip of my tongue. As I get closer to my husband, I see Dec is not next to him. I quickly look around. Panic rises with him nowhere in sight.

I run, shouting at Rick. "Where's Dec?"

"I don't know. Wasn't he with you?"

What the what?

Pulling my hair, I do a full 360, scanning each and every square. No sign of him.

"I left him with you. Damn it, Rick, what the melon?" I scream at him, hot rage taking over. My breathing is rapid, my body trembling, and all I see is red. Every single muscle in my body is tense, and I'm burning up.

Unbelievable.

"Why are you yelling at me?" He pulls back, looking at me with an empty expression. I blink, clenching my hand into a fist to restrain myself from choking him. I'm really struggling here. And to think that a mere minute ago, I had it all together.

"Seriously?" My cheeks are burning, and I reach for my chest. It hurts. It hurts so fucking much. And yes, I am fully cursing now, despite having controlled myself for three years straight.

Damn him for this.

"Nora, what's wrong?" Luka's voice somehow instantly calms me down.

"I don't know where Dec is," I shudder, feeling my hands shake.

"Shit! Nora, I'm sorry. He is inside; he's ok," Luka reassures.

"What?" I meet his kind face, and my lungs are thankful for the breath I finally inhale. "You were with him?"

"He's on the couch reading. I just came to get him some snacks."

Why doesn't it surprise me that Luka took the reins? Again. How can a stranger care so much for a kid when his own father can't be bothered?

Luka nods, his hand brushing my upper arm, soothing. I want to lean into his touch, but I settle for the fire that spreads through me instead.

"He got a bit agitated when the kids brought out water guns and started screaming. Rick didn't know where his headphones were, so we just went inside."

My eyes snap to Rick. Of course, he doesn't know where his headphones are. It's not like they haven't been in the same bag since I bought them for him. Shutting my eyes to contain this boiling rage, I heave, "Are you fucking kidding me?"

"Nor, don't put this on me; you told me nothing about his headphones. I don't pay attention to that."

Right. What was I thinking?

"Maybe you should start," Luka thunders, knitted eyebrows, nostrils flaring, jaw tight. He looks so intimidating, and for a beat, I'm scared for Rick.

Rick brings out his chest, barking back. "What did you say to me?"

This is not happening.

"You heard me," Luka snarls, getting in his face.

"Please," I beg, stepping between them. A scene is the last thing I need, especially on such a celebratory day.

"What is your problem?" Rick lashes out at Luka, ignoring me.

This is turning into a *Fall Out Boy* song, and we'll definitely be going down swinging. Especially due to Rick's loaded God complex, one second away from cocking and pulling it.

"I thought it was obvious, but let me paint a picture. You are my problem. Declan deserves better," he finishes on a high note.

I want to hug the man and punch him in the chest for doing this to me. I know he means well, trying to protect me, but I don't need him to fight my battles, been doing just fine on my own.

Yeah, in keeping quiet.

"Luka," I sputter, demanding his attention. When I get it, instant regret washes over his face.

He steps in front of me, saying his piece, "One thing worse than a single parent is a married single parent. You're better than this, Nora!"

With that, he storms away, while I stand there frozen, watching his back get further and further away. Numbness consumes me, and my heart disintegrates.

Chapter 37

Luka

Fuck!

I just had to go and open my big mouth, making everything worse. It's not like I could help it, not after the way that asshole raised his voice at his wife, like she was the one to blame for his egotistical nature. My chest tightens with guilt and frustration, but I hide it behind rage, desperate to protect her from my own internal chaos.

With each step, my anger grows; the voices behind me fade into obscurity. Clothes be damned, my charger too; I can borrow Mak's. Whatever... Nothing in that place matters anymore.

That's a lie, and you know it!

Damn my mind, or is that my heart speaking to me?

"Luka Elias Hart." That does it. No matter my mood, hearing my full name from my mother instantly grounds me.

It's a thing in our family; we have this way of communicating without words. Just one look is enough to carry out an entire conversation. Right now, her expression is telling me that I'd better sit my ass in the passenger seat and calm down while she and Tristan get our shit and join me. I am not a mama's boy, per se, but saying *no* to that woman—impossible, trust me. Sure, she has a good person aura about her, but no one has wrath like Eva Sophia Hart.

Yup, I am that petty and will be using full names from now on—or at least until I cool off.

The car door opens, and Tristan Cade Hart slides inside, grabbing the wheel. My mother's hand on my shoulder offers a comforting sense of support.

It takes her about five minutes before she finally speaks up, "Ok, I think I've given you plenty of time to wallow. Now I need your words, feelings, and all."

You wouldn't think that her words are demanding by the tone, all gentle and soft, but her eyes, man, those are out of a detective movie, made for the interrogation room. I can feel the weight of her gaze, sharp and unwavering, pressing onto my chest, making it hard to breathe, as if her eyes see right through my defenses.

That's when a motorcycle passes us by, accompanied by the sound of a horn and two waving hands. Frankly, I'm the least bit surprised that Mateo and Sabrina left to follow us. We're that all-in, ride-or-die, anytime-and-anywhere kind of family.

I pull out my phone and type a quick apology text to Ryan. He answers right away with nothing but a wink emoji. Tessa, on the other hand, follows up with a threatening text that ends with a heart emoji. I don't even wanna get into that right now. I've got enough on my mind.

"I'm sorry, Mama, I know you must be disappointed by the way I acted, but I just couldn't stand it anymore."

"Oh, my boy," she sighs. "If that's what you truly think, then you don't know me at all. I've never been prouder of you."

"What?" Both Tristan and I yell in shock.

She scoots over, placing her head between us, and gives my shoulder another gentle squeeze.

"You love her and that boy. Hell, I fell in love with them as well. I think I've loved them since you came home from work that day with the biggest smile."

That gets me to choke up. Her eyes fill with tears, and her words evoke all the simmering emotions in me.

"What am I supposed to do now, Mama?" My voice cracks. "She loves him."

I could see it. The love she felt for her husband, which concealed the anger, overshadowed the disappointment. But I also noticed something else, something undeniable in her eyes.

Turmoil.

A silent struggle.

I want to believe I had something to do with it. But I know better. She doesn't know how her touch, her gaze, sends me ablaze. She doesn't see me like that; she only sees him.

"Just let her find her way."

"I don't think I can," I admit weakly.

"You want my two cents?"

"Do I have a choice?"

It might as well be a rhetorical question. Tristan gets on the interstate and speeds up, melting into the traffic. The sun is high above us, not a cloud in sight. I turn up the AC, feeling sweat bead all over my button-down.

"Never," she deadpans.

"Then why ask?" Tristan points, and she smacks the back of his head, scolding, "It's called buildup."

Mama clears her throat. "The way I see it, she's too good

for her own good, and she gives everything into that family. She desperately wants all the pieces to fit, and will keep trying to polish the one that doesn't quite match. Regardless, Nora needs to grasp that her piece is perfect, and you need to let her achieve it, because only *she* can do that. When she's ready, then you'll do the finishing touch and complete the picture with your interlocking one."

Now that's some profound shit right there. Notice how she said 'when' and not 'if'? Yeah, me too.

"What's with the puzzle analogy?" Tristan grills.

"I find it fitting," she shrugs, and he chuckles. I, on the other hand, turn to the window and watch the trees we pass by as I reflect on her words.

I said my piece. Both she and Declan deserve better, and I hope with every fiber of my being that she will open her eyes and realize it.

Today only confirmed my doubts, the real reason behind Nora's pain. My blood boils thinking about how Rick wouldn't even bat an eye when Declan got agitated over the noise. That amazing boy who looked at me with eager eyes while opening his arms for me, as if he were inviting me into his world. I finally got the chance to try this joining thing I read about. It's a part of a son-rise program I found interesting. The way Nora interacts with her son, I'm pretty sure she is using it as inspiration for their relationship. The broad smile and belly laugh melted my heart as I held him tight and spun him around in circles. When he let go and started shaking his hands, without a second's thought, I mimicked his action. That was when he looked at me, entirely and deeply, making everything around us irrelevant.

Later, when the kids started screaming, his hand went to his ears, and I covered them with my own, shielding him from the noise. I looked around for help, but Nora was nowhere in sight. The only logical thing for me to do was to approach Rick. When he shrugged his shoulders after I had asked about Declan's headphones, anger culminated, but I suppressed it for the sake of the boy, for the sake of her.

Having no idea what to do, I got us inside. We took a seat on the couch, and I pulled out my phone. It took me a minute of scrolling to find the right soothing song. Declan smiled at my choice of African beats and relaxed into me.

I smile at the memory, the way his soft hair felt between my fingers as I ran my hand through it. Then my heart cracks a bit more, mostly because in that moment, I wished more than anything that he were mine.

Chapter 38

Nora

You're better than this, Nora!

The drive home is silent.

You're better than this, Nora!

After the Harts left, everything turned into a shit show. Rick ended up punching Ryan, Declan started screaming, and I wanted to do the same. It took Dec a long time to calm down, and when he finally did, I apologized to everyone, and before I knew it, we were on the road. I'm driving, since Rick's hand is swollen, and he's still heaving. Dec fell asleep two miles in, thankfully. So now, it's just me and the road. Since there's barely any traffic, we get home in less than an hour. I park the car, step out, and open the door for Dec to jump out. I grab his backpack when I notice Rick is not following. Instead, he maneuvers to the driver's seat and, without a single word, backs out of the driveway.

You're better than this, Nora!

We enter the empty house, and my Bug runs straight upstairs. He knows the drill.

In the bathroom, I let the water run until the tub is half full. There's a fair amount of bubbles going, so I help Dec out of his clothes before he gets in. Motor sounds escape his mouth as he plays with a toy boat. I'm on the floor, keeping an eye on him while ignoring the vibrations of my phone. I know everyone is calling, texting… everyone, except my husband, that is. Oh, and Luka.

What am I thinking? He doesn't even have my number, so there's no point in waiting to hear from him.

Stupid! Stupid woman!

I watch the last bubble dissolve, then I stretch out my hand. Dec takes it, and I help him out of the bath. He doesn't have many sensory issues, but he is very particular about the thread count of his towel. So, using his favorite blue one, I dry him off, head to toe. By the time we get dressed and head downstairs, it's already time to eat.

Rick is still AWOL.

I fix up a quick sandwich and watch as Dec devours it. After dinner, I brush his teeth and make the mistake of glancing up at the mirror. I look like shit, and that is putting it mildly. Shaking it off, I hand Dec a glass of water and wait until he's done gargling. I'm pretty sure he already peed in the tub, but I set him on the toilet just in case. Three long minutes of foot tapping later, I finally hear the sound I've been waiting for. I flush, then kneel down so he can jump for his piggy ride to his room.

While I grab a book, Dec is shuffling into his bed, fluffing his pillow the way he likes it. I take a seat next to him and read the story of the day. This is my favorite of his books. You have a story for every date of the year, so it's a new adventure every night.

While my mouth voices the story, my mind shouts at me.

You're better than this, Nora!

I get back to the task at hand, Dec's breathing my focal

point.

"The end," I whisper, pressing my lips to his forehead. He's out cold, and I get it. It's been a day.

I slowly get off the bed, lingering a bit to watch him like this, so peaceful. I slide the book back onto the shelf, switch the big light for the nightlight, and walk out of the room.

You're better than this, Nora!

Downstairs, I sit on the couch and wait. And wait. And wait.

Irritation strikes, and I grab my notebook and start writing. I have a good flow going, words pouring out with ease. They are angry, dejected, heartbroken... But they're here, and I need them out. As ten years unfold, not a single tear comes. The numbness subsides, and something else fills me. Maybe it's hope. But if I'm being honest with myself (and I am trying), it's indifference.

You're better than this, Nora!

I press the pen, ending with a dot-dot-dot. Then, I take a deep breath and read through all the past letters. A lot of them are me repeating myself, so I pick the ones I think have the most impact. I find the one from a year ago, the last time we were intimate. However, I wouldn't call it that. There was nothing intimate about it. I remember that day so clearly. I felt like an inanimate object, a freaking blow-up doll. That day was a hard one. Dec was extra moody, kept jumping on me, and I was so damn tired and overstimulated. All I wanted was to soak in a hot bath.

I was beyond worn out, but did you care? Of course not! Because it's always about you. And then you had to pull out the 'you never feel like it' card. You had to bring out the big guns and make me feel worthless—again. So I hope your dick is happy fucking a corpse because while you pounced into me, I felt nothing. Thankfully, you did so from behind, so you didn't see the tears.

Funny thing, that day we didn't even kiss. The last time our lips touched was weeks before.

You're better than this, Nora!

I can't get Luka's words out of my head. They follow me, so loud, so clear. I fold the letter down with the other five I chose and shove them in an envelope.

Then I hear it. The worst sound possible.

My life is giving me another test, in the form of my son's scream. I fly to his room, falling to my knees by his bed. He's covering his ears, sweat dripping over his pale face, screaming his lungs out. It's one of those piercing sounds that has one mission—to break my heart. I cradle him and hang tight, giving everything I have into soothing him. It's not working. He keeps on screaming, piercing my eardrums to a breaking point right beside my bleeding pump. Pointlessly, I ask what's wrong, and like always, I get no answer in return.

This is that part of this damned diagnosis, the label, that I hate most. He's in pain, and I can't pinpoint the source, and that right there cuts me like a blunt knife.

Remembering Rick has taken the car, I grab my phone and call for a cab. By the time it gets here, we're dressed and ready.

The driver speeds to the hospital, unbothered by Declan's loud shrieks, and I'm thankful. When we arrive at the ER entrance, I thank the man and pay well over the price before I run inside with Dec in my arms. I explain everything, that he's autistic, that he can't say what hurts, and that it will be difficult to check him up. I also refuse to let them take him, not without me by his side, holding his little hand. Where he goes, I go.

I am his voice; he is my heart.

I am his voice; he is my heart.

I am his voice; he is my heart.

Chapter 39

Luka

My family won't leave me alone.

They are hovering, in silence, agitating me. I think they're scared to breathe out loud, thinking any sound will break me. *It might.*

Why couldn't I keep my stupid mouth shut?

No. I did what I had to do, even if it was a push in the wrong direction. His direction.

Another mug filled with coffee appears in front of me. I absentmindedly take it, bringing the warmth to my mouth. I won't be able to sleep anyway, so what's a little more caffeine?

My phone rings, shaking the table with the vibration. We all share a look.

Who is calling at this hour?

I lean over, and when I see Ryan's name, I answer and put it on speaker before full panic can take over.

"What's wrong?"

"Declan is in the hospital."

I freeze, my chest cutting off any air flow.

"Which one?"

"Mass General," Ryan answers, and I hang up.

I don't even blink. I am out the door so fast that I have to turn back because I forgot my keys. Mateo blocks my way,

Mak next to him, shoulder to shoulder, dangling my keys. "You're not driving."

"I have to go," I bark.

"I didn't say you can't go. I said you're not driving. I am. Come on."

I slide into the passenger seat, leaving Mak to take the reins. Other voices murmur around me, but I can only register the one in my head.

Declan is in the hospital.

My truck pulls up to a stop at the parking lot where Mak works. A hand reaches out to pull me outside. I don't even remember the drive here. I feel two strong holds on each arm as we walk somewhere. When the sliding door opens, it all hits me at once, and I turn feral for a mere second before I collect myself into a sane person with a hefty dose of panic. I approach the information point and ask the kind lady where Declan is.

"Are you family?" she asks, her tone as lovely as it is professional, but her words strike deep, knocking the breath out of me, and my knees wobble.

"He is." Bianca steps to the counter, giving the nurse a soft smile.

What. The. Fuck?

"Thank God, you had me worried there for a minute." Ryan strides toward me, pressing his hand on my shoulder. "You hung up on me."

That's when I see he's sporting a black eye.

"What happened?"

"Rick happened," he deadpans. "Anyway, we're still waiting to hear from the doctor. They are running all sorts of tests. He was screaming and kicking, so they had to put him down."

The knot around my chest tightens, making it hard to breathe, and I can feel my palms sweating.

"And Nora?"

"She's with him, wouldn't let them take him without her."

The velocity at which my heart is pumping is downright alarming.

I scan the waiting room. Everyone is here, even Elle, sound asleep in her car seat, spread out on the small table. No Rick in sight, though. Ryan must notice my annoyance, so he leans in to whisper in my ear, "His phone is turned off."

"I hate that guy."

"You and me both."

This is the second emergency where he's unavailable; that I know of. God only knows how many times something like this has happened.

"Bianca said I was family."

"I heard."

My best friend clears his throat and pulls me aside, my guess is so no one can hear him. "Bianca loves Nora. She loves her son too, but she also knows him. You know, she told Nora not to leave Canada for him?" That makes my eyebrows skyrocket.

"Yeah, she told her not to give up on her dream, that she doesn't believe Rick is worth it, that he is too much like his father."

"What?"

I don't know the details regarding Bianca's first husband, only that he was abusive. If Rick showed any violent inclinations toward Nora, I don't think he'd be breathing. Plus, I would've seen it in him. I know firsthand what abuse looks like, feels like, and what it does to a person. So I am sure his abuse isn't physical—it doesn't make it any less, though.

"But you see, Nora was desperate for a family. All she ever wanted was to be a mother and a wife."

"And then she got exactly what she wanted," I bewail, exhaustion taking over my heavy heart.

Maybe Nora should've been more specific with her wishes.

While I am busy piecing it all together, working on a better understanding of Nora's mindset, she appears through the sliding door, making everyone close in around her. She looks downright desperate, beaten down, and strong all at the same time.

"It's an inner ear infection. They gave him antibiotics and will keep him overnight. He's still down and probably will be for the night, so you don't need to stay. Thank you all for being here." She examines all the faces and starts nodding when she realizes the most important person is not among them. How is it possible to have your heart broken over one person over and over again? Hers over Rick and mine over her.

After some protest, the waiting room clears. Mateo stays with me; the rest of the family takes Mak's car. As much as I don't belong, it's the only place for me to be.

Before he left, Mak made sure Declan got the best treatment and secured a bed for Nora so that she wouldn't have to leave his side.

So when I finally decide to go to Declan's room, the last

thing I expect is to find the two of them sleeping. I quietly sneak in and grab the remote to turn off the TV. I stare at her, crunched in the chair next to the bed, holding onto his little hand like it's a lifeline, and in many ways it is. She opens her eyes so slowly and blinks a couple of times, each time making her eyes widen, like she doesn't believe what she is seeing.

"You want coffee?"

"That would be great," she mutters, her voice shaky, eyes puffy and red… she must've been crying all day long.

"Have you eaten?"

She shakes her head hesitantly.

"I'll get you something."

"Thank you," she mumbles.

It's the least I can do—the bare minimum, in my humble opinion. But I know better now. For her, it's so much more.

The cafeteria is closed at this hour, so my only choice is the vending machine.

Full arsenal in hand, I open the door and sigh at the sight. Nora is grunting, trying to unfold the bed someone must've brought while I was getting her food. I place all the stuff on the table in the corner and walk to her. I grab the clasps to free the thing when she mutters, "I can do it myself."

"I know you can," I seethe, "what pains me is that you can't seem to understand that you don't have to."

I set up the fold-out bed next to Declan.

"Eat. Please," I beg, pointing at the table. She nods, and I linger, hesitant to leave. I take one last glance at the patient. One look at him is all it takes. I give him a soft kiss on the cheek, and without another word, I walk out.

I know what I have to do, and the way my heart aches only makes my choice that much easier.

When Mateo notices me, he reads my mind and follows me to the truck. With eyes fixed on the road, I feel my brother's stare, but he remains silent.

When we reach the blue townhouse, I park my truck behind the SUV and rush to the door. I don't knock; I pound. It swings open, and I come face-to-face with the man who has everything I ever wanted.

"What do you want?" he hisses, and I have to restrain myself from punching him.

"Your son is in the hospital, and your wife needs you. Get dressed and get in the truck."

He opens his mouth, but I stop him with a bark, "You have two minutes!"

Turning my back on him, I beeline to my truck. When I slide inside, Mateo looks at me with so much sympathy and respect that I am a second away from combustion.

"I'm proud of you, big brother," is the last thing he says before a stowaway joins us.

Chapter 40

Nora

The first time I ran away from home, I was four years old. Ok, I didn't technically run away; I locked myself in the bathroom. My purple butterfly backpack was filled with my favorite snacks, which I had stolen from the kitchen, the ones my mother always hid from me. I took a pillow from my room and used the bathtub for a bed. I was excited, as weird as that may sound. I couldn't wait for my parents' reaction. Much to my dismay, I got none. They didn't notice till morning, when mom had to get ready for work and couldn't get into the bathroom. Talk about feeling like nothing.

That's my life for you. And it just went downhill from there. And to this day, I blame myself, thinking that if I did my chores, was the best student, they would love me more. If I were the best, they'd care enough to show up. My parents never came to any of my recitals, not even the one that made the national news. I was featured in the newspaper as a prodigy, a once-in-a-lifetime talent, at the age of ten. Even though I was labeled as impressive, I still felt like I didn't matter.

Ryan was the first person to accept me so effortlessly. Around him, I didn't have to try; I just was.

I depended *sur moi*, provided for and took care of myself. Got emancipated at sixteen, found a job, and truly started living on my own with a simple smack of the judge's gavel. When Rick joined the picture, I was still that person, until we moved to Boston. That's when everything changed.

My family noticed it before I did. They tried to tell me, but I couldn't see it. Wouldn't see it. Refused.

One thing worse than a single parent is a married single parent.

Luka's words are like a knife to the chest that keeps on twisting. He wasn't wrong. When it comes to Declan, I am the one who does it all, without a break. My only free time is when I sleep, if we can even count it as such. It's exhausting, being in charge of everything, carrying the load, all the while catering to all my husbands' and child's needs. Not only am I a single married mother, but I am also a single married woman. I have no partner. I have a roommate who sees me as nothing more than his maid. That brings up the question: Who takes care of me?

I can't even take credit for that one. Sunny asked it in our Discord session last night. After Rick came to the hospital, I couldn't look at him. Sleep wouldn't come, so I sent out an SOS. It didn't take long for my online shrink to go deep. When I told her that I felt like I had to wait on his hand and foot because he was the one working and providing for us, she turned on the caps.

Sunny: *ELEONORA GRACE TREMBLAY, YOU LISTEN, AND YOU LISTEN GOOD! Or read, I guess...*

Sunny: *Marriage is not about guilt-tripping or about compensation; it's about mutual trust and compromise, about doing it all together, distributing the weight. It's not always fifty-fifty; sometimes you take on more, other times he should do the same. It's about finding common ground—together. Maybe you let his actions happen, but he was the one who made them.*

I reread her words for the umpteenth time, then scroll down to the last messages, where she made me realize that the reason why I haven't spoken to Rick's family about our problems is that I am scared to lose them.

Sunny: *Was it worth losing yourself?*

Me: *I am not important*

Sunny: *And who is?*

Me: *Declan. Rick. They are my everything. My son's happiness is the most important thing to me. After him comes Rick*

Sunny: *And what about your happiness?*

Me: *What about it?*

Sunny: *Where does it come in?*

Me: *As I said, I'm not important*

Am I truly living? I'm going through the motions, doing what I'm supposed to do, and plastering on a smile when needed. And I honestly believed I could keep on going like that, I really could. But at one point, it feels like I'm watching my life from behind a glass. Everything feels different, distant. I'm merely existing. I have no spark, no value, no joy. Stuck in the same loop, wondering when I'll start to feel alive again. I got so accustomed to taking care of everyone else that I didn't even realize I disappeared.

Crisser, I forgot music. I forgot my dreams.

I've become a background character in my own life. I don't know how to get *me* back or if that version of me still exists. But I do know I miss her. I miss feeling more than what I do for others. So now the question is… How do I get her back?

Chapter 41

Rick

I'm losing her.

No, you stupid idiot. You lost her a long time ago, to the point where she's unrecognizable. My wife used to smile, sing, dance… I used to enjoy the melodiousness of her voice.

After a sleepless night in the hospital, Declan was finally released this morning. Nora didn't yell; didn't fight, and for the first time, I am scared.

She comes in front of me, disrupting my view of the TV. I see the suitcases in her hand, but I say nothing.

"We're going to the cottage. I think we both need some time apart to think. Breathe."

"Wow. How cold. You made your point, Nor."

I'm a jerk. Yet, I can't help it.

"And what point would that be?"

"You win; lesson learned."

"Rick, I am not walking away to teach you a lesson. I am leaving because I finally learned mine." And with that, she walks right out the door.

There's this recurring dream that woke me up on god knows how many nights. It's one where my son and I have a conversation. That's it. That's the dream. The worst part is that I haven't done a thing to make it a reality. It's all Nor.

She's the one doing everything possible for our little guy. I know it, am aware of it, but am too proud to show it. I stare at the envelope she left on the coffee table. I know what's inside.

I open it and slide the first letter out to unfold it. It takes me some time to go through them all. There are a couple of songs in here, too.

Some words are repeated multiple times, such as undervalued, unappreciated, and alone... One that hurts the most: UNLOVED.

For fuck's sake, she feels unloved... it was a major fuck-up on my part, and I was so oblivious to it. I know how good I have it, and I took advantage of it, but at her expense, at Declan's. I never made an effort for either of them, and the realization of it consumes me with guilt. Honestly, I don't understand why Nor hasn't left me years ago, and yet I can. It's the woman she is, big heart and all. The most compassionate person ever to exist. She faded away right in front of my eyes, and I? I was blind to see it. Like a bystander, I read her words over and over, thinking back on how it all went down, my perception way off.

Not for one moment during my childish behavior had I thought about how it would affect her.

I reread the last letter, remembering the day as if it were yesterday.

Something nudges me, and I jolt upwards into a seating position. Nor is in her pajamas, hair disheveled like she's been tossing and turning all night.

"What?"

"You forgot." It's not a question. I'm still half asleep, so I

have no idea what the hell she's talking about.

"I'm really hurt, Rick. I know that my birthday is not a big deal and I never expected some grand gesture… but when you didn't even acknowledge it, it felt like I didn't matter."

What is the big deal? We haven't bought each other presents since we moved here. If she were expecting a gift, it's her fault for having such expectations.

"There you go again. You're always starting fights over nothing. I was beat; every muscle in my body hurts. If you want me to keep working and giving you everything you need, you wouldn't be nagging me about a date on a calendar."

Her face falls.

"It's not nothing. It's my birthday. Was my birthday."

I grab the remote. I'm awake now; might as well catch up on the latest podcast.

"I never said that. You're imagining things again, twisting it around."

"So I imagined you not doing something?"

"Don't be so dramatic. It's your insecurities playing with you. Last week, you said I was controlling. Now, I'm what? Forgetful? All you do is criticize me."

Tears fill her eyes.

"Oh, look at that. Playing the victim with your tears. It won't work."

I get up, tossing the blanket on the floor. "I'm done with this conversation. I'm going out."

Without giving her a second glance, I storm out.

I drank myself stupid that night. We ended up not talking for three days, and it wasn't for lack of trying on her part.

The doorbell rings, and I jump to my feet, hoping she has come back. Then I think better of it.

Why would she ring the bell?

I walk to the door and swing it open to find none other than my mother.

"Not now, Mom. Nora left."

"I know. That's why we need this talk."

I step aside, giving her room. My mother goes straight to the couch, pulling out a bottle of Jack from her purse. I bring two tumblers from the kitchen cabinet and take a seat next to her. Without asking, she pours both glasses to the brim. I take mine and gulp the entire thing down. My mother does the same.

"You know I love you, right?"

Yeah. This is not a good start. I'm about to get served. I deserve it, though. I nod, filling another glass, leaving the bottle in the air with the question. She bobs her head, and I fill hers as well.

"I also love Nora. And I need you to stop this. Let her go, son."

"I can't."

I'm selfish, I know. And it's for all the wrong reasons. I'm too dependent on her, too comfortable in the way things are. Were. Even thinking about doing it all by myself irritates me. That right there is the reason I am everything Nora put to paper.

"Yes, you can. Keeping her in your life is ruining her. And I can't watch her lose herself any longer."

That brings up the question. Could I? I've been doing it so far without a care in the world.

"I love her."

"I know you do. That is why you have to do what's right for her. She needs to come first; you need to make it happen. She won't do it; you know she won't."

I down another glass, mulling it over. Nor won't leave me; she loves me.

She loves me.

She loves me.

Unloved.

Fucking hell!

Narcissist

You act superior, think you're special.
Diminishing me and my succession
With your critical gaze, you look down
At me, my life, tossing away my crown

You like your power, have your success
You forgot I know how to play chess
This queen won't bow to admire
My king, this awakening will be dire

Admit it, without the need for a twist
Allow the notion you're a fucking Narcissist
Overreaching and egotistical
Not enough to describe what is critical
Admit it, see what you've missed
Let it sink in, you're a Narcissist

My voice does matter.
You just don't like to hear it
Maybe I should change the key
Tune it so you can clearly see
What was in front of you all along
The love, heart beating so strong

You like your power, but I will take it
Make it clear, maybe even shake it
This queen will not bow to admire
My king, this awakening will be dire

Lena Knight

Admit it, without the need for a twist
Allow the notion you're a fucking Narcissist
Overreaching and egotistical
Not enough to describe what is critical
Admit it, see what you've missed
Let it sink in, you're a Narcissist

Dear Rick

July 21st 2024

I spent the day crying in Dec's bedroom while he played beside me. You just told me I was not a good mother, and I tried my best not to have a complete meltdown in front of the kid.

We both said things neither of us wanted nor meant to hurt each other, but you know, just as much as I do, that words tend to make the deepest of cuts. Your snaps at me are always around the belt, but this time you went below it, and I can't say it didn't kill a part of me. Of all of the statements you could've hurt me with, for you to choose this one is beyond reason. I honestly don't understand what I have done for you to hurt me like that, for you to say those things.

All because you got mad for putting a temporary tattoo on his forearm. Seriously? I don't understand the problem, nor your reaction, and yet here we are. You are on the couch, not giving a single fuck, and I'm here, breaking apart in front of our son. I'm thankful for his autism right now, considering he's oblivious to my pain. The worst part is that even though you don't deserve my pain, here I am feeling every shred of it caused by your words and actions.

I love you

Dear Rick

September 3rd 2024

So, another day, another cold shoulder. It must be the theme of the month. Honestly, I forgot what we were even fighting over. Must be another thing I did wrong, like always… what was it this time? Lunch was not salty enough, or did I forget to wash the car? Or maybe it's the more obvious one, I didn't spread my legs when you demanded? No, that was two nights ago… I know, I didn't jump as high as you wanted.

God, I am sick of this - I am barely holding on, my strength is fading away, and you're there, without a shred of remorse.

Why can't I do right by you? Why is it that every move I make is the wrong one when all I do is everything for you? I accommodate your schedule, not the other way around.

I love you!

Dear Rick

October 15th 2024

I am so lost right now. I've been sitting on this empty bed for the past hour rewinding our entire argument, trying to pinpoint what I said or did wrong. I honestly don't know if there is something seriously wrong with my brain, but I can't seem to find any logical reason for your outburst. I sometimes wish you would stop and listen to me, rather than twisting my words to suit you. And even after I had apologized AGAIN for the stupidest, smallest thing a person could get angry over, you still didn't even flinch. And now I'm sitting here in the dark, wondering how you can soundly sleep while I am breaking apart. I conclude that you don't care! You never did. How can you stand by and watch me tear myself apart and not give a single fuck? Only an egotistical person can do that... But that's not who you are, right? You can't be that cold… I refuse to believe it. So I'm begging you, desperately begging you to snap out of it and come back to me. Please let me know what to do so that we can make it work. Please..

I still love you!

Dear Rick,

November 1st 2024

    I am so pissed right now. I was sick, wiped out by the stupid flu, and all I needed was rest. Would it have been so hard for you to say, 'You rest, I have him'?

    You do know that he is your son as much as he is mine, right? Funny thing about it is that I always have to ask you to watch him, correction - I always have to ask if you can watch him. Like you're his babysitter and not his parent. I blame myself for that one as well. Fuck I blame myself for everything. It's the one thing you taught me, the one thing you engraved in my brain. That I am in the wrong, that I am the one to blame all the time. Congratulations!

    Blame me, what's one more???

I still love you

Dear Rick,

March, 13th 2025

Happy birthday to me!

I don't know anymore!

Chapter 42

Nora

Having free time to think is a pain in the ass. And that's just my humble opinion. My brain physically hurts with all the running around it's been doing.

And what do I have to show for it?

I am even more confused now than I was a week ago. My talks with Sunny took a toll on me. I learned that hyper-independence is a trauma response. That was her take after I talked about my childhood. She also said I was emotionally numb and in survival mode. I had to Google it, because frankly, I didn't understand half the words coming out of Dr. Sunny.

One question she let out in the universe still haunts me.

Do you see love in his eyes, or do you see the reflection of yours?

Another thing learned: manipulation is a form of abuse. That conclusion came after she pointed out his most frequent type of manipulation, his focus on how I reacted rather than how he treated me.

I honestly believed that if I just tried a little harder, it would somehow work itself out, thinking love was enough. I thought I was enough.

I've been dealing with my problems alone, with stuff

others would break down a long time ago. I learned how to smile while crumpling on the inside. He called me cold, and maybe that's true, but only because I've been burned too many times.

It took a Dove Cameron song to finally see that I wasn't a difficult person to love. That one's been playing on repeat, a true eye-opener. Not only regarding my life with Rick, but also how another person made me feel. How acts of kindness brought me out of my shell. It's as if I'm seeing it all for the first time… the way he looks at me, how a single touch brought me back to life. We all know there is another person worth the space in my head, and his name is Luka. He doesn't live on the second floor; he's squatting in the abandoned place that is my heart. It wasn't supposed to happen. And yet… I allowed it. I gave a piece of me for him to take, all the while he ever so slowly took his own place within. Engraving himself in my flesh.

The full moon casts light on the table, highlighting the newest product of my turmoil. Solitude I am used to, but being here, under the moonlight, I don't feel lonely. The stars are my companions, carefully listening to my strums. Playing helps me explore my options and think about possible outcomes. Rick is the one who has to make a choice. The ball was left in his corner. Fight or flight—his choice—my undoing.

Luka's words appear in the forefront of my mind like a neon sign.

One thing worse than a single parent is a married single parent.

You're better than this, Nora.

You're better than this, Nora.
You're better than this, Nora.

But am I? Do I honestly deserve more?

The hairs on my neck prickle, and as if summoning him with his own words, I feel him behind me.

"You can't be here," I gasp.

"I know." It comes in a whisper, flying through the air, reaching to that part he's taken over.

I missed his voice. And I hated every second of it. I tell myself that I shouldn't ask, that I don't want to know. The question slips out anyway. "So why are you?"

"Just wanted to make sure you're ok."

"I'm always ok."

That's all I ever allowed myself to be. Chills take over, and I hug myself, knowing dang well it has nothing to do with the fresh air.

"I don't doubt it." He comes beside me, but I don't lift my head. I can't look at him. I'm not ready.

"How is Declan?"

He cares. Oh, how this man cares. I can hear it in his voice, and it intensifies the ache. One positive aspect of being here, away from all my problems, is that Dec's been thriving. I've never seen him so happy. And that alone is worth all of it.

"Sleeping," I mutter, my fingers grabbing the pendant around my neck, the feel of it distracting, soothing.

"I am sorry, Nora," he falters, and I can't take it; that crack in his voice hits somewhere it's not supposed to.

"What you said was cruel," I lie. Sure, his words cut deep, but they came from a good place; they have been looping ever since they left his beautiful mouth.

"I am not sorry for what I said."

What the melon? My jaw drops. "But you just..." He doesn't let me finish, his tone firm and steady. "I am sorry for hurting you, not for speaking my mind."

That confession hits me like a punch. I turn to face him. The dark circles under his eyes stand out in the moonlight. I feel the weight of my guilt mixed up with the longing.

"I don't know your story, but I know you. You are not happy, Nora. You're so far gone into this role you think is the only definition you have of yourself."

I am going to lose this battle, I just know it. Luka makes me weak, and that's saying something.

"You're wrong," I thunder, standing up to make a point.

Wrong move.

I've been on the receiving end of belittlement, degradation, and indifference, and not once have my knees wobbled. But now, with Luka so close, I don't think I can even stand my ground.

"You're only fooling yourself," he scoffs, shaking his head.

I want to tell him he's far off, except I can't. And he knows it.

"He loves me," I croak, trying my best to believe those words.

"I don't doubt it. Who wouldn't? But you and I both know that sometimes love isn't enough. I know you love him, and I know he loves you too, but not in the way that you need. Not in the way that you deserve."

My heart is pounding so fast that it might actually burst. I can't take it; it's too much. All of it is overflowing, slipping out, and I can't do a thing to stop it.

Deflect. We need to deflect.

"You don't know me," I wail, "You don't know what I do or do not deserve."

"I may not know your favorite color or your favorite movie, but I do know your soul. The one that aligns perfectly with mine. I know your heart, Nora, the pureness of it, the love beating out of it so loud that it's impossible not to hear it. I know Declan is your life, and so is music. You wear it all on your sleeve, but you hide the pain because you're scared of losing the people around you if they see it. I know you play with your pendant when you're nervous. I know you have six tattoos, even though you told me you only have five."

I gawk at the man, unfathomable to scale, and I know my face can't hide any of the erupting feelings. How on earth could he possibly know that? I hid it even from Ryan. I don't dare ask, even if not knowing is all but killing me. And now my stupid palms are sweaty, and I can smell my armpits, and not in a good way.

"You sacrificed enough, and even without your sacrifices, I know you deserve the world."

As much as his words weren't intended to hit, I can't help but feel them punching hard, depriving me of air. For the first time, I don't want those words to come out of someone else's mouth. So much is running through my head. Questions of the heart are taking over. Should I listen? I haven't so far…

For the longest time, I've been walking a specific line, and even though it felt like nothing was lost, something was missing. My inability to decide what's wrong or right, which way to go, or when to stop is frustrating. I know my heart is trying to tell me something; I only wish I could figure out what…

A slight gust of wind passes by, causing me to shiver. Or maybe it's because Luka is standing in front of me. Close. Too close.

I look up when I feel his hand moving. He cups my face, his fingers soft, heavenly, even with the blisters. Panic takes over, my entire nervous system malfunctioning as his eyes pierce through me. Tears emerge, and I flinch when I think he's about to kiss me. Not because I don't want it, but because I know it will be my undoing.

"No, Nora. I would never do that to you."

I gulp. Swallow, embarrassment going straight to my cheeks as I avert my focus to the ground. So I read that totally wrong. No biggie. It's not the end of the world.

Stupid, stupid woman!

Heart pumping vigorously, I take a breath in an attempt to compose myself and fail.

"As much as I want to kiss the hell out of you, claim you…" There's a fair share of desperation in his voice, triggering my quiver. "Show you how and what I feel; I know it will only result in your guilt, and that is the last thing you need."

Oh.

Claim? How he feels? He said that, right? I want to ask, get it out of him, but as expected, words fail me. I can't articulate, not even for all of it to stop. That stupid guilt takes over yet again, eating me on the inside. I am feeling too much, breaking at the seams.

He brushes past me, but before he reaches the corner of the house, he turns. "I do know your favorite flower, though…"

I wait for it, holding on to my pendant like it's a lifeline, the only thing keeping me grounded.

"Daisies. And I bet the reason is that it was the first flower you got from Declan."

It's the first flower I got, ever. But I don't tell him that. I do watch him walk away, leaving me standing alone, with nothing but the darkness around as my only comfort. I hear the car door slam, followed by the rev of the engine, before it fades away. The man just took out the pin and disappeared before the grenade that is my life exploded.

You'll get through this.

My mind tells me, and I have to trust it. As confused as I am, I have to have faith that it will get better. Maybe not today, perhaps not tomorrow. But one day, between laughter, crying, and washing dishes, the pain will stop, and I'll be ok. Maybe even better than I ever was. I have to give myself time and trust the process.

Detonate

Talk to loud, I went silent
Act too soft, I went strident.
I go left, you turn me right
You retrieve, but I want to fight

You like red, I become it.
You hate blue, I dissolve it.
You like gold, but I'm allergic
Still, I wear it, make it liturgic

No more hovering, tossing the shields
No more evading the minefields
I welcome the blast
Forgetting about the past
Ready to detonate, no questions asked

Walk too fast, I slow the pace
Don't like makeup, so I wash my face
Don't like it long, I go short
Everything about me becoming a fort

You like the sun, I love the rain
Forget about happy when you like the pain
You like chess, made me your pawn
Too bad my faith has already been drawn

No more hovering, tossing the shields
No more evading the minefields
I welcome the blast
Forgetting about the past
Ready to detonate, no questions asked

Chapter 43

Nora

What the melon was that last night?

I am still not over Luka's little visit. As if I needed another sleepless night on my bingo card... So, if you're wondering why I'm on my third coffee at eight in the morning, there's your answer.

My notebook is on my lap, a timeline of my life, my marriage, mocking me. I take another sip, smiling as I watch Declan play in the lake.

You know what's really funny!? Of all the expectations I had for this place, not missing our home wasn't one of them.

I open the last empty page left.

Reading the damned thing over and over again only made my stupidity shine through the pages. Everything about it unnerving. If I didn't know I wrote it, I'd be screaming at the woman who had, with a full-on rant. But alas, I am the one who put the pen to paper in an attempt to recover something figmental.

This whole thing would be so easy if I didn't love him.

How messed up is it that I wish I didn't love my husband? Don't answer that. Let me give you something worse. There were times I wished he had cheated so I'd have a reason to leave.

Yup. That'll get you to hate me. Well, join the club. And you know what? I don't even care. Gone is the feeling of guilt. Gone is the fear. All that is left at this point is emptiness.

The war raging between my heart and my head lasted for far too long, with my head winning most of the battles. Now, the tables have turned. I can feel it in my bones, feel my heart embracing the challenge.

When there's no drop of coffee in my mug, I sink back in the chair, feeling the sun peeking through the branches. The birds' chirping feels like an invitation.

Without a second's thought, I pack a small backpack with all the necessities, get Declan dressed, and we're off on an adventure. Okay, it's not that poetic; it is only a simple hike in the woods, a mere five-minute walk from the cottage.

Halfway up, I curse under my breath. I did not pick the best part of the day for this; good thing I brought enough water. Dec whistles, or tries to, then starts singing his ABCs, and keeps on smiling. We find a large clearing overlooking the lake, and I hold my breath.

Is this my '*The Wild*' moment?

No, it's more the '*Fall*' episode Lorelai moment... An epiphany...

My entire life flashes by, all the times I felt like nothing, all the times I was put down, just whoosh past. In my mind, it all plays out in black and white, as if my inner recorder were trying to tell me those were the darkest times. Then colors appear, and all the good things in my life come together. First, Ryan and our friendship; then music; followed by the birth of Dec; and my family being with me. As the memories unfold, the colors grow increasingly vivid, with some standing out in stark contrast. When the last good memory flashes, it lingers a bit longer than the others before it, too, dissipates. I am left with a view of the sun, the green scenery, and the unmoving water. I inhale, long and hard, before I let it all go with one strong breath.

Right there with the sun at its peak, the greenest of grass surrounding us, I do the only logical thing... I scream!

For the record—it feels liberating!

Chapter 44

Luka

Six months later

Standing on the platform overlooking the building rising in front of me, I feel as empty as ever. The project I worked so hard on is staring right at me, finished… I should be proud, happy even, but instead, I feel nothing. Days went by slowly, lost without this sense of fulfillment.

Watching my life pass me by, as people around me tried their best to cheer me up and fill a void, took its toll. Nothing helped. I drifted away, closed myself in a room so tight it sucked all the air right out.

It's pointless, and I'm aware of it; still, I can't help it—the pull is too strong.

I don't know where I'm going, but I have faith that I'll eventually find my way. It's the solitary path that I try so hard to avoid. No matter how much I wished for them to show up here, like that first day, to bring my heart back to life… It never came…

And despite it all, I'm still not giving up. There's some hope left, barely flaming, but it's there, always present—the one thing I can never let go.

Life moves on around me; I'm the one standing still, stuck in that last moment, the last time I saw them. The smell of strawberry on his light brown hair, the softness of his cheek, the way his hand felt in mine... the freckles on his mama's face, those hazel eyes that have the power to stop time. Every detail occupies my very thoughts, and frankly, I didn't do much to make it stop. My hands feel empty without theirs to fill them, much like my heart.

I can't tell how many times I got behind the wheel and drove to them only to turn the truck around. Ryan's been no help, refusing to give me any information. Being around them has become difficult, so I started making excuses. The only place I feel safe is at home, even under Sabrina's scrutiny.

I want Nora to have her happy ending. She deserves to be happy, even if it's with him.

"Boss, we need to pull the platform down," Peter, my second-in-command, reminds me.

Looking at my wristwatch, which marks the end of the workday, I nod and step down from the platform when it reaches the ground. All the work stress is irrelevant, making it even more productive. All my sites are working like a well-oiled machine, reducing my headaches.

"Have a good one, Pete," I say, and he smirks at me.

"You too, boss." He gives me a wink and disappears around the container. What's with the eye twitch?

I go through the site, making sure everything is ready for tomorrow, when all the tools and containers will be picked up. I lock my office, walk to the front, and have to rub my eyes when I get to the gate.

Am I going insane?

Maybe it's a mirage. Surely my imagination can't be *that* good. More rubbing, along with intense blinking, occurs, but the image before me remains, growing clearer.

Right there, holding two cups of coffee, is the incarnation of every figment, every fantasy. Sneakers on her feet, legs covered by a beige maxi dress, and a jeans jacket keeping her warm. Her hair is longer and lighter, falling to the center of her breasts, and that freckled face glows back at me with a smile so wide her eyes match it. The wrinkles on the sides play around, pointing out the twinkle that's hitting the center of my chest. She looks happy, peaceful somehow, without that pained look I was accustomed to, and it makes my heart sink.

I take slow, decisive strides until I come face to face with her, my head tilting down as hers lifts, for the full effect of our staring. That scent of hers wakes up every fiber that missed the hell out of that narcotic aroma of hers.

"Hi." Butterflies fly at the mere sound of her soft voice.

"Hi," I parrot, still unable to grasp the concept of her being here.

"Black, no sugar, still hot." She offers one cup and takes a sip from the other.

"What are you doing here?"

"Came to see you," she deadpans, tilting her head and biting her inner cheek.

"Why?"

"Do I need a reason?"

Yes! No! Maybe!

Not knowing what to say, I go with a more obvious question.

"Where's Declan?"

"He is with his dad."

I swallow the lump that tries to choke the life out of me

and nod, overdoing it.

"It's his week," she states, like it's a passing thought.

Come again!

"We got divorced."

Please, God, make what I'm hearing be true.

I cast my eyes downward, my heart still as I inspect her hand. Then I see it—her empty, very much bare ring finger. Something in me sparks to life, much like the first time we met, and my heart goes into overdrive.

"When?" I mutter, barely hearing myself from the loud pumping happening right there, in the center of my chest.

"Five months ago," she falters.

I should be happy, right? So why am I on the brink of fuming? My hand tightens around my cup, and my chest starts to heave.

"I ordered Ryan..." she stops, correcting herself, "Everyone, not to tell you."

"Why?"

"Because I didn't want..." she cuts herself off, her cheeks turning red. One shake of her head with a deep breath is all it takes for her to get it together. "I needed time to work on myself, to get to know me, find the person I lost, rediscover, and all that before I..." she trails off, nervously biting the corner of her lips. I understand it all completely. In her mind, all she's ever been is a mother and a wife, so naturally, some heavy growing and self-discovery are all but expected. And as much as I want to hear about her journey, I need to know the reason she's here more.

"Before you?" I prod, all eager and hopeful, like a puppy at the pound.

"Let's go for a walk." She ignores my question and refuses to look at me, and that knocks the hope right out of me.

I lock the gate and join her side, though keeping a respectful distance. We cross the street when I utter, "Give me the rundown of the last six months."

I'm too eager to know. How did it go down? How bad did it hurt? And I know it did. It's Nora we're talking about. She's an emotional woman, taking everything to heart, so I am sure it hasn't been easy.

"You want the bullet points or a full audio description?"

"The full please," I politely mock.

She starts softly, mostly telling stories about her and Ryan growing up. Then she talks about her parents, about the lack of affection, attention, and love. She tells me how she finally broke away from them and began to live. Her smile grows big when she talks about college and music. About the songs she composed, the lyrics she wrote. She had a dream of playing in a big orchestra and was a breath away from making it come true.

Enter Rick.

At first, it's a story of acceptance, about finding a home and a new family. She spends more time talking about Tessa, Bianca, and Jack than she does about Rick. I'm not sure whether it's for my benefit or if there's something more to it. Deciding on the latter, I continue listening closely as she describes her life in Canada before she moved here. Her expression changes right about the time she mentions the move. She gives me more insight into the story Ryan has already told me: she was the provider before, only to become dependent on someone else. My pulse rises when she goes on about feeling guilty for it.

The sun is now hiding behind a family of clouds, making the air around us chill. We take a turn into a quieter one-way street with barely any cars passing by.

Her face lights up when Declan's name escapes her mouth. She reveals that she'd forgo the birth alone, not because Rick didn't want to be a part of it (though I doubt that), but because she was used to doing everything on her own. She starts crying when she describes what Declan looked like when they placed him in her arms, how she felt, and how the world made sense at that moment. Then my heart breaks again when she reveals that Rick first held his son ten days after his birth. It keeps on breaking the more she tells me about her marriage, Declan's diagnostic journey, and motherhood.

By the time she finishes, there's nothing left to be broken. That fact alone makes me reflect on how strong she actually is. How much she has carried around for so long, and yet has never complained.

"I don't know what changed, but it was Rick who served me the papers."

That little declaration doesn't hurt as much, only because Rick finally put her first. A part of me is sad that it took him so long; the other, the selfish part, is grateful that he let her go, knowing if he didn't, I wouldn't have a chance.

I'm not sure I have it, anyway.

"I thought it would hurt, but all I felt was relief."

She plays with her fingers around the cup, not looking at me, like she's ashamed to admit it.

"Look at me," I demand, wrapping my hand around her wrist, and we both stop. She does what she's told, bringing those glossy eyes to meet mine. "Never feel guilty for how you feel. Especially not with me, ok?"

She nods. We toss our empty cups in the trash and continue walking.

"What was it like being away from Declan?" I'm digressing, I know, but I think she needs the diversion.

"Weird," she blurts. "The first day, I didn't know what to do with myself. I barely slept that night, thinking over worst-case scenarios. The next day didn't go any better. Then Tessa called and yelled at me, so I went for a walk alone." She lifts her brows at the last part, almost as if in horror. "I ended up at a small bistro and drank coffee in peace, and I loved it." She closes her eyes, smiling, "until guilt took over."

"Don't do that to yourself."

"It's hard not to. I enjoyed time without my kid. I'm a terrible person and an even worse mother."

"Nora," I reach for her hand, and she immediately locks her fingers around it. "You are an amazing mother. Declan is lucky to have you," I speak from the bottom of my heart. It's the first thing I noticed about her, the reason I fell in love with her. She drops her head, letting me know how much she doesn't believe my statement.

"Remember when we met?" I wait for an acknowledgment. She nods, and I continue, "I noticed how easily you shared that he had autism, without a single restraint, like you're proud of it."

"I am. I never hid from it, never played it down. I just…"

"Embraced it," I jump in, causing her lips to curve further.

"Yeah, I guess."

"And when we were up in the crane when Declan said it was a spaceship, you didn't correct him, you just played along..." Her eyebrows wrinkle her entire forehead, making that V, begging me to get to the point.

"You honestly think that solely on those two points, you are not on top of the best mother billboard?"

"There's no such thing," she brushes it off, downplaying herself.

"You need more? I got more... like how you understand his intention before he even makes a step, or how you scan every new place to seek out all the possible hazards, or how you don't eat ice cream so that he can have two." I can't figure out why I'm getting aggravated by this. I'm supposed to convince her how amazing she is, not get angrier by the word count.

"I'm sorry."

"Fuck, Nora, stop apologizing. Just hear me out, listen, and let my words sink in. Believe them, believe me. You are an amazing mother," I say, determined. This time, she doesn't protest, doesn't shake her head. She just stops to stare at me. I follow her lead, planting my feet across from her.

"Repeat after me, I'm an amazing mother," I challenge, knowing damn well she needs this little nudge. It's she who said it was a talent of mine, so I have to use it; it's only fair.

Chapter 45

Nora

"I am an amazing mother," I repeat, and he cracks a smile.

"Again."

"I am an amazing mother," I state, letting it sink in. At this point, it's impossible not to feel the impact of what this man said. Those eyes alone have the power to make me a true believer; the only prophecy that matters. To me, at least.

I spent so many sleepless nights fighting the demons, mostly those who kept telling me I was not a good mother. Those fears, tumbling in all directions, self-reflections, and other bullshit that wouldn't allow any sleep.

I walked a long time without a compass, and it took me longer to realize I was rehashing old wounds when I should have been following my instincts. Those thoughts kept coming back to me over and over again, like they were trying to tell me something. And I finally listened. I wasn't going weak; I just stopped agreeing.

"Don't ever doubt that, if not for your sake, then for Declan's," he insists, his eyes glinting in the daylight.

"Where were we?"

I go on, talking about therapy and how well it's been for me. For Rick.

I recall the last time the two of us had a heart-to-heart.

"Do you think we'll ever be ok?" Rick asks, his voice cracking. I take a deep breath.

"No matter what happens, we once were us. And no matter how many times you've hurt me, crushed my love, I am thankful for every moment," I tell him, grabbing his hand. I press it to my chest when I see tears in his eyes, and for the first time in ten years, I see actual remorse. *"You are and always will be important to me, so yes. I think we'll be more than ok."*

"I am so sorry, Nor. I wanted to give you all the love you never had; instead, you got pain you didn't deserve, and I didn't even realize it."

"It's as much my fault as it is yours. But I forgave you a long time ago. It's me I have trouble forgiving." I'm not there yet, but I'm working on it, knowing I have a long way to go.

"You deserve to be happy, Nor. More than anything, you deserve to be loved."

I sigh, "That's the last thing on my mind right now. Kinda need to learn from my mistakes."

"Love is never a mistake, and not every guy is a stupid ass like me."

I smile, but it's tamed, hiding the ping that hits my chest.

Our eyes lock, and I see it… our entire past unfolding right there in front of me. He brings my hand to his lips and gives it a gentle peck. "I do love you, you know that? Always will."

"I know."

Our love was childish. Crazy. Ready for anything. To fly or fall. And I fell, the crash so painful that I barely got up, thinking there was no moving on.

"The more days passed, the more I kept missing something. Someone. Someone who knows my touch, feels my smile. Sees my soul…"

Our eyes lock, his hitting deep, to the center of my being. He sees me, knows me.

"But I wasn't ready, still had issues to solve with myself. It was when Rick told me what you did, back when Dec was in the hospital, that I couldn't do it anymore."

I still can't wrap my head around it. How selfless Luka was to go to Rick and drag him to the hospital, showing how much he cared by putting my needs first. It was then that I knew what true love was. Is.

Luka clears his throat. "I'm sorry, it wasn't my place," he starts apologetically, and I lift my hand for him to stop.

"No, Luk. What you did…" I hesitate, taking a breath, "God, you have no idea how much that means to me." Dropping my head, I sniffle, "You put me first."

No one, and I mean no one, has ever done that... This taught me a good lesson. And from then on, that is exactly what I've been doing. It took a while getting used to, but I started living by being number 1.

Rick and I got close in a different kind of way, more open. He's in therapy, as am I (with Sunny, naturally), and we're both working on being the best versions of ourselves. When it comes to Dec—he's happy, thriving, and enjoying the extra attention. And that's exactly what I tell Luka, down to Rick encouraging me to apply for a job.

At this point, I am bawling, full-on sobbing. Replaying all this over is spiraling my emotions, and I can't stop them from overflowing.

"So I sent my resume to this Art school, and they called me for an interview."

I dig my employee ID out of my purse and hand it to him. He looks it over, and when his gaze meets mine, his eyes flare. I am now part of the faculty—my title: music teacher. I have a title and a job. I scan his face, mapping out his reaction. The smile he gives me is the one I've been dreaming about my entire life. That happiness filled with pride practically screams out of him.

"I'm so proud of you," he gushes, and I feel his words in every fiber of my being.

"Yeah?" I wheeze, itching to get closer.

"Fuck yeah," he shouts, and I giggle.

"I'm proud of myself, too."

"As you should be."

"I'm a teacher," I rave, my heart ready to burst.

"I see that." His eyes, God, those eyes of his will be my undoing. He looks at me with so much affection that it makes my heart ache.

Without another word, we round the corner, and I start laughing when a familiar, colorful sign comes into view.

Shaking my head, I quip, "You sneaky little…" I eat up the last word that would automatically follow. It's not who he is. Not by a long shot.

And here I was thinking I've been guiding the way this entire walk, but nope. Luka had his own agenda, and it's called ice cream.

Like a true gentleman, he opens the door for me, the little bell above us chiming with its salutations. I enter the small space, flashing Luka a smile, and he follows behind me. A young teenage boy greets us from behind the counter, and we greet him right back.

I scan the selection, humming as I contemplate what to get. I can't even remember the last time I ate an actual scoop of ice cream, so I don't actually know what flavor to get. Luka doesn't rush me, just watches patiently.

"Oh my God," I gasp when my eyes land on something unexpected. Luka leans over, searching my line of sight, and his proximity causes chills. His woodsy scent runs through my respiratory system, replacing the oxygen I no longer need. All I need is him.

"What is it?" he rasps, and I chuckle.

Pointing at the far left end of the fridge, I explain, "That is a Canadian specialty." Then I order two scoops of Tiger Tail and start clapping my hands like I'm a kid having her first ice cream, which is not far from the truth. Luka orders a Mint chocolate chip, and we both snort out a laugh. He doesn't fight me when I insist on paying; he just lets me have it, knowing how important it is to me to maintain my independence. Plus, I get to pay with my own paycheck. How awesome is that?

Chapter 46

Luka

I almost forgot how easy everything is with Nora. How natural.

We circled back to the site, the streetlights and moonlight replacing the sun. I'm sure my feet are done for, but I don't feel a thing. All I feel is her. The smile, so lively, full… Perfect.

I hear a familiar ringtone, but it's muffled, and that's when it hits me—I left my phone in the container. I smack my forehead. Hard.

Idiot.

"Everything ok?" Nora asks, rocking back and forth on her heels, brows furrowed.

"I left my phone inside, and my family is probably blowing it up," I reckon, working the lock. Nora follows me as I rush inside just as the ringing stops. I grab my phone in time to see the latest text come in.

Mak: *Everyone is freaking out. Where are you?*

Shit.

I really hope they didn't tattle on me to Mateo. I don't have any missed calls from him or Sabrina, so I think I'm in the clear. He and Tyler lost their parents in a car crash, and it left them with hidden wounds, more so on Mateo. He'd start to panic if any one of us was late without notice. I get it. And I feel guilty about worrying any member of my family.

Me: *Sorry, left the phone in my office. Nora's here*

His reply is immediate.

Mak: *Enough said. I'll hold the fort*

Me: *I appreciate you*

I pocket my phone and turn, leaning my ass on the edge. Nora hasn't moved from the door, arms behind her back, ankles crossed, keeping the distance. I want to close it.

"I'm sorry," I mutter, not sure what to do next. Should I offer her a ride home or suggest we order dinner?

"Never apologize for loving your family."

I cock a brow at her odd response, but it eases when I realize what she means by it. It's endearing how she sees it now, understands what acts of service stand for.

The pendant around her neck gets trapped between her fingers; her subtle way of telling me she's nervous. But that's not what's causing my heart to somersault. She's looking at me the way she does in my dreams, like I am the only thing she sees.

Could it be?

There's only one way to find out… here goes nothing…

"Nora?"

"Hm?"

"Why did you come here?" I don't stutter; my voice is firm,

with no hitch in it whatsoever. She gulps, her hand trembling around the silver daisy.

"Ryan said you're not seeing anyone?" It comes out as a question, and I can't help but smile. Every part of me is jumping in excitement, my hopes already up, even though they probably shouldn't be.

"I wasn't sure if you…" Her shoulders sag, her expression panicked. Nerves take over me as well, sweat breaking out.

I want to lay it all out in the open.

"No, Nora, I'm not seeing anyone. Not when there's one woman who occupies my every thought, and she's not even real."

I haven't even bothered seeking out someone else's company, knowing damn well no one could fill the hole Nora left. Maybe it was foolish of me to think that one day my wishes might come true, but it's been the only way I could cope. Not a second passed by in the past six months that her beautiful eyes or Declan's smile didn't flash through my mind. She stole my sight so I couldn't look at another woman, robbed me of my hearing so I wouldn't hear another's whisper. She took my heart, but what she doesn't know is that it went willingly, knowing its one true owner.

Her eyes widen, mouth agape as she releases a soft gasp.

"Well, in that case…" she hesitates for a beat, then lifts her chin; those hazels piercing through me, a new set of confidence in them, one I've never seen before. "I came to claim you."

Damn, that sounds magnificent! Almost unreal. But she is here, beautiful as ever, if not more. Definitely more, because her smile is reaching her eyes, no sign of the pain behind the sparkle.

"What are you waiting for, then? Claim me!"

She bites her lower lip, sending some signals down south, but doesn't make a move. She averts her gaze to the floor, and panic strikes. Did she change her mind? Did I read this all wrong?

"Nora?"

She lifts her lashes, those golden halos around her pupils lighting up.

"Yeah?"

My galloping heart goes frantic, and I swallow. "Claim. Me!"

She snaps out of the intensity of my gaze and looks around, her brow furrowing. She strides to me, pulls out a chair from under the desk, and steps on it. It's cute that she thinks a bit of height advantage is needed to make her point. I would easily go down on my knees if I'd known her intention.

I close the gap between us, lifting my head just as she drops hers, and then she makes all my wishes come true. Our lips collide, fireworks fly in my mind, my body, my soul.

What is happening?

The best damned kiss of your life, that's what.

Finally!

It's as soft as it is hard, filled with need and desperation. Nothing ever felt so right, so good, and I never want it to stop. It's a life-altering kiss, the one for the books, reach for the stars, knock it out of the park kind of energy that we exchange. I feel it all, the pain, the agony, the tears shed… It all vanishes, and pure bliss takes over. Something so fragile, yet powerful, is happening right in front of me, a healing process… All the unknown, all the uncertainty now irrelevant. Everything ceases to exist; only the two of us remain in this time loop that I want to keep on repeat.

My soul fell in love and waited, because it knew where it belonged… Right here, wrapped around hers…

Chapter 47

Nora

This is really happening…

I am in a lip lock with a man stealing my breath away.

Songs were written about this feeling; books even tried, but in any case, they all failed… There's no way to describe this in a way that gives it the justice it deserves. I feel so alive, wrapped in the safety of his strong arms, with his lips telling me how much he wants me, with mine reciprocating it right back.

Suddenly, I am being picked up, my feet dangling in the air before they meet the floor.

"What are you doing?" I pipe over his mouth.

He pulls away, framing my face with his warm palms. Our eyes lock, and I lose all of my functions.

"Doing some claiming of my own."

Oh God.

I can't think straight, see straight… captivated by this man, the way his eyes beam at me, with such intensity that it is almost palpable.

His container, or better yet, office, is small, and it smells like him. It's neat, everything in place, no clutter, just order. My eyes land on his desk, and I bite my lower lip.

"Want me to do the move?"

God, he reads me so well.

I turn into a bobble-head.

Chuckling, he turns to his desk, and in one quick swoop, it's wiped clean. I press my thighs together to ease the throbbing. It's no help.

He turns to face me, his eyes playful, that stupid smirk of his turning all sexy. This is escalating quickly, and I can't say I saw it coming. Before I can grasp this concept, I am being lifted, like I weigh nothing, and my ass collides with the wooden surface. His hands are everywhere, covering every inch of my body with gentle strokes as he moves from my ankles, up my thighs, over to my waist, where one settles with a firm grip.

He brings his mouth to mine while his other hand holds the entire back of my neck, twisting me to the side for an inviting angle. I forget how to breathe altogether, but I open, allowing our tongues to meet for a dance-off.

He pulls away, and our eyes lock. It's a hard thing to describe, the lustful and hungry look that screams from his eyes. The color of amber, but I do prefer whiskey since they are so addictive and have the power to make me tongue-tied, crazy, and reckless, much like the real deal would. Shimmering and bright, like the blend of the finest gold. This light catches them perfectly, reflecting the shade of red mixed with yellow, much like when a single drop of hard liquor glides down a tumbler, all smooth, slow, and captivating.

I always notice how bold the features on his face are, the way his outline forms a unique shape, something between a square and an oval, or how tight his jawline is. As I look at him, it's as if certain parts demand my attention, making everything else fade. It's so intense that my heart rate, not to mention my breathing, would be considered life-threatening. My hands get sweaty, my heart pounding so hard I fear it will jump out from under my dress.

Though his tough exterior might lead people to think he's all hard, his eyes stand out the most, revealing everything there is to know about this man. Solid, tenacious, vigorous, soft, resilient, strong, warm and fuzzy, protective, honest, sexy as hell, and so lovable that it hurts... There are a lot more adjectives I can use, but it would take forever; plus, I presume you can catch my drift.

Where was I?

Oh, right—the eyes... Well, we can forget about the eyes since I am now all into the lips. He firmly presses them to mine. His kiss is nothing short of flawless, dominant, hard, but also soft, starved, and generous... His tongue swirls around mine, like the most harmonized, seductive dance, spot-on breathtaking.

My hands start to move on their own, sneaking up his muscular arms. I feel the shiver, the slight vibration his body makes in response to my touch. I did that, my fingers did that, and it kicks up my confidence enough for me to spread my legs and pull him closer, right there in between.

He's hard. Rock hard.

That gets me to Earth, like an ice bucket.

"What's wrong?"

'It's too fast' is my first thought. People go on for years before being remotely ready to get back in the saddle or whatever you want to call it. So what does that say about me?

"I… I…" I stutter, "I didn't think this through. I came here without any expectations…"

Hopes, sure. But expectations, none. All I know is that I haven't stopped thinking about this man in front of me, nor can I ignore the ache in my heart any longer.

His face softens, and he whispers, "We don't have to do anything." Even his tone is patient, and it only adds to the pool forming between my thighs.

"I want to. God, do I want to… It's just…" I hesitate, too mortified, not to mention scared… It's been so long, and what if… No. I'm not gonna ruin this with overthinking.

"I'm not prepared," I splutter, to which his brow jolts upward.

"What?" he quips, pulling back just a little so he can get a better look at me.

Embarrassment takes over, and I spill, "I didn't… landscape?" My whole face cringes just as my cheeks flush; I can feel the warmth, the stupid tattletale.

The smug son of a biscuit laughs.

"Don't laugh at me." I push at his chest. He doesn't even flinch. I mean, why would he? He's all muscle wall, hard pecs, I'm not even ashamed to admit, have invaded my dreams on the regular.

"I can't help it... Landscape?"

"What do you want me to say? I didn't get a chance to groom it?"

That sends him overboard, into a full-on belly laugh, his head thrown back, and his teeth on full display. It makes my heart jump up before it sinks into humiliation.

"Nora, look at me." My name has never sounded so good,

but I can't look at him. I'd rather dig a hole and hide in it.

He gently pinches the tip of my chin between his thumb and index finger, slowly lifting my head. My eyes follow, meeting his, and fudge, what a sight. Did I mention Luka is gorgeous?

"Don't deny me," he pleads. I can hear it in his voice, the need, the heat. "I want you, every part of you, groomed or not." His voice is all rugged and husky, making it hard to think about anything other than ripping all these textile barriers separating us.

"We don't have to do anything. I am perfectly happy kissing you and owning that beautiful mouth of yours."

A mixture of a gasp and a moan escapes me, making his eyes widen.

I want to recoil, but instead I straighten up and clear my throat.

"I come with a lot of baggage," I start under my breath.

"I can share the load," he assures without hesitation. And I have to hand it to him; he doesn't look the least bit worried or panicked.

"I'm a mess, but I am working on it. I also come with a son and an ex-husband, with whom I share custody. Meaning Rick will be a part of our lives, and I know it's all complicated and shit, so I am giving you an out, no judgment, no resentment. Right here and now, this is your chance to tap out."

He backs away half a step, locking eyes with mine, going so deep, landing in my soul. He places his palm over my heart, gushing, "Do I get this?"

"You have to share it with a five-year-old daredevil," I lift my shoulder.

"Do I get the other half fully?"

"Yes," I breathe it out.

"Mine?"

"Yours," I gulp, the warmth of his palm reaching a place that has been deprived for far too long.

"Then that's all I need to know," he states, like it's that simple.

"Just like that? I don't want you to feel stuck."

"Nora, I tossed the key a long time ago. There is nowhere else I want to be than with you. Now I have a confession of my own to make," he husks, his hands disappearing out of sight.

"I'm starving."

"Oh," I mumble, unable to hide my disappointment. "There's a nice pizza place around..." but I don't finish, because he drops to his knees.

Oh.

Oh.

His calloused fingers drag across my dress, the fabric sending a tingling sensation as they graze my bare skin. He leaves the dress wrapped around my hips, leaving my legs exposed, his hands covering the thickness of my thighs. With a soft tug, my legs spread wider before he disappears between them.

He pulls my underwear to the side, and with what I can only imagine as his tongue, he introduces my south to a whole new sensation. My tongue-virgin clit goes straight to heaven. The movements, so meticulous, slick, hot, and cold at the same time, are confusing the hell out of my entire body.

One flick sends impulses to my toes, making them curl, and when his finger slips inside, every part of my whole being comes to life. Another finger joins, and they turn at the right time throughout every thrust, making my breath frantic, desperate for more.

"You taste so good!" he mumbles, and I gasp.

"Really?" escapes me, making him pull away. My clit throbs at the sudden departure, and in the blink of an eye, his lock with mine. With my chest heaving and my heart seconds from bursting at his gaze, one I can only presume to be the reading kind, he husks, "Your fingers or mine?"

Words fail me; my mind goes blank, a full-on tabula rasa. He takes my hand in his, separating two fingers, and slides them inside me with a growl of his own. His eyes never leave mine as he brings them to my mouth, and I take them, my tongue circling the tips, looking straight at his lips before they press onto mine. I shove my tongue and dance around his, hungry as ever.

"You like that? Tasting yourself on me?"

I hum into him, the concept of it so possessive and greedy.

"Tell me, what does it taste like?" His forehead rests on mine, and I can feel the heaviness of his breath.

"Like mine," I rasp, and he growls, the sound making my pussy clench.

"You damn right I am," he agrees.

I'm having trouble grasping this side of him, almost animalistic. Can't say I hate it, though.

"Say it," he demands, hoarsely and so beautiful doing it.

"I'm yours."

"Fucking finally."

Chapter 48

Luka

Mine.

No word has ever sounded so good. The need for her to repeat it over and over is turning me into a caveman. I want her to scream out my name, for nothing else to exist except the two of us.

"Fuck Nora, I was yours since the second I laid eyes on you," I profess, wanting it to sink in.

"I'm sorry it took so long." She lodges her lips on mine, and I take them.

"We have forever to make up for it."

Forever, now that has a nice ring to it…

I slide my hand in her underwear where my fingers find the warmth inside her, and my thumb takes over the sensitive place my tongue had parted. I want to watch her fall for me. This woman drives me insane, yet keeps me grounded. That fire in her eyes is my undoing, the starvation that only I can fulfill. Slowly, I sink back to my knees and go all in. My cock is desperate for attention, but he has to take a back seat; this is about her. My eyes widen at the sight of her pussy, the way it glistens for me. My fingers move in and out, twisting and turning as my tongue flicks over her pulsating clit. I can feel the rise, the way she clenches around me, so I curl them up, making her body go rigid. Her nails, though short, dig into my shoulders, a clear sign of her surrender.

"Luk, you need to stop. I can't… It's too much." I lift my gaze, finding her head shaking.

"Just ride it, baby, I've got you."

"Fudge," she mumbles, and with one hard dig, she's done for, combusting right there with my fingers and tongue working in sync. I don't stop, riding it out with her all the way.

"What. The. Fuck?" She breathes between each word. "It. Just. Keeps. On. Going." She moans through heavy breaths, and when it's over, she goes limp. I suck in her slickness, savoring it before I straighten up, finding her dazed. I must admit, it looks so fucking good on her.

I take her mouth again, and her hands fly around my neck. She's so responsive to me, almost as if she's as desperate as I am for this connection.

"Want to keep this going at my place?"

I swallow; my head drops as I pull away.

"I live two blocks from here," she quickly adds, obviously understanding my hesitation.

The pressure in my chest subsides. "What?"

"Neither Rick nor I wanted to stay in that house. We both found something near Dec's kindergarten, thinking it'd be easier on him to stay close."

That gets me to perk up.

"He's in kindergarten?" Pride mixed with excitement surges through me.

Nora nods, beaming at my reaction. "Yeah, three months in. He loves it, and so far it's going great."

She knocks the top of her head three times, and I chuckle before doing the same. Superstition be damned.

She waits while I close up, and we start walking. I don't know why I'm so nervous. I'm a grown man, for fuck's sake. Her hand finds mine, the contact sending electricity through my entire nervous system. Our fingers intertwine as she leads the way.

I set a quick text to Mak, letting him know I'll be late. He responds with a wink emoji.

Five minutes later, we arrive at a small apartment complex that gives off a suburban feel. She opens the large gate, and I stay behind her as we walk through a courtyard leading to her front door. She unlocks it, and we step inside.

I take pride in being a patient man, but that person flew out the window the moment Nora showed up at my site.

"C'mere," I whisper. The door hasn't even fully closed behind us, and my lips are already pressed to hers. The keys fall to the floor with a clunk, and she jumps into my arms. I hold her tight; she does the same, hands flying to grab my hair while her ankles lock around my waist.

"First room on the left," she murmurs into my mouth, and I carry her to the bedroom. As much as I want to take in my surroundings, see her place, I am too focused on her. I gently lower her onto the bed and admire the view. Biting my lip, I join her and bury my face in the crook of her neck, making sure to hover so I don't squish her.

"Please tell me you have a condom," I exasperate.

"I have an IUD..." she hesitates, "I haven't... we haven't..."

I use my elbows for support, my palms framing her face. Her freckles are dancing in front of me, and slowly her cheeks turn pink. My need to wipe off that embarrassment of hers is so strong that I press my mouth to hers with so much force I think I might break her. Her hands find the back of my neck, and I wrap my own in her hair, tangling my fingers in the locks.

"I might not be good." It comes out so nonchalantly that I have to chuckle.

"Stop laughing at me."

"Stop saying stupid shit."

"It's not stupid."

"You felt that kiss? I'm not alone in this, right?"

She stays silent.

"Nothing about us can be short of perfect."

That sentence makes her whimper, and fire ignites in her eyes.

I plant my ass on my heels, and she sits up, tugging her jacket, shoulders swaying as she slowly pulls it off. Next, she brushes the straps of her dress, letting them fall down her shoulders. I swallow, unable to look away as she slides the dress down to her waist, giving me a front row seat to a simple white bra molding around her breasts. My clothes are discarded in mere seconds, until I'm in nothing but my boxer briefs.

Her soft palms cover my chest with sloppy movements, stopping at the waistband. One finger slips inside, just at the hem, and grazes over the whole length of my stomach. Her lips are on me, working over every inch of my chest. There's no rush in her torturous kisses, like she wants to retain each contact. Her tongue comes out next, tracing the center line from my Adam's apple to my belly button, her hands retracing the steps, nails scraping my skin.

She tugs my boxers, and with one quick swoop, my cock jerks up. Her eyes widen as she takes it in before she gulps, "We should call that thing *The Hulk*."

This is the worst time to be laughing, but I can't help it; she has that effect on me, hopefully always will.

She falls back on the bed and lifts her hips, and I take it from there, dragging the fabric down the rest of the way. I make sure to trace her sides with my fingertips, leaving goosebumps in my wake.

Our eyes meet, and within a beat, our tongues are working around each other.

"I'm clean, we do regular checkups every six months," I speak with my mouth on hers, but it makes her pull away, her face so hopeful. If she thinks I could even think about any other, let alone be with someone else, she has another thing coming.

"Only you, Nora." That's all I say, and it's enough.

She spreads her legs for me, and I hum when I find her soaked. I rip her underwear and take my hard-on to cover it with her glow. My tip presses into her opening, waiting. One look is all I need before I slowly slide inside to the only place I'll ever belong. She stretches around me with shaky breaths, and I need a minute to get myself in check. It feels too good, too much. Never have I felt such a deep connection with anyone, bare, and somehow it only intensifies the feeling of her, of us. My hand takes her breast, her nipple spiking out, begging for attention. I give the other my tongue, making her gasp out my name. One slow pull out, deep breath in, and I plunge, ramming her wall. The pace shifts from fast and hard to slow and soft, repeating this pattern in circles. Her hands grab onto every surface of my body, from my biceps to my ass.

She curses at the lack of hair on my head, yelling at me, like it's my fault she has nothing to pull on.

"Say it."

No thinking, no analyzing my question; she knows what I need right there as our bodies become one.

"I'm yours," she screams, making the effect of the words echo deep.

"Wholly?"

"Everything I have is yours." Her hazel eyes meet mine, the look like a stamp, the gavel marking the case closed.

"Fuck!"

Chapter 49

Nora

You know... I've read about it, over and over... I listened to audiobooks that sold out on smut and spice. Honestly, I thought it was made up, being fiction and all. Boy, was I wrong.

The moment he hit that wall, I was sent into orbit, maybe even beyond, somewhere unknown. I never knew sex could feel so good, so possessive and addictive. We're not even done, and all I wanted is more of it. When I came on his mouth, it was like nothing I have ever experienced, something so dirty about it, but also so cosmic. And then, when I felt the thickness of his cock fill me up, a whole new world opened up.

He's looking at me like I am his everything, feeling so wanted; it's what pushes me over the edge. His eyes don't leave mine as I ride the wave, and I feel the tears trying to emerge. I let them fall, let him see me. I'm safe; he's taking away all my insecurities. My body is not what it used to be, and yet, I don't feel a shred of shame, only appreciation. It's pure worship, the way he devours my core... Taking the life out of me only to push it back in.

"Give me one more!"

"Fuck Luk, I can't."

"Yes, you can! I've got you."

"I…"

"I'm right there with you."

That does it; those words with that husky voice, desperate for me, send me overboard. Every muscle in my body goes stiff with full-on body spasm as I scream his name.

Bear with me here; since I only know how to express myself through music, this is the best way to describe it. He plays me like an instrument. The way he fiddles with me, pulling each of my strings, all the while making my G note sing with each movement, pumping in and out like staccato, making smooth motions that tie it all together into legato. And when he finishes, it's with a grunting vibrato.

My God… I am gone.

His strong body collapses on top of mine, his face falling next to mine, as we both try and fail to catch our breath…

I've obviously had sex before; Declan is proof of that. It's just that Rick was a selfish lover. He went in and out. No preparation beforehand, no cuddling after. I orgasmed a handful of times, in the bathtub, using my fingers, only to feel guilt after, like I cheated, which is stupid, I know… It's how my brain works.

Not now, though. Now my brain is in a state of bliss, as is my entire body. Luka made love to me, took care of me, made sure I'm satisfied first… Nothing has ever been like this. I want to tell him as much, but my lungs won't let me. He jumps in, reading me, like always.

"I know, baby, I know."

And it's enough. More so.

"I'm definitely calling it *'The Hulk'* because that thing sure can smash!"

A full body shake happens while he lies on top of me, both of us laughing, wrapped around each other.

He's still half hard when he pulls out. I, on the other hand, can't move, spread across the bed, limp. The soft caress of something warm has me lifting my head. Luka, on his knees, taking care of the mess our action created between my legs, is a sight. I prop up on my elbows, enjoying his focused gaze as he soaks it all up with soft dabs. With each swipe, he makes my heart melt. This man, with his rugged exterior, is the most caring, attentive, and gentlest of souls, and he's all mine.

"You know what's funny?" I singsong when he finishes wiping me clean.

"What?"

"We did some heavy claiming right there, and I don't even have your phone number."

It's almost laughable. We jumped right into it, and I should be panicking, but I'm quite the opposite. There's not a shred of guilt; it's overpowered by this strong sense of elation. I just might be on cloud nine, and it feels right.

"That is not funny; that is just terrible judgment on your part."

"My part?" I gawk, pressing a hand to my chest, offended.

"Yes, considering I do have yours."

"No, you don't. I never gave it to you."

"You didn't—" he winks "—Ryan did."

"Traitor," I bark, taking a mental note to kick Ryan right in the balls. He's got enough kids, so I don't think Tessa will mind.

"Technically, I took his phone and copied your contact information."

"Sneaky," I drawl, wiggling my brows.

"I have my moments."

"You never used it?"

"I wanted to, but…"

He doesn't need to finish. I know. He respected me too much and wanted me to reach out. And I admire him for it. It's then that I notice that I am still very much naked, without a shred of discomfort.

What is this man doing to me?

My life has sure done a 180, and while I did work hard on rediscovering myself, it took one look from this man to bring me back to life.

He collapses on the bed next to me, and I take advantage of it, lying on top of him. Channeling some newfound confidence, I lick his bottom lip.

"If you keep on doing that, I will never see what your apartment looks like," he says in this deep, husky voice that gives away a sexy vibe, almost making me explode all over again.

I pinch my thumb and my pointer, dragging it over the length of my mouth, zip-locking it, all the while my eyes dare him. I'm not a person who does these kinds of things, this teasing, alluring, or whatever movements my eyes are making. But Luka brings out this hungry side of me, and all I want to do is test his limits while testing my own. I don't shy away, bringing out the seduction, not afraid of it one bit. And when he whimpers, I'm already halfway there.

He's roaming through every square foot, taking in every detail. I am sure, now more than ever, that he has done the same thing back at the house, only when I wasn't there to witness it. It would explain many details he knows about me that I haven't shared.

He stops in front of the bookshelf Ryan built specially for me; it's shaped like a heart, and it's the best part of the home I made for myself and Declan.

"How did you know that daisies were my favorite flowers?"

I come behind him, and he barely turns, scanning me over his shoulder from the corner of his eye. I can't see his mouth, but I know he is smirking.

"Your necklace," he confesses.

I look down at the pendant between my fingertips and smile. Now I feel stupid, because... Duh. Closing in, I press my cheek against his back and wrap my arms around him. They're not long enough to fully lock around him, but the embrace is no less powerful.

"And the tattoo?"

That one bugged me for the last half a year. I regret not asking him about it that night.

"Ryan told me you got emancipated when you were 16. I figured you marked it somehow." He says it so matter-of-factly, blowing me away. He's also right. It's the first thing I did after I exited the courthouse.

I unwrap my arms, and he turns to face me, those eyes filled with wonder and affection, making my heart skip a beat. I walk backward to my couch, and he follows me. When I sit down, I lift my right foot, giving him the perfect view of my past. It's a small drawing of a family tree burning with a phoenix rising from the flames.

"Why there?"

"To remind myself not to get stomped on," I chuckle at that one, knowing the irony behind it fully.

"You should've looked at it more often."

Don't I know it.

I smile at him, going for a heavy once-over.

His left brow lifts, and I bite the corner of my lip. Standing up, I extend my hand. He takes it, no hesitation, no question, just holds it tight as I guide him to the bathroom, my newly discovered filthy mind screaming with excitement.

Chapter 50

Luka

The warm water adds to the steam already forming between us. Nora's naked body on full display is like a dream, but better, because it's the best kind of reality.

At first, she was hiding from me, but it didn't take her long to get comfortable, something I take as a good sign. Her body is a work of art, and I'm enjoying myself far too much admiring it. The way her freckles dance over her skin, her shoulders, between her perky breasts... the stretch marks over her stomach tell a story, down to those thick thighs I can't seem to get enough of... the way they mash in my tight hold. Every part of her is perfection.

With the yellow loofah filling my hand, I slowly circle it over every inch of her body, front to back. Even with the water sedating her skin, she still shivers with every touch, and I revel in it. I've never had this... This comfort... The degree of freedom one feels in someone's presence. It calms my nervous system as much as it electrocutes it.

The shower barely holds the two of us, but we move around each other with ease. When I finish covering her with foam, she takes the loofah and starts her torture over my hard skin. Except, under her mercy, my skin is anything but. She's turning me into the softest version, both mentally and physically. I identify even the gentlest of touches, down to her breath on my skin. With her, I feel immortal and so alive, and I never want to let go of this feeling.

All rinsed off, we take turns drying each other before we take over the bed, fully naked.

"Luk, I'm hungry," she wails when I attack her neck.

"So am I," I whisper right under her ear, and goosebumps spike out all over her.

"I need substance, energy, and water mixed with a heavy dose of caffeine," she whimpers, her back arching while I lick the length of her neck and collarbone. I know I should feed her, but I can't control myself. Not after I've tasted her, felt her around me… I want to consume her whole.

She stays quiet when my tongue descends to her center, only moans escaping her. Her body is more than ready for me when I slide my hand over her wet opening.

Just one orgasm, and I will feed her—I tell myself.

Her skin is still overstimulated from the shower, so I have no doubt it won't take long. My fingers dig into the warmth, pumping in and out, twisting with each move. She breathes out my name with each flick of my tongue over her clit, and when I pull it between my teeth, she is done for. Every muscle in her thighs stiffens, and she screams through a full-body shiver. The vibration spreads across her stomach with her climax.

"Fuck Luk, the things you do to me," she gasps out, her eyes cutting through mine.

I slide my tongue over the space between her legs one last time to savor the taste. My eyes lift, blessed with a view of a delighted Nora. I decide it's my favorite version of her.

"What do you want to eat?" I ask, then plant a soft kiss on

her forehead.

"Whatever you want, I can whip up something quick," she tries to pull herself up, her breath still shaky from the aftershock.

I shake my head, and our noses graze at the movement.

"You will stay here, rest, while I make us something. Just tell me what you want," I demand, though my tone is far from it.

"You don't have to do that."

"I want to; there's a difference. Now this is the last time I'll ask…" I growl at this point, "What do you want?"

"I can go for French toast."

That makes my smile widen. There's nothing I want more than for her to find her voice, to state her claim. With that, I give her a hard kiss and beeline to the kitchen.

I find everything I need easily, roaming through her kitchen as if it were mine.

I love what she's done with the place. It's colorful, just like her personality, with no coordination in sight. Every pillow on her small beige couch is a different color and pattern, and they cover the whole damn thing. A small white coffee table centers the room, its top covered with candles of various shapes and sizes, set atop a circular jute table mat. The walls are filled with pictures of Declan and a few from Elle's baptism. There's a big one with all of us on it. Something about me being there on her wall gives me comfort, even though I share the frame with Rick.

Ten minutes later, a tray in hand, I freeze at the door. My insides flutter at the sight of her peacefully snoozing. A chunk of her hair hides her face, so I place the tray on the nightstand and take a seat next to her, then gently pluck it away. Her mouth curves into a broad smile, melting my heart.

"I smell bacon," she wheezes, sniffing the air audibly. I chuckle and graze my fingers over the constellations covering her flushed cheeks. She gasps, her exhalation one of pure bliss, and I lean in for a kiss. She takes it, converting it from a peck to a full-blown make-out session. Her arms lock around my neck so fast I lose balance, my elbows flying to the bed on instinct to save her from getting smushed. I shake my head, chuckling in her mouth, and she hisses when I try to pull away. The fact that I am physically stronger plays no role in this scenario, since this woman has me. Owns me. In every sense. Weak can't even cover what I am around her.

"I thought you said you were hungry." I manage to loosen her grip and pull away enough to meet her frown.

"I think I need you more than food."

"Do you now?"

She hums, her head bobbing.

"Well, I need you healthy and well-nourished first," I retort, sitting up and looking down at her.

She whines, pouting her lips, looking like she's one wrong move away from a tantrum. Though cute while doing it, the sulk has to go, so I grab one piece of bacon and tauntingly wave it through the air around her nose. I airplane it to her mouth, and just when she opens, I detour it to mine, folding it in one quick bite. The show continues with my loud moaning and humming, and I deliberately leave some grease on my lip before I rid it with my tongue.

She gives me one hell of a death stare, then gulps the entire plate in record time, hoses it down with a glass of water before she, without warning, jumps on me—literally. It's like a scene from Planet of the Apes.

"I hate you," she growls, pressing her glossy mouth to mine. I bite her lower lip, snarling right back at her with, "Wanna try that again?"

"I said what I said." She tilts her chin up in pure provocation, her eyes flaring. That does it. I'm taking out the big guns. And by big guns, I mean my fingers dancing under her armpit, on the side of her waist, and wherever else I find her ticklish zone. She collapses on the bed, now locked between my knees, each one placed around her hips. Her body tries its best to dodge, escape, and endure my torture, but it's pointless. The best song echoes through the room in the form of her laugh.

"Ok, ok…" she gulps. "You win," she admits defeat, and I raise my fists in the air in victory.

"What did I win?" I look down at her; she's still panting.

"What do you want?"

"You."

"You already have me," she bubbles. Add to that the sparkle in her eyes, and it's everything.

Chapter 51

Nora

"Sooo," I drag it out. "He cooks, he reads, and knows how to use his tools—" I wink "—pun intended."

I am plastered on his chest, my chin digging into the back of my hand, palms overlapping, covering the lower end of his sternum, arms spreading over his ribs. His legs are wrapped around my lower body, our eyes locked, giving me the full view of my addiction.

"Is there anything he can't do?"

He's drawing circles from the top of my shoulder down to my elbow and back, perfectly matching both sides with the speed, pattern, and intensity. Every hair on my body dances, letting the room know my skin is in heaven. And so am I.

Luka sucks in a breath through his teeth. "I'm not a morning person."

I give him a pointed look, and he gawks at me, grinning. "I need a full cup of coffee before I can function. Just because I'm awake doesn't mean I'm ready to do shit, you know?" he quips. I like this version of him, unfiltered, serene, and maybe it's selfish of me to think that I have something to do with bringing it out.

His hand slowly glides to my upper back, making a whole mosaic between my shoulder blades. It's then that my eyes decide to let out some uninvited tears. Luka freezes at the sight, propping himself on his elbows. I shake my head, smiling as he stares at me, slanting his head like a confused dog.

How do I tell him that he just made my dreams come true with a simple touch? On a scale from meh to weird, how eerie would it be to admit that this simple act of affection is it for me?

Before I say something I probably shouldn't, I detour. "I'm happy," I blurt out, my heart pumping fast. My palms are sweating, and I think I'm going to vomit. I cuss on the inside, because what the hell is wrong with me? I almost told him I love him. It's too fast, I know; that's why I deviated. The fact of the matter is that I know what it feels like now. I'm older, wiser, rediscovered. I can't deny that for the last six months I had nothing but Luka on my mind. Longer, if I'm being totally honest. It's the way my entire being comes to life at the mere thought of him, the way my heart beats to the rhythm of his name... but mainly, it's the way I am around him. Not only alive, but truly myself.

"You better be, I'm not planning on going back. Fact."

"Oh?" I feign confusion, but he hits me with his dimpled smirk. I have the privilege of seeing his dimples more often, and at this point, I might start complaining because, frankly, those things should be illegal.

He maneuvers me with ease, dragging me over his body until my lips meet his. His erection presses into me, or rather, I push into it since I'm the one on top. His hand finds the back of my neck, the thumb slowly tracing the line of my cheekbone. The intensity in his stare is almost palpable. He sees me. Knows me. It stops every organ in my body from functioning.

"I'm happy, too," he proclaims, his voice so melodic I can see the notes forming on a scale.

"You are?"

"You doubted?"

"Maybe," I mumble.

"Don't ever do that again."

I shrug, and he sits up. Straddling him, my legs go around his waist, locking him in. I'm transfixed by those whiskey eyes piercing into mine.

"Baby," he drags, revealing a taunting smirk that has no right to melt me into a puddle, and yet, I'm mush. "I thought my tongue, fingers, and my dick's actions were self-explanatory, but maybe it wasn't clear enough," he drawls. I open my mouth to protest, but he cuts through gritted teeth, "Now, I want you to ride me, take me, and show me how much you want me!"

I swallow, unable to breathe. My body decides to accept the challenge before my brain even gets the chance to contemplate it. My hips start moving, the length of his cock perfectly placed under my center. I ride him like a cowgirl, feeling his foreskin following every move. He groans, putting his hands on the sides of my hips, and the sound only makes me race harder. His erection is covered with my arousal, practically drowning in it. It's too much, yet not enough. The friction, the tension itself, is making me crazy at this point. So crazy, I don't even recognize myself. His grip tightens, like he can sense the tension building… and my, is it building. I feel it all, every single particle feels it. This is a new kind of high.

Perhaps it's because I'm the one on top for once, or maybe it's because I am taking what I want. It all comes down to—it's simply the man. This perfect specimen, with his massive, strong arms framing a torso eight-pack hard, it might as well be a brick wall. His deep V, which has no business being there, points at the massive package he has been gifted. This man, who can easily ruin me, all the while making me believe he would never dream of it. If there's a way to materialize the word 'perfect,' it would be Luka Hart.

"Fuck, Nora," he growls, that husky voice finishing off my crescendo. When I calm down from this new peak, I glance down to inspect the damage my juices caused, only to find his in the mix. My cheeks blush instantly, the warmth spreading over the apples, and the bastard grins. Then he raises one eyebrow, almost as if challenging me, but to what?

"Own it," is all he says before he scoots me up and carries me to the bathroom. This little condo has one flaw and one flaw only—no bathtub. Plus, the shower is on a smaller scale. Still, the two of us, despite his massive body frame, fit inside. We shower under a warm spread, hugging and kissing the entire time, a bit more PG-13, minus the naked part. All dried up, my body finds his cradle, and he carries me to the bed, tucks me in, and spoons the hell out of me. His nose digs into my neck, and his breathing tickles all the surrounding area.

"Wanna go with me somewhere over the weekend?" he speaks in the crook of my neck, and I hum. At this point, I have no energy to speak; dreams are calling me, but his voice is impossible to ignore.

"I plan to be glued to you this entire week," I sing-song,

and it makes him chuckle. Without another word, he scoots me closer to him, my back to his chest, his hands locking around me. With two more inhales, I'm gone, knowing my dreams are now my reality.

You have my word

I'm holding all the strings
With both my hands tied
Cuz for what's right you have to fight
For a love so grand, even in the night

My heart is on my sleeve, I'm holding it out
Here, just take it, guard it tight
The look in your eyes means it's worth it
Cuz it runs so deep, and you deserve it

No matter the weather, even through a storm
I won't let a single raindrop fall
You have my word, I'll keep us safe,
away from all the clouds that may come our way

When all the stars align,
When the moon lights up the sky
We'll get lost in a world
Made just for us

We'll dance under the moonlight
To the beat of our hearts
A melody so sweet,
Fighting against all odds

No matter the weather, even through a storm
I won't let a single raindrop fall
You have my word, I'll keep us safe,
away from all the clouds that may come our way

Chapter 52

Nora

'Slow motion' by Jonas Brothers blasts from the speakers of Luka's truck. The man wouldn't let me sit by the window, no. He made me sit in the middle so that I would be closer to him. It was too cute, impossible for me to deny him. His hand rests on my knee, my head on his shoulder, making me feel protected. He doesn't complain about my singing, we don't fight, and he can't keep his hands off me.

We've been glued to each other this entire week, and even went on dates, like we're teenagers. On Tuesday, he took me out to dinner, and on Friday, we went to see a movie, though I don't recall what it was about. Our nights are spent under the blankets... we talk, make love, do it a bit dirty, cuddle, and enjoy the silence while wrapped in each other. I know we dove in, but it's a different dynamic, one I can't help but wish to continue.

When he takes the next exit, leaving the interstate, we enter a port town I've never been to before. I'm not even sure if it's a part of Boston. The truck turns onto the last street, and I take in the row of houses, all on the smaller side. So much greenery, trees, and flowers around every single one of them. Yards filled with trampolines, swings, slides, and bicycles in different colors on the lawns. It somehow reminds me of my hometown. Although Broumont is a mountain town with a lot of surrounding greenery, it's the warmth of its streets that makes it feel like home, just like this place. Luka never mentioned where he was taking me, but I saw a sign that said 'Welcome to Neponset/Port Norfolk.' I'm admiring the tree line when he pulls up into the driveway of a yellow, two-and-a-half-story house with an elevated front porch. I can't help but smile when I see a tire swing on the tree covering the end of the front yard.

He brought me to his home. I gasp, and he tightens his grip around my knee, not saying a word. He gets out of the car and holds his door open for me to get out. I slide out, and we start walking when the front door of the house opens.

"Oh my God," Eva screams and starts running toward me. Not her son, but me. I am wrapped in her arms within a breath, and everything about her embrace feels like home—warm, accepting.

"I am so happy to see you!" she exclaims, and I gush, still locking her in.

"Me too." She pulls away, her hands finding my shoulders, her head bobbing as she gives me a once-over. There's a twinkle in her eyes, like maybe she is satisfied with what she is seeing. Something about it makes me want to shy away, but I choose to own it. She grabs my hand and drags me inside. Luka hasn't moved, still by his truck, frozen. "What am I? Chopped liver?"

"Sorry, honey, but I saw you yesterday. I haven't seen this one for way too long," she shouts over her shoulder, leaving poor Luka in the dust. I can't stop laughing.

The moment I step inside, I hear a loud shriek, "No way!"

I recognize the voice immediately, Sabrina. She moves the crowd away and chokes me with a hug of her own.

"I can't believe you're here," she whispers in my ear, and there's nothing I can say or do at this point. Tears start to flow on their own, impossible to stop.

"Let the woman breathe," I hear Mateo say, but Sabrina won't budge, and I love her even more for it. She pulls away only to hug Luka, whose face is filled with content.

"Oh, Shrek, does this mean what I think it means?" Sabrina asks him. "Scratch that, I don't need the answer; I see the dimples," she bubbles and hugs him so tight I fear his eyeballs might fall out.

Two unfamiliar faces stare at me, and I wave at them, unsure of what my next move should be. It's Mak who steps up, obstructing my view and opening his arms. "We meet again."

I take his offering, chuckling under my breath, "Under better circumstances this time."

He's about my height, with dark hair and warm, latte skin tone. His stylish, kind of retro eyewear suits him perfectly, and I gotta say, he has a dashing smile completing the look. He's cocky, I know that for a fact, since I saw the way he engaged with his female coworkers, but deep down, I know he's kind. The way he took care of me in the hospital is proof enough.

A tall, athletic Mateo look-alike shoves Mak aside and opens his arms. I burst out laughing. "You must be Tyler, nice to meet you." He mumbles a thank you in my ear. Not sure what he's thanking me for, I nod anyway. His girlfriend, who is fit, tall, and gorgeous, steps in. Her blonde hair is up in a ponytail, and she's wearing baggy clothes that somehow suit her. We embrace each other, and I squeeze tight. "I'm Nora."

"Oh, I know," she says in the same tone Sabrina used when we first met. "I'm Maddison, but you can call me MJ."

I nod, noticing the absence of one Hart, so I wonder, "Where's Tristan?"

"Practice. He'll be home soon," Mak answers just as Sabrina snatches my hand and hauls me to the couch.

I'm sandwiched between her and MJ, both of them giggling. Luka gives them a sidelong glance. "Don't scare her away, please. I've become attached," he jabs.

"Wouldn't dream of it," Sabrina retorts. I, on the other hand, turn into a puddle.

I take their home in. It smells like coffee, and that alone makes me love it. The living room is colorful, alive, and screams family. I thought I was a knick-knack hoarder, but seeing this place, I am an amateur. I think Eva has kept every single thing these guys ever made. I see macaroni art on the walls, so many family photos, and books… lots and lots of books.

"Is this happening? Are you two together?" Sabrina asks, looking between Luka and me. I don't know how to answer that. Fudge, I claimed the man five days ago, and now I'm too chicken to say it out loud.

"Yes," he answers for me, "She's all mine."

God, how I love hearing that.

All the women in the house squeak, and I shake my head, not a shred of embarrassment in sight.

"Where's Declan?" Eva asks, taking a seat in a rocking chair across from us.

"He's with his father." The room goes silent.

"We got divorced five months ago." I swallow a nonexistent lump. I don't know why talking about it is so hard, like divorce is a failure. Maybe because, for a long time, I believed it was. "We share custody, and it's his week."

"I know I should say I'm sorry, but... I can't," Eva blurts out, a full-blown smile covering her face.

"Me neither," Sabrina speaks next, and everybody follows with nods, smiles, and words I can't quite single out, due to them overlapping in various tones and voices.

And just like that, they welcome me in, giving me the sense of belonging I've been craving.

I meet Luka's intense gaze, that spark in his eyes loud just for me, and I smile so wide that it physically hurts. So this is what it feels like to have your dreams come true. Dang, my imagination did a poor job, because this right here... It's better than I could've ever envisioned.

Chapter 53

Luca

I have a confession… I am scared shitless.

There is no way a person can be this happy.

My brothers are in their making fun of me mode, poking at my obvious grin. I can't help it; it's all-consuming. I never felt so fulfilled and so blindsided. I don't show my emotions so easily, since I don't tend to wear my heart on my sleeve. It all changed when Nora torpedoed my life. She turned me into a gushing, stomping, stupid, walking, talking cheer.

"Who are you and what have you done to our brother?" Tristan teases, slamming his hand between my shoulder blades. The collision stings, but I laugh through it.

After our youngest brother got home, the household was divided into two groups. The girls are inside while we men are in the backyard preparing the grill for later.

"Yeah, what happened to *The Hulk*?" Mateo jumps in next.

It fucked my women into oblivion.

I choose to chuckle instead of saying that out loud.

"You look happy," Tyler beams, coming to my side and handing me a cold beer.

"I feel happy. I *am* happy," I emphasize.

"No one deserves it more than you do, brother," he says in a hushed tone.

My brothers were never only my brothers. Growing up, I was their provider as much as Mama was. Although I wasn't the oldest, I felt most responsible for all of them, including our mother. I started working at a young age and learned the value of money, saving every dime. It was always well spent, whether it was for Mateo's new bike or Tyler's new shoes; it didn't matter. They had everything they needed. I made sure of it.

Working hard was never an issue; I enjoyed the work, the control, and the ability to provide for my family. That was my purpose. Somewhere along the line, I started saving for my future, with a family of my own in mind. As more time passed, the more that dream started to slip away. I held on tight to it, though, the string unbreakable. Nora made me want to pull on it. I want to test the waters to see if the dream is still possible with her and Declan in the picture. As if reading my mind, Mateo clinks his bottle to mine, "You gonna take her there?"

I nod, "I'm planning on it today."

"You gonna tell her?"

"I'm not sure yet. I want to see her reaction first." I tilt the bottle, chugging half of the cold liquid down my throat. "How are you and Sabrina doing?"

"Great, she's killing it, making a name for herself in the courtroom," he says proudly. Sabrina opened her law firm at the beginning of the summer. Her brother, Simon, works there as a legal investigator. She does a lot of pro bono work alongside her high-profile cases. My brother also made headlines. After completing a summer internship at ENOVA, he secured a permanent position in the development of innovative medical equipment. They are currently working on a cheaper, rapid diagnostic machine that combines CT and MRI. Mak is helping him with that one, utilizing his medical skills.

"I'm proud of both of you!" I exclaim, giving him a quick smirk. He opens his mouth but closes it, and just as I am about to pry it open, Mama opens the back door.

"Book club time?"

We all nod and rush inside.

There's not enough seating, so both Nora and MJ take the floor. The house is getting too small for all of us, but I guess that's the point. Our family is growing, and I wouldn't have it any other way. I'm excited to have Nora be part of this-to see our dynamic in action.

"So, since it's Nora's first time here, let's give her the basis," Mama announces. "We are discussing *Drive* today. It was MJ's request."

"Stella is my favorite FMC of all time," Maddison explains to Nora, who nods in understanding.

"Did we buy our car just so that she can yell 'Get in my Tahoe'?" Ty jumps in, "Yes, yes, we did."

"Hey! You love that car!" MJ screams at him with heart eyes. My brother shrugs, changing the subject. "If you, by any chance, read the book, feel free to get in on the discussion."

"I did it on audio last year," Nora mumbles.

"I loved *Reverse*. Joe Arden, am I right?" Sabrina wiggles her brows, MJ joins in, and all three of them blush. I share a look with their significant others, and I can say for certain that we are all getting jealous of a fucking voice.

Mak saves us all with an over-the-top clearing of his

throat.

"I'm just gonna put it out there…" he pauses for dramatic effect, then quips, "I hate Crown."

All four women have their hands over their chests, letting out loud, dramatic gasps. That turns into a whole new argument, so I sit back and enjoy the show.

Tyler excuses himself, leaving for the bathroom just as Tristan claps his hands. "All this book talk is making me hungry. Who's up for pancakes?"

All the women scream, "Noooo!" simultaneously.

What the actual hell?

Tristan's eyes go wide; he looks like a deer caught in the headlights. Also, I think he's shaking. Their loud outburst scared the shit out of him. I want to laugh, but then my eyes bounce from one woman to the other, all sharing the same teary-eyed expression.

"What was that for?" the youngest of the bunch practically wails.

"If you know, you know. If you don't, consider yourselves extremely lucky," Sabrina relates, adding to the confusion.

Tyler walks back in, reading the room.

"What happened?"

Mateo fills him in, and then our little brother shares some light. "It's a dark romance thing. Never, and I mean ever, mention pancakes." He shakes his head like we're the idiots, then adds, "Oh, and also cookies and cream ice cream."

Since none of us read that particular genre, at least not that I know of, my curiosity gets the better of me. I lean in, whispering, "Care to expand on that a bit for us?"

Mateo follows my lead, and so does Tristan. We're all

ears, waiting for Tyler to blow the lid off.

"All you need to know is that one causes instant tears, the other may involve gagging, and not the good kind."

Mateo swings an arm around Tyler's shoulder, going for a subtle chokehold so he wouldn't draw any attention. It takes our little brother three seconds to cave, just like I knew he would. "Okay, okay. I'll send you the titles. Sheesh." He wiggles out of the hold and gives both of us a little push. I chuckle, Mateo snickers, and Tyler… he blows a raspberry in our direction—the big baby.

I turn my gaze to Nora, locking eyes with her perfect hazels. There's an intensity in her stare that causes me to lose air.

Now is as good a time as any, I tell myself as I walk toward my girl.

I lean in, bringing my lips to her ear. "Wanna go somewhere with me?"

She nods enthusiastically, so I take her hand, giving my family a look. With their approving nods, we go outside, meeting the sun.

Chapter 54

Nora

It feels like I am in the middle of a Hallmark movie. Luka's by my side, holding my hand, our fingers locking the grip. I hear the soft melody forming to the beat of our steps. His one giant one mixed with my two quick short ones. I listen to the violins in my head, the piano notes, the whole song developing, down to the birds chirping. We walk by the water, between houses, and he shows me his elementary school, the playground where they played as kids. Next is the basketball court where Tyler learned to play the sport he now excels at. Then, all of a sudden, there's a small clearing, and I have to stop in my tracks. I pull him back, and he loses his balance a bit, but says nothing.

"Wow," I gasp, and he chuckles.

"What?"

Before us is a one-story house in the making, with a large yard and immense potential. The roof is just being put up, and by the looks of it, it will be a hip one—my favorite type. The house itself still has a lot of work to do; there are no windows or doors, but I can envision it all. I love that it's not positioned directly by the street, but rather farther back in the yard. The only downside is the lack of a fence surrounding it, but that's a me problem. I stare at it a bit longer before I finally speak.

"It's *the* house," I marvel, "I hope they don't ruin it."

"*The* house?" he asks, and I laugh.

"Yeah. When I was younger, Ryan and I drew up our dream homes. His was this Victorian mansion with a fudging tower, and mine was something just like that one." I point at the house ahead of us. He's grinning and cute doing it. I bite my inner cheek. "What?"

"How would they ruin it?"

"Pick the wrong color, door, frames, etc.," I state with a shrug.

"What would you pick?"

"White facade with anthracite windows matching the roof, and a wooden door, maybe rustic oak…" I trail off, then another idea hits. "Oh, and I'd frame the corners of the house with the same wood."

"You know your construction?"

"Blame Ryan for that," I muse.

"I should thank Ryan for that."

"What do you mean?"

He shrugs. "I can talk to you about my work."

"You can talk to me about it regardless. But, yeah. I know my way around wood," I wink, "pun intended." He wraps his arm around my shoulder, bringing me closer. I melt into him, breathing in his scent.

"What else?"

"Hm?" I mumble, lifting my head.

"About the house?"

He seems genuinely interested in my opinion, so naturally, I perk up. My eyes take it in, ideas floating in my head with ease.

"I'd keep the grass, pave the driveway leading to the front door, and have a separate garage. I can't see the back of the house, but if it's not done, a small, enclosed glass patio would be great. And maybe hedges around the entire property."

"Is that it?"

"Yup," I pop the P.

What I keep to myself is how I imagine the front yard: a swing set, a trampoline, a pool, and a slide; a gazebo somewhere in the corner; a grand piano inside. A girl can still dream, can't she? Just when my mind has constructed a picture of Dec running through the yard, Luka takes my hand, gives it a little squeeze, and we continue our walk.

As we close in on Luka's home, we hear voices echoing from the back, so naturally, we follow the laughter. An impromptu potluck is in full bloom. A wooden table and some of my favorite people around it, with a feast spread across the entire length of it.

"Oh, good, we can eat," Tristan yells when he sees us coming.

"You didn't have to wait for us," I say in a lower tone, but Eva steps up with a wave of a hand, "Nonsense, honey."

That's when I see a familiar face that wasn't there before, and I shriek, blowing my own eardrum, "Larry."

I'm frozen in place, blinking profusely. "What are you doing here?"

Sabrina is the one to answer, "This one likes picking up strays," tilting her head in Eva's direction.

I can't believe my eyes at the sight of him, all put together. He's got clean clothes, no holes in them, a shaved beard, and a nicely trimmed haircut. I don't think I've ever seen him without his hat, so I didn't even know he was blond. I don't think. I run and jump into his arms. Larry takes me in, and I can feel his smile even though I can't see it.

When we pull away, I feel Luka behind me, so I turn. "After you told me his story, I figured he could use a friend who'd understand him."

Somehow, my heart knows who he's talking about, so I shift my gaze to Eva. I see it, right there in her eyes, the same hurt I saw whenever I looked at Larry. She loved once, lost it, and never recovered. She gives me a barely noticeable nod, and I give one right back in understanding.

Larry moves for me to sit next to him, and Luka takes the vacant seat at the end. Larry offers me his hand, and Sabrina from my other side does the same. I take them and bow my head, allowing Eva to say her prayers before we all finish with an "Amen."

The men attack the meat tray, grabbing and shoving each other as if they were fighting for gold or something. Sabrina shakes her head, and so does Eva. MJ and I join in a full-blown laugh. Luka takes my plate and fills it up for me. My jaw drops when he sets the overflowing plate in front of me. The man was fighting to get me the best meat, not for himself. Mateo and Tyler follow their brothers' lead. Tristan winks at Mak and gives him a big-ass steak. It's endearing how close they all are.

I talk with MJ about school and basketball, though I don't know much about the sport beyond Michael Jordan playing it many years ago. Sabrina retells a story about her latest court case, and Tristan replays his game for the table. He's now a freshman at Temple University, and they play against Yale tomorrow, so he gets to spend the day with his family. Getting to know them, their stories, backgrounds, dreams, and aspirations is easy. Each is unique in its own way, yet they come together to form a perfect whole. They are each other's biggest fans and supporters, something I admire. I want to be a part of it, to see their games, to see Sabrina dominate in the courtroom. I want it all. And I want it with Luka.

Just as I start to think about how Dec would fit in, Eva comes from behind me, placing a hand on my shoulder, leaning over. "Next time, bring Declan. He can play here; it's gated and safe for him. Maybe Luka and the boys can build him a swing here in the back. The tire swing is old, still standing for sentimental purposes only." She smiles, with that wide, sincere grin that makes me all warm and fuzzy. She's a dream mom, one I aspire to be, and I'm glad that she chose Luka and the rest of them to raise and guide.

"That sounds great. I'll make sure to bring him," I say with a smile. Sabrina resolves then to clear her throat and walk to Mateo's side.

"I have our next book recommendation." All eyes snap to her. "It's about this crazy couple, a lot of smut, a lot of love." She smiles down at her husband, and his eyes are firmly locked on her. Tears are forming there, and he seems nervous. "The FMC is a kick-ass lawyer, and the MMC is a big-shot engineer," she keeps going, while all of us share confused looks. "And they're expecting a baby," she finishes with the biggest grin, impossible not to see from space.

Eva stands up first, hands covering her mouth, happy tears streaming down her face. In a matter of seconds, everyone is on their feet, circling both of them.

"I'm gonna be a grandma?" Eva shouts, and Sabrina starts leaking (her words, not mine). It turns into a major sob fest on all fronts, mixed with a lot of clapping and jumping. I join the massive group hug and cry like a baby. The huddle drags on for long minutes before everyone finally gives the happy couple breathing room. Sabrina comes to me, whispering, "I'm gonna need advice, the motherly kind, and a lot of it. So don't you dare leave that man."

"Never planning on it," I whisper back.

"Good. Welcome to the family," she simpers, and the only thing I can do is cry some more.

Chapter 55

Luka

By the time moonlight shines upon us, the backyard is all cleaned up, and everyone is in a relaxing position. Tristan went to the hotel where his team is staying. Mateo and Sabrina took over the loungers, Mama her swing chair, leaving Ty and MJ the only available place—the ground. Tyler finds a blanket and spreads it over the grass, and MJ happily lies down.

I am in my hammock with Nora in my arms. My leg is hovering over the side, allowing me to swing us. The clear sky is filled with stars, offering a stunning view. Nora's soft fingers brush over my chest in slow strokes. If this is not heaven, I don't know what is. Ok, that's not entirely true. Declan here with us would be absolute heaven. But I'll settle for this one for now.

"When do you get Declan?" I dip my chin. She lifts her head, giving me the full view of her beautiful face.

"I pick him up at three on Monday," she answers with a confused expression.

"Can I go with you?" I swallow, unsure why I am so nervous. Her lips turn upward, and her palm flattens on my chest, right above my frantically beating heart.

"Are you sure?"

"I miss him," I admit, trying to imagine how much he has

changed in the half a year I haven't seen him.

Is his hair longer, darker?

Did he grow taller, skinnier?

Does he have more freckles now?

Does he still remember me? I hope he does.

"What about your work?" She swings her leg over my knees and leaves it there to lock me in.

"I got a good boss; he'll let me out early."

"Wow, lucky bastard," she leans her head back on my arm.

"You have no idea," I whisper, placing a gentle kiss on the top of her head.

Soon, yawns echo the night, starting with a more obvious one coming from Mama. It's our cue to leave. After hugging it out, Sabrina and Mateo straddle his bike and whoosh away. I open the door of my truck for Nora while she's still locked in with my mother. The sight of them hugging will never get old. When I told Mama I'd be spending the night at Nora's place, she cupped my cheek and said that wasn't news.

Even in the dark, I can see all the emotions circling in her eyes. Sadness, loss, happiness, pride, and love. She lets love and happiness shine the most, and it's greatly appreciated. It feels like leaving the nest, even though it's far from it. And as much as it saddens both of us, we can't be happier. Nora allows us to have a moment by sliding into the truck, and I hug my Mama as tightly as I possibly can. This woman is one of a kind, with the biggest heart and a tender soul. Irreplaceable and the first person I truly loved, the first person who truly loved me. The next thing she tells me proves it. "She's the one, son, I knew it from the first time you came home with the biggest smile on your face. Take care of them," she sniffles into my chest, and I can't help but crumble.

"Thank you, Mama," I whisper, "I love you so much."

"I love you, and I love her."

Wiping her tears, she motions at a waiting Nora, and I backtrack to the truck. When she gives me her signature beaming smile, I get inside and start the engine.

"We don't have to go." Nora takes my shaking hand. I didn't even realize it was trembling when I white-knuckled the steering wheel. Nora, noticing, makes me love her even more. She understands me, the importance of my family, and our connection. She also understands my mother, and something about it eases the anxiety. I shake my head, turning my palm so we can intertwine our fingers. With one hand, I maneuver the truck in reverse, and with my eyes focused on my home, I back away, knowing it will always be there for me.

Waking up with Nora in my arms is a dream come true, even if her hair tickles my nose, ears, and chest. It's all over the place, and yet, I wouldn't have it any other way. Plus, she's naked, and that is a big factor in my not caring about anything else. The entire room smells like her, but it doesn't stop me from inhaling the real thing.

"You turning creepy on me?" she mumbles into my chest.

"Maybe," I drag, then yelp when she pinches my side. "What was that for?"

"No idea," she quips, propping her chin on my chest to look at me. "Seemed fitting."

"You always this spontaneous?"

She tilts her head. "No. Not usually. But it's easier lately. Feels like…" she hesitates, "life's asking for something different."

"Different how?"

She thinks about it for a second. "Less perfect. More real."

I am struck stupid. God, this woman. This side of her, so open, free, is doing wonders to my crotch. She notices as much.

"You can't be hard right now," Nora slurs, her eyes widening.

"And why not?"

"Uhm, your brother's game," she reminds me. I check the time, then face her with a daring stare.

"I thought you were not a morning person," she snarks, and I purse my lips, cocking my brows. "Luka, no!"

I wiggle them a little.

"Don't you dare," she threatens, pressing her lips together to stop a smile from happening. I go all in, showing her those dimples I know she likes so much.

"Damn you."

"This is all your fault," I drawl, flipping her on her back. She bites her lip when I pin her, her wrists captured above her head.

"How is it my fault?"

"You're irresistible," I admit, brushing my nose against hers.

"Dial the charm, mister. We have to leave in thirty minutes," she points out. "We're far from ready, plus, need I remind you, we haven't had our caffeine fix yet." She's right. We both know it. But there's also this thing called fashionably late. So with my mind made up, I lower my lips to her neck, pressing a soft kiss that makes her whimper. My tongue darts out, tracing the length of her collarbone. I'm rewarded with a moan, my cock hardening at the sound.

She gives in, her legs falling to the side. I take advantage, pressing kisses all over her body until I reach the motherland. Her hand finds my hair, gripping and pulling the moment my tongue flicks over her clit. Her hips react, pushing upward. I smirk. My baby is greedy.

"Luk, please," she begs through another whimper, and I revel in it. I had a plan to play, tease, prolong, but I am a weak man. For her.

I slip my fingers inside and move in the rhythm I learned she likes, while my tongue circles around her most sensitive part. It doesn't take her long to peak; I can tell by the way she's trying to suffocate my digits.

"I need you," she moans.

You see what I mean?

All she has to do is ask, and I'm there.

"I'm all yours," I murmur; voice sultrily.

It's safe to say we are definitely going to be late to the game.

Chapter 55

Luka

The sun is shining, cars are zooming past, and I am smiling. Skipping early from work, I met with Nora at her school, and now we're walking to pick up Declan from kindergarten, hand in hand. We're a freaking postcard. And I love it.

"How was work?" I ask when we round the corner.

"Great," she deadpans, one shoulder shrugging. It's a nice spring day, though it hasn't officially started. Usually, this time of year, the weather likes to play a roller coaster, but so far, over the last couple of days, it has been warm and sunny.

"I kinda need more than that."

She slows her steps, and her hand twitches in mine. "What do you mean?" There's hesitation in her tone, and I don't like it one bit.

"Like, what did you do? Did any kid piss you off? Did you inspire them? There's so much to go on." Somewhere in the middle of my babbling, she stopped walking. I look at her, confused.

"What's wrong?"

"Sorry, I just…" she sniffles, and I pull her into my arms. Then it clicks. I feel stupid for not realizing it sooner. She's not used to this. I plan to mend that. Not intentionally, but full on naturally. I mean, I can listen to this woman count, and I'd be mesmerized by it. We start walking again, and to ease her tension, I begin talking about my day, glad it was a good one with few hiccups. I'm boring her with the endless emails that never stop coming, but her focus remains on me. When I'm done, we're both smiling.

"I think I might do some production for the school. A musical, maybe," she chirps, all the emotions screaming out of her, enthusiasm taking over.

"That sounds interesting. Does that mean you would write the whole thing?"

"Yeah, the music, the lyrics, the dialogue..." she trails off, then titters, "I'm excited."

"I can tell. It suits you."

"What does?"

"Excitement. I like it on you."

"You do?" she doubts, and I hate it. I get it, but I hate it.

"I like everything on you." I stop our walk, framing her face before I claim her mouth. She opens without hesitation. In the blink of an eye, I'm pinning her against the building wall, my hands roaming all over her body while our tongues dance. It takes all my restraint to pull away, especially when I see her mouth swollen and eyes hungry. She's heaving, and so am I. We both take deep breaths, without blinking, before I take her hand, allowing her to guide me the rest of the way.

Declan's kindergarten is colorful on the outside, with rainbows and flowers painted on the walls. We enter, and I take my time scanning the place. There are five different groups, each with a distinct color theme. Declan's group is blue, and I don't know why, but it suits him. Nora knocks on the door and swings it open. I find him instantly, playing with the blocks in the corner. A blonde lady shouts to Declan that his mother is here, but he doesn't react. Only when his mother speaks up does he perk up. He runs to us, and Nora squats to meet his hug. He turns to me and yells, "Crane," before he lifts his arms in invitation. Tears might be falling down my face as I pick him up, and I am proud of each and every one. I hug him tight, then give him a once-over. His hair is shorter and a bit darker. He grew an inch and gained approximately a pound. A part of me hates that I missed it all, but I know it had to be this way.

I help him put on his shoes, then pick him back up, giving him a little twirl that makes him giggle, the sound sending my heart into orbit. I mouth the word 'ice cream' to Nora so that Declan won't hear me, and she nods. I refuse to let him down, despite her every protest.

We turn around, and I finally set him on the ground. He takes my hand like it's second nature, and gives Nora the other one. With one happy Declan between us, we walk into the sunset, or at least it looks like it in my head.

It's then that the woman of my dreams decides to give my life a whole new, different meaning.

"I love you," she declares, and my heart stops beating altogether.

"Say that again."

"I. Love. You," she repeats, her eyes shining right at me.

I was wrong. This is the best song, music to my ears.

Chapter 54

Nora

It's been a little over five months since I ambushed Luk at his site. During the time we have been inseparable, practically glued to each other's hips. The only time we were apart was when we were working. Even then, on our breaks, we talked on the phone. Luka and Dec got close to a point where I started feeling jealous, but in a good way; if that's even a thing. He calls him father, as he does every other male person in the world. He calls all the women mama, so we're not reading much into it. Luka and Rick buried the hatchet, leaving no animosity between them whatsoever. They even coordinate pick-ups together to make it easier on me. Rick's been proving himself time and again, and Declan thrives because of it. He works with him at his place and takes him to therapies without complaint. We've entered a new dynamic and formed a new kind of friendship. For the first time, we have mutual respect and validation. He even suggested we take a vacation and that he would take care of Dec. We still haven't taken him up on it because of our busy schedules.

Now that you're all caught up, let's get to it.

We just finished our book club session at Luka's house, and now we're walking the same route he took me when we first got together. I stop in my tracks when I see it. The dream house, all finished… Painted white, anthracite frames and windows, with an oak, rustic door framed to match the rest. My jaw drops when I see the roof of the gazebo, in the shape of a hexagon. The pillars and fence are the same color as the door, and the roof matches the house's. A paved driveway leads up to a small garage, a mini replica of the house itself. In the yard, there's a colorful playhouse, combining a swing, a slide, and a sandbox.

I feel Luka's eyes on me, so I meet them. I stare at his knowing smirk, my state somewhere between wanting to slap it away and kiss it at the same time.

"What?" is all I can think to say. He takes my hand and guides me over the paved path. I hear the sound of keys dangling when we reach the front door. He's smiling, hand in the air, holding a key with a metal key chain shaped like a daisy. There's a fifty percent chance I might be having a heart attack. I gulp, my shaky hand taking the key. Speechless, I slide it into the lock and turn at the same time as I twist the black round knob. The door swings inward of its own accord, and I can't move. Luka places a hand on the small of my back, slowly giving me a push forward. My feet move, but my mind stays outside, not catching up with my body. Again, I feel Luka's gaze on me, but I don't turn to check. Not when my eyes are busy looking at the interior.

I walk through the small hallway with a shoe cabinet, a wall-mounted rack, and a shelf above it holding three boxes. He pushes me in further, and with a couple more steps, we enter the living room. It's unfurnished, but there's so much light streaming in that the hardwood floors look all the shinier. Luka's hands find my shoulders, and he guides me to the dining room slash kitchen. A large oak table, matching the front door, with black legs, takes up most of the space, surrounded by black chairs with beige cushions. Eight of them, to be exact. The kitchen is enormous, featuring a large island at its center. The lower portion is anthracite; the countertops are oak; the upper portion is matte white, with a couple of cupboards covered in smoked glass. I remain speechless as he advances me further. He shows me the pantry and the guest bathroom, then stops before the master bedroom. I walk in, taking in the large space.

There's a king-size bed with a white leather headboard in the middle. Two nightstands on each side, a TV mounted on the opposite wall. I take a few steps and find a huge walk-in closet leading to an en-suite bathroom. My mouth starts to drool when a bathtub comes into view, big enough for two. My fingers itch to touch the ceramic, but instead, I turn to Luka. He's leaning on the door across the master bedroom, and I don't even fight the pull that makes me join his side. It's a children's room, with a bunk bed, but instead of the lower bed, there's a desk. A closet fills the other wall, next to a bookcase stacked with books and stuffed animals, all Disney. The floor is covered with a Dumbo-shaped carpet.

I'm a sob fest, not even bothering to stop my sniffles. But he's not done. Nope. Luka takes me to the next room, which he says could be a playroom. We don't stay there long since it's empty, and he takes my hand and drags me to the back of the house. And sure enough, there's a glass-closed patio, fully furnished—a mixture of metal and wooden chairs, a big table, and a swing lounge.

"Luka, I…" He brings a finger to my mouth, stopping me. I

glare at him, furrowing my brows.

"There's more," he whispers, and I shake my head. "I don't think I can handle any more."

He cups my cheeks, those ambers sparkling with so much love, I can hardly breathe.

"You can handle anything. You're Eleonora Grace Baker."

I don't know what I did to deserve this man, his heart, but I thank God for him every single day. He takes my hand, brings it to his lips, and plants a soft kiss on my knuckles. I shiver at the contact, reveling in the current of electricity running down my bloodstream. I don't even realize we're moving when he stops in front of a closed door.

"You ready?"

I shake my head because no, I am certainly not ready. I might flat-line when I see what's waiting for me on the other side. He swings the door open and steps aside. One step in, and I am in heaven. My feet move on their own accord, my eyes widening at the sight. A grand piano sits in the middle of a large room. There are three different guitars mounted on the right wall. Posters of musical notes, sheet music, and instruments cover the walls between the two windows. There's a small recording station set up in the corner, with tech I've never seen before. And even though everything in this room is breathtaking, it's the piano that has me crying.

It can't be.

My hand grazes over the top, then I open the cover to reveal the keys. I glide over each note, goosebumps erupting with harmony. I take a seat at the bench and stare at the closed music sheet book in front of me. Luk takes a seat next to me, but I can't face him. Not yet, at least. If I do, a full-blown meltdown would surely happen.

"Play me something," he whispers, his lips grazing my ear, sending shivers down my spine. My hands find the first position with my eyes closed, and I start slow, getting the feel of it first, reconnecting with my old friend. I hunch down to confirm and gasp when I find my initials carved on the bottom.

"How?"

"Ryan," he blurts like that's enough of an explanation. Spoiler alert, it's not, and I tell him as much.

"I'm gonna need a bit more than that."

"Our best friend told me where you pawned it, so we went there. The guy found the receipt, and we tracked down the owner. When we told him the story, he got all soft, and he sold it to me."

I fall apart.

"What, what about the house?" I stutter, sobbing each word.

"I bought the land two years ago. I started building the foundation last year."

"I don't understand." And I mean it. Confusion is all I have right now.

He has this look, something between content and hope, I think. I don't have it in me to figure it out at the moment. I swallow, and he must notice my nerves because he takes my hands and holds them over his thighs.

"I got tired of waiting for my soulmate, so one day, I decided to build a house, hoping I'd find her in the meantime."

That gets me to pull back a little. My breath catches, and for some stupid, weird reason, I turn jealous. It's silly, I know, but I can't help it. Not to mention, it's hypocritical. A year ago, I was married to another man, so I have no right to act this way.

"At one point, I gave up and decided to sell it," he discloses, and disappointment washes over me. Sadness comes next. I see it so clearly: the want, the need for family.

I finally bring myself to ask, "When was that?"

"The day I met you."

I gasp in disbelief.

"That morning, I contacted a friend who works in real estate and told him to put it on the market," he clears his throat. "I called him back the same day to pull out."

"What?" I wheeze, grasping for air.

"You brought light into my life, and I guess I got hopeful, knowing you'd probably never be mine."

Be still, my heart.

"You never acted on it," I surmise, knowing dang well what kind of person he is, thinking back to the time at the cottage, when he told me he wasn't going to kiss me for my benefit.

"I'm not built that way, and you know that."

I nod, take a piece of paper from my back pocket, and place it on the music rack. I take a deep breath and start to share a part of myself, a part of him, through the notes that have been playing in my head ever since I first truly saw him.

Angel Guarding

In my head, on my shoulder
There you've been all along
By my side, all the way
You were there

Without a say, without a word
You said more than anyone ever could
With just one look, I knew it all
The secrets, the stories that mark my fall

I sore to crash, crash and burn
Only to get your faith in return
I rose high again with one blow of your wings
The angel guarding all my most valuable things

You gave me time, you gave me space
Allowed me to find my own place
Even after I'd fallen from grace
You took it all, slowing your pace

With just one look, you said it all
In my corner, you left the ball
My choice and mine alone
You waited for me to come back home

I sore to crash, crash and burn
Only to get your faith in return
I rose high again with one blow of your wings
The angel guarding all my most valuable things

Chapter 58

Luka

Don't cry, don't cry, don't cry.

Fuck it, I'm crying. Sue me.

I'm gonna turn into a blubbering mess because this amazing, beautiful woman, with the voice of an angel, wrote a song for me. And it's not just that the lyrics hit deep, or how the melody plays with my heart… It's the date in the corner. She wrote it back in August. I was important to her back then, and I still am today—hopefully, will be for the rest to come.

Right now, as much as I want to lift her and take her to the bed I hope to be ours, I am as impatient as a man like me can be. There's a well-laid-out plan at play here. Days spent getting every detail right, sleepless hours working through every thought. It's all pointless now as the air fails to reach my lungs. And when she hits the last note, I am already on one knee. Her eyes are closed, her breath trying to catch up with a long exhale. She smiles when her fingers leave the keys, and when she turns to face me, I see her crimson-covered cheeks. Her head immediately starts shaking, eyes watery. I reach into my pants pocket to retrieve a small bag. I had to get it out of the box solely to avoid suspicion.

Enthusiastically, she turns into one of those bobblehead toys, not even waiting for the words that I prepared in my head. I give her a pointed stare, the one that practically demands that she indulge me. And she pulls away just a bit, enough to provide me with the podium.

"Don't worry, I got everyone's blessing."

"Everyone's?" She tilts her head, pursing her lips.

"I asked Declan first, and he gave me a high five." She chuckles, and I tell her about sitting her entire family down, including Rick, and how they all gave me their approval.

You know, it's funny, the term 'right person, wrong time'… but that's not what this is. This is the right person, right time; it just happened under the wrong circumstances. Right time because if we'd met before, Declan wouldn't be in the picture. We found each other when it was meant to be—at the time when I almost gave up on the notion of a soulmate, and when Nora was ready to face her reality.

I take a deep breath, barely getting over my words, and she chuckles. "If you think it's soon, let me tell you why it's not." I start stronger this time. "First, I waited my whole life for you. Second, I knew from the moment I met you and Declan that I wanted to be a part of your life. Third, I don't want to waste another day without us living under the same roof, sharing the same bed. I never want to wake up without you by my side. It's the first thing I'm asking. Move in with me here, in the house that I built for us even before I knew you. And then, marry me, on your terms, whenever you want, however you want, just fucking marry me and spend the rest of your life with me because it is the only life I want to live." I finish with a sharp breath, finally easing my lungs, which have been in agony throughout the entire proclamation. Her hands find the sides of my face, and our eyes meet, both pairs filled with tears. Her nose wrinkles, and her freckles dance with her grin.

"Let me tell you why it's a fucking yes. First, you are the most amazing person I have ever met. Second, you deserve so much love, and I am going to give you all of mine. Third, I had this exact dream when I first ran away from home. This life, right here with you... It was a dream that seemed so far away, and now you've made it come true. I love you. And I will marry you today if you want."

And then she kisses me. The kind of kiss that makes all the stars align. That life-altering thing you can only read in books. The kiss I never knew to be possible. But I feel it, every particle of it sending the sparks of love between us. I never want to let go of this feeling, of this person, of this life. This is it for me. Just last year, I gave up on this notion, of this possibility. I had given up hope for this life, and now I have it. I am the luckiest man alive, and I can only hope she's as happy as I am. I am going to make her happy every hour of every day... love her, cherish her, and respect her... Value everything she is so much that she'll never doubt herself again. Her strength is her power, and she is finally shining the way she was meant to. She thinks it's because of me, but it is all her. She has the power, and she is my weakness. And I am willingly giving it all for her to take.

Epilogue

Luka

A year later

I hate working late. What's funny is that I used to love it. Now I hate working altogether because my stupid job is keeping me away from my family.

I met with Rick right after I'd finished damage control: two workers had gotten into a fight and knocked over an entire EPAL pallet of tiles, breaking every single one. I arrived at his apartment, and when he swung the door open, he gave me a knowing, condoling look before Dec ran over to me.

We're good now. He's showing up for his son and stepping up. A part of me is sad that he didn't come to his senses while he still had a chance with Nora, but the selfish part of me is thankful he was too late. Perhaps it was always meant to be this way. Declan, the main reason why.

He gives me a quick rundown of Declan's week, and we then turn to discussing his new job. He stepped into the latter, running his crew in a new electric company. Less stress and more freedom with his hours, something he demanded for his son. He hands me Declan's bag, and I pick the big guy up in my arms. He leans over to kiss his dad on the cheek, and Rick gives one right back before we wave goodbye.

We take the stairs down and get to the SUV. I am now a

proud driver of a fully equipped family car. With Dec safely secured in his seat, I bring the car to life and turn on my boy's favorite mix—Disney songs.

I am fluent in everything Declan-related. We have our unique form of communication, something Nora is definitely not jealous of (wink-wink). Thankful for the lack of traffic, we're home in record time. I park the car in front of the garage so that I won't waste more time. Dec unbuckles his seatbelt and jumps out when I open his door. We both run inside to find the house empty. Declan goes straight to his books (he tends to check his stock) to make sure everything is in place. I envy his memory sometimes; he knows every single book he owns, down to the number the title belongs to.

While he's busy roaming through the shelves, I head straight for the back patio. The back door is open, and I lean on the frame, crossing my ankles. I have the best view in the world right now. My girl is holding ours, singing her the lullaby she wrote when we found out she was pregnant. She rocks the bundle to the sides, swaying, still not noticing my presence, or at least not acknowledging it. I slowly walk to them, coming behind my wife, before I wrap my arms around them. I dig my chin in the crook of her neck, and Nora leans into me. I can feel her lips curving as she continues to hum. I look down at a sleepy Daisy and smile. She's a month old, still has barely any hair, honey eyes, and her mother's lips. I have a feeling she'll have her mother's freckles too. There's some of me in her as well, but I'm happy she took most of Nora's beauty.

"How was your day?" Nora mumbles, turning to face me. She motions with her chin, and I follow her to the nursery.

She gently places Daisy in her crib and turns on the baby monitor. We both go back to the porch and sit in the bench swing, my hand going around her shoulders. She leans against my chest, and I tell her about my messed-up day. She kisses it all away, one of her many superpowers. Her kisses silence the world around me.

"How are you doing?" I ask, my hand grazing over her upper arm.

"Good. I'm waiting for the other shoe to drop. She's too good a baby, Luk, that's not normal." She lifts her head so we can look at each other. The place between her eyebrows wrinkles, and I have trouble believing the thought that went through her mind. I can't stop my chuckle, and she slaps me on the chest.

"You want some good news?"

"Always."

"I met her."

"Nooooo," she gasps, sitting up. I give her a quick nod, and she sighs. "I hate you. I wanted to meet her first," she whines, making me laugh even more. Only Nora would get jealous of me meeting her ex-husband's girlfriend before she did.

"Does she seem nice?"

And there she is. The Nora we all know and love. The one who thinks about others. She wants this for him, for Declan as well. But mainly for Rick, to find someone who'd bring out the best in him.

"You're gonna love her," I admit, and the statement eases her up, her shoulders relaxing.

"I want him to be happy," she confesses, and I smile.

"I know," I say, cupping her face with my palm. She leans into my touch, then swings one leg over mine. I blink, and there she is, straddling me, her knees framing my legs. She grazes her fingers through my hair, making me groan. Our lips meet, and I pull her closer. I feel her brows go up when she feels me underneath her. One grin, followed by the biting of the lower lip, and then she's staring at me, love pouring out of her.

"I'm happy."

"Yeah?"

"So fucking happy."

"Then I am happy too."

Her eyes narrow.

"I said what I said," I conclude and kiss her again, harder this time.

Our puzzle is complete. A perfect fit. And I'm as happy as a man who has gotten everything he ever wanted could be.

Chapter 1

"Come on, dude, you've got 2 minutes to shower, and we need to sprint out!" Ben yells as he breezes by me to get the first empty cubicle.

"Where's the fire? The class is not for another…" I look at my watch: 35 minutes.

"Yeah, but theirs is still going on, so we have to hurry!" he shouts back. The room is filled with the whole team, each under a showerhead, scrubbing at full speed.

"Whose?" I remove my shirt and toss it on the bench by the wall.

"The girls, dumb-ass," someone screams from the showers.

Now it all makes sense.

"You guys are crazy." I shake my head, turning on the water, setting it to just the right of lukewarm.

"Trust me, Ty, you *want* to be there," Cole says, his brows dancing up and down.

"I am nothing if not a team player." I give in and join their fast pace.

"That's the spirit," Parker yells from across the room.

"I thought you were gay?" I quickly work, scrubbing my hair, loving the sensation on my scalp.

"True, but I am nothing if not a team player!"

"Touche!" I holler back.

All at once, as if an alarm has gone off, we turn the taps and start getting dressed. The next thing I know, we're power walking to the performing arts hall.

"Thank God it's still not over," Ben sighs with relief the second we get in the hall overlooking the large mirrored studio, filled with girls in the middle of a dance. The entire Basketball team is glued to the glass, focusing on said girls. Amused, I join them, allowing my eyes to be blessed by the view. Girls in short shorts, tights, tops, tight shirts… Girls with different body types, hair colors, all hot in their own ways… following Ms. Lynch at the front.

The team is well acquainted with Ms. Lynch, the woman assigned to carry out our punishment for the fight we caused during the first game of the season. The only thing the coach could think of to punish us was to embarrass us; his words were around *'If you can't act like men, then maybe I should indulge you'* right before he laid out his master plan.

Subjected to two and a half months of dance lessons, all so that we can perform a formation-type choreography in front of our friends and family at the Christmas benefit. For the last month, we've been practicing the cha-cha twice a week, and today is the day we're supposed to have our first practice with our forced-on dance partners.

Right now, I am looking at all the potentials focused on their reflections.

Well, all except one.

Love at first sight. I've heard of it, read about it, seen it on multiple screens, and witnessed it happen to my brother. On the other hand, I haven't had the pleasure of experiencing it. That is, until I laid my eyes on a blonde wonder.

Right there, overlooking a crowded room with bright lights and loud music, I get struck.

Experienced symptoms: all-around butterflies, shortness of breath, stopping of the heart, stiffness of the muscles, chest pains, temporary focused blindness (as in - not able to see anyone or anything else other than her), tightening of the throat, arousal, and spiking high temperature. To sum it all up - the whole nine yards.

A special kind of lighting strikes me, and my body goes into shock. It's that kind of thing that no doctor can fix, no remedy for the illness, no cure, no way of ever going back. In all honesty, I'm not planning on going back. I like the feeling, the moment it has its hand in consuming me, I am done for. The problem is that I want, need, and am determined to get more.

The entire room blurs out, making her the sole focus of my view. She is the only one not showing off her body, wearing a loose t-shirt with her sleeves pulled up over her shoulders and basketball shorts. Her blonde hair is tied in a ponytail, swinging from side to side. Her mouth opens to the lyrics, and she moves in sync with each beat. It's as if she's feeling the music, immersed in it with closed eyes, all the while nailing every step. I forget how to breathe, looking at her, transfixed, and I swear, time stands still for a moment. A bit of frustration comes over me due to her closed eyes, making me desperate to see them - the color, the shape, her soul.

Noticing the direction of my stare, Ben snaps me out of the trance. "Don't even think about it, man."

"What's the story there?"

Ben takes a deep breath, the warning kind, before he says, "That's Maddie, the volleyball captain, and you don't stand a chance. No offense."

"Some taken, but tell me more," I demand, intrigued.

"Look, Johnny, trust me when I tell you, don't go there."

I chuckle at the name drop from before either of us was born and fight the urge to sing out the timeless tune.

"Points for the reference, but if you don't mind, indulge me." I am practically begging, ready to go down on my knees even.

"Fine, your funeral," he gasps, then gives me what I need, placing his arm around my shoulder. "She's the all-around player of the year, number one in the state, and doesn't do basketball players. Trust me, we all tried and failed miserably."

Of course, she isn't going to make it easy, and we haven't even met.

"Minor setback," I deflect. "Keep going."

"You have a death wish, I see," Ben sighs, shaking his head. "She got here on a basketball scholarship."

"But I thought you said she plays volleyball?"

"Patience, brother, patience, I was about to get there." He rolls his eyes for emphasis.

"Did you ever read about a big-shot high school player that all the majors wanted to draft, and she turned them *all* down?"

"Yeah, from Chicago, Stevens something."

I stare at the beauty, her eyes still closed, entranced in her world. She looks breathtaking, and the info dump I was just overstimulated with makes her unreal. But there she is, flesh and bone, intimidating and inviting all at once.

Ben squeezes my shoulder and points at the person I'm developing an obsession with. "Meet Maddison Stevens."

"Damn," I mutter.

"Yeah, bro," Ben agrees, praising how she quit basketball and turned to volleyball to keep her scholarship. He didn't say anything about the reason she quit basketball, only how she spent the summer training for a whole new sport before trying out for the volleyball team and making the second string. By the following season, she was crowned captain.

Impressive is too small a word to describe her.

The music stops, and all the girls scatter to the corners, grabbing their towels and bottles. I check the time; it's probably just a break, since there are fifteen more minutes till our torture starts. Unable to look away, I soak her in, and the switch. Taking a place in the right corner, she grabs a blue bottle and chugs it right before she spits some of it out, bursting into laughter over something a tall redhead says. Her smile is even more captivating than I imagined.

The clapping of Ms. Lynch's hands gets all the girls to momentarily stiffen before they go back to their former places. The redhead and Maddie do a cute handshake with wiggling fingers and their tongues sticking out right before they take their positions. Her eyes close the moment the music starts, and her fingers start drumming to the beat, tapping the side of her thigh, and when she begins her steps, I can't look away. Diverging from the dance before the break, she moves more sensually, swaying her hips, deep diving into the salsa rhythm, and it is the worst - slash - best thing any man could witness.

"Does she have a boyfriend?" I turn the question to Cole.

"Are you deaf or just need an ear cleanse?" It's Ben who drawls, "It doesn't matter; she does not do basketball players."

"Not what I asked, Ben."

"As far as I know, she's a free woman."

That she sure is!

Mateo

The roar of my engine used to be my favorite sound. That first spot on the list was replaced by a voice coming from a shitty, barely functioning Jeep. My feet holding the balance, I found myself next to it at the red light and couldn't help but turn my attention to the beautiful creature entering another dimension. With her eyes closed, she belted out a song I've never heard before, but would surely Google later. Head banging in each direction, hands flying, and fingers wiggling - not a care in the world. My eyes traced the length of her braided hair, one loose strand dancing in the wind, dark, thick lashes, and when she opened her eyes, I forgot how to breathe. The most beautiful set of green eyes stared right at me, hitting me right in the middle of the chest. Those full, red lips pulled into a one-sided smile, and I flipped open my visor, but her focus went to my bike. With all her glory, she slowly raised those greens to meet my browns before giving me the middle finger salute, making my jaw drop, not that she could see it, but I was damn sure she could feel it. The moment the light switched to green, her tires screeched, and she drove off. Without blinking, I shifted into gear and stayed behind her, never losing her out of sight until she finally parked in front of a small café. My spidey senses told me she knew I'd been following her all along and that I just took the bait. So without any hesitation, I parked next to her, took off my helmet, and tapped on her window. She rolled it down, the old-fashioned way, I might add, before she turned to me, revealing her smirk.

"Stalk much?" One cocked brow followed by crossing her hands over her chest. And yes, I paid very close attention to all the body language.

"I believe it's called serendipity," I said, giving my most innocent look.

"Uh, I love that movie, but I don't think that's it…"

Mental note: watch the movie Serendipity.

"And what do you think?" I asked, amused by her whole allure that wouldn't allow me to blink, let alone breathe. What the hell was this girl doing to me?

"There *is* this possibility of a certain motorcycle driver following me for the last…" she checked her empty wrist - "I don't know - ten minutes."

I opened my mouth to play dumb, but she cut me off. "It's not like you kept a safe distance for me *not* to notice," she hissed, and I swallowed hard because I honestly thought I was being all smooth and inconspicuous.

"But I guess the joke's on you," she added, making me shift my weight from one side to the other.

"Meaning?" Narrowing my eyes, I tried to make my voice all husky, but it came out more stuttery than I anticipated.

"Meaning you're not so bad to look at." She finished it with a wink, the sight making my insides flutter. Crossing her hands over the window slot, she leaned over, slowly studying me from head to toe. I allowed it, doing the same as I placed both hands on the roof, and bowed down to her eye level.

"So, what's a fancy girl like you doing driving a beat-up piece of shit like this?" I wondered, bewildered by the fact that she looked like someone who wouldn't want to be caught dead near the thing, let alone in it.

"Please don't insult Rusty." She stroked her hand over the steering wheel, shushing it, like I somehow offended the thing, then continued with an upbeat tone, "I have things to do, errands to run."

"Errands?" I pumped through a laugh. For some reason, this girl looked like she had never run an errand in her life, too polished, all the while giving out the opposite vibe. I wasn't sure which version was the right one, but I surely hoped the bad girl screaming out of her eyes was the real one.

"Yeah, just your regular side hustle." With a shrug, her chin found her forearm to lean on.

"Care to be more specific?"

"Not really." Another shrug. Guess she was determined on staying evasive, but I had to hand it to her, she was cute doing it.

"Fair enough." I let out a sigh, giving up, for now.

"So Rusty, ha?"

"Suits him, doesn't it?"

Sure did by the amount of infestation.

"Oh, look, a coffee shop…" Her eyes flicked toward the terrace, her voice obvious with taunt. "I sure could use a cup of coffee, but damn..." One quick snap of her fingers. "I don't have any cash, and I don't see an ATM." She pretended to look around, not even trying to act subtle, biting on her lower lip. Her insinuation brought a new smile to my face, my response a grin. "Darn."

She brought her eyes up to mine, flashing those thick lashes at full speed.

Hoping out loud, I played along. "I was about to go get a cup for myself, if you would like to join me."

"Well, if you insist." Nonchalance was this girl's forte, I was sure, but I saw the way she eagerly grabbed her bag. I opened her door, staring at her while she slid outside with elegance. Like a real gentleman, I let her lead, my gaze dropping to her swaying hips and that tight ass that begged to be looked at.

"Do you want me to slow down, give you a bit more time to stare before we sit down?"

Fuck. Was I really that obvious?

I dragged a hand down my jaw.

We found an empty table in the corner, and I slid a chair out for her. With a quick nod, she took a seat, and I followed, taking the chair right across from her. At the same time, two packs of smokes hit the table, gliding to meet in the middle. We both grinned, and she took one cigarette out and slowly brought it to her mouth. In a quick whoosh, I took out my Zippo and placed it at the tip.

"You sure you want to do that?"

I paused for a second, puzzled, but she didn't leave much time to mull it over.

"Where I come from, when you light someone's cigarette, you owe them seven years of pleasure." I didn't even flinch before I sparked my lighter, and she took it, dragging the poison in, curving those full lips.

"And where is that?"

"Somewhere far, far away." She gave me a side smile and more evasiveness. Lighting up my smoke next, I relaxed in the chair as the waitress took our orders - a double shot with cream and two sugars for The Vamp, and a plain black for me.

"So what's the deal?" I skimmed over her presence, taking note of the details of her appearance. Her whole graphic screamed designer. While my eyes roamed over her exterior, 'Miss Independent' played at the back of my mind.

From her knee-high black boots to her dark leggings, tucked in, and a black t-shirt, which covered her curves just right. Long, oval-shaped nails, not polished with color but shiny. Even her porcelain skin caught my attention. When my eyes rose, she smirked, green eyes slicing through me. Those naturally full, delicate lips and dimpled nose perfectly mirror the image, with one beauty mark on her left cheek disrupting the symmetry of her face. She was a fucking Goddess, Femme Fatale personified, sent from hell to torture any man in her vicinity. Her body: a weapon of mass destruction.

"Don't make me ruin this with a cliche." She couldn't hide her amusement.

"What? You'll have to kill me?" I quipped, and she let out a soft chuckle. Everything in me tingled at the sound.

"Something like that."

"How about a name?"

She gave me a look, a mix of intrigue, surprise, and a bit of relief. But then she puffed, "How 'bout no?"

Her tongue stuck out, slowly grazing over her upper

teeth, the sight of it sending an impulse thankfully hidden under the table. The more I looked at her, the more nervous she seemed, but something told me it had nothing to do with me. Maybe it had everything to do with the side hustle she was hinting at before.

She smiled and thanked the waitress who set our coffees on the table. Dragging another nicotine-infested breath, she eyeballed me, and I followed. The smoke we both exhaled collided in the center, as if our breaths had a mind of their own. My phone buzzed; I ignored it, knowing it was Ty calling to find out where the hell I was. I was determined to block out everything around this fucking enigma I desperately wanted to solve.

"You live around here?"

"No."

Well, she wasn't gonna make this easy.

"Got any brothers or sisters?"

She took a moment, contemplating, maybe. I couldn't get a good read.

"Nope," she popped the P, narrowing her eyes.

"Favorite color?"

"Seriously?"

Well, this was going nowhere.

Where the hell has my game gone? And how do I get it back?

The sound of her feet tapping was the only thing I could hear, and the more the seconds passed, the more she fidgeted. I tried my best to keep it cool, but the pumping in my chest wouldn't allow me.

When I opened my mouth to ask another question, she

looked at her nonexistent watch, then back at me, chugging down her coffee, mumbling out something I couldn't quite pick out, but it was definitely not English. She stood up, taking something out of her back pocket, husking, "Sorry to make this short, but I am on a tight schedule." A couple of bills flew to the table, and she turned to walk away.

No cash my ass!

I jumped to my feet, the chair shrieking with the push.

"Can I have your number?" I could hear the desperation in my voice, but I didn't even want to hide it. I wanted to see her again, to get to know her, to kiss the hell out of her.

Not bothering to stop, she said over her shoulder, "I don't think so."

I ran around her and blocked her car door before she got to it.

"What can I do to change your mind?" I uttered, making her captivating eyes face me.

With confidence, she slowly took a step closer, grabbed the lapels of my leather jacket, pulling me to her, our mouths inches apart. I could feel her breath, the smell of nicotine, and temptation. Our lips met in a gentle peck, and she pulled away too quickly, finding my ear with a whisper, "Let's just leave it to serendipity."

Frozen in place, I watched her slip inside her car, my lips pulsing from the small contact. The exhaust popped when she turned the ignition, followed by a squeaking noise that made me turn. From the frame of her rolled-down window, she rasped, "Word of advice, grow out your hair a bit, give 'em something to pull onto."

In one blink, she was gone.

Fucking Vamp!

I got on my bike to follow her, but the vibration nudged me to answer my phone. "Be there in five, little brother, sorry."

Also by Lena Knight

Brick-ed series
Averted
(Sabrina & Mateo)
Anticipated
(Aria & Cillian)
Allured
(Nala's story - coming late 2026)

Fostered H(e)arts series
Nothing's fair in Love & Basketball
(Ty & MJ)
Nothing's fair in Love & Marriage
(Luka & Nora)
Nothing's fair in Love & Cardio
(Mak's story - coming late 2026)
Nothing's fair in Love & Formation
(Tristan's story, coming early 2027)

About the Author

Lena is a wife and a mother of two, and somewhere along the way, she lost herself in her roles. She has a master's degree in Physical Education, but after her son was diagnosed with autism, she proudly pulled on her stay-at-home-mom shoes. She rediscovered herself through books and the new worlds they opened up. Reading turned into writing, and a new passion was born. Lena grew up never believing in herself, but thankfully, there are people in her life who gave her the push she needed to try… so this is her… trying.

You can find her on:
TikTok -   authorlenaknight
Instagram - authorlenak

Acknowledgements

First, I want to thank my only support system—my husband. Without you, I never would've taken this step. Thank you for believing in me and being my rock.

To my kids who made my dreams of becoming a mother come true… Mommy loves you the mostes.

To my beta readers and editors for helping me improve the story.

To BookTok, for getting me back into reading, which led me to write.

And last but not least, I want to thank you, dear reader, for giving my story a chance.

Lena